A.S. McMillen

The Seventh World

BATTLE FOR ANTILLIS

- BOOK TWO -

Illustration by Antonello Addipietro

Publishing Services provided by Paper Raven Books LLC

Printed in the United States of America

First Printing, 2022

ISBN 978-1-7355932-2-7 Paperback

ISBN 978-1-7355932-3-4 Hardback

Dedication

To all those who always encouraged me and believed in me when nobody else did. That belief is the reason I never gave up. Especially you, Kerri Jean (and your big, beautiful, wonderful, amazing, nerdy, weird, and accepting heart—the greatest friend an odd-ball like me could have ever dreamed of!)

And to Fritz (my Ellis) and Monica. You guys are amazing and the best friends a dreamer could have.

Also, to my wonderful husband and best friend, Shane. Thanks for always listening to my crazy ideas and dreams and helping me follow them.

And, as always, to my companions near and far—to my Sammi, Luna, and Hulk!

Acknowledgements

Thank you to my wonderful editing team and publishing team for making my dream come true.

To Martin Miller (Marty), thank you for helping me with my website and other tech issues.

To my parents, Tom and Sandy. There aren't enough words to express my gratitude. But thank you for the hard work it took to raise a child with her head in the clouds and supporting the grown-up child who still marches to the beat of her own off-tune drummer.

Acknowledgments

Table of Contents

Part Three: The Resistance Begins

Glossary

Prologue
HISTORY OF ANTILLIS AND ALDERBARD

There are several galaxies throughout the universe and several planets in each system. Many galaxies are new and have no life, while others are so old that life has expired. There is a belief that there are at least one hundred galaxies in the universe where life thrives. However, with the mother's gift of connection she gave her children, each galaxy with life has only seven inhabited planets—seven sibling planets. This is also true of the Devas galaxy. The seven sibling planets in Devas are Antillis, Alderbard, Canopiuis, Alpharman, Regulusa, Sirios, and Terran.

Camulos took over every other galaxy in the universe with seven sibling planets and is now in Devas attempting to take over or destroy it (if he can). Although the Devas resistance is small, they have been able to keep Camulos from accomplishing his goal for over a thousand years. However, they have been fighting for so long that hope is now getting thin. But Callais hasn't given up. He believes if he can gain back control of at least two planets, there might be a chance that they could rescue the others and hopefully defeat Camulos. These two planets are Antillis and Alderbard.

Antillis is at the heart of the Devas galaxy, centered between all planets in the system. The star closest to Antillis is an older star and is much smaller than the stars surrounding the other planets in the Devas system. Antillis only has one large moon that controls the waterfall from the sky and the groundwater on the planet. This provides Antillis to be lush with thick forests. The elements on Antillis that are most revered are flora and fauna, which are teeming across the planet. The dense forest provides food and coverage for many animals and beings on this planet. The dark depths of the trees also keep many things hidden and many things that still must be discovered. A rare plant found on Antillis, called Desmodias, is used to craft almost indestructible fabrics. This fabric is used for several things, but mostly for the sails on the Devas ship and the sacred relic… the Fabric of Space and Time. Because of the flora and fauna that cover the dense forest, the three elements most used on

Antillis are air, water, and earth. These elements are often used for healing purposes and can enhance a variety of spells if used properly.

Magnus wasn't only the head keeper of all of Devas, but also one of the original head keepers on Antillis. Magnus and the other keeper, Constantine, had knowledge (and passed down this knowledge to others) on how the plants and animals could be used for healing. This knowledge they passed on also contained sacred spells that required plants and animals needed to protect the Devas system. Magnus and Constantine trained many keepers (and some worthy of this knowledge) to be healers. Once the training was completed, many healers were stationed on other planets throughout the system to heal the sick or help the keepers that needed wisdom about plants or animals. Magnus also noted that Clara was one of the greatest healers he had ever trained. So, Clara was often sent on healing missions, more than any other healer. This gained her a deep knowledge of healing and of the planets that other healers (and even keepers) would never understand.

Although Magnus was the head keeper on Antillis, since he was also the head keeper of all of Devas, he traveled a lot. Because of this, Constantine mainly was the head keeper over Antillis. Constantine stayed on

Antillis for many years, but he eventually left Antillis when Callais set up his base for the protectors (long before the Camulos invasion). Callais also chose Antillis as the protector headquarters because of the planet's central location and the elements found there that were beneficial in creating protector spells. After Constantine left Antillis, he made his way to Terran. At the time, Terran was one of the youngest planets in the Devas system and wasn't very populated. So, Constantine decided to start his own work on Terran training healers, thus, leaving Callais and Magnus Antillis to train protectors and healers. After the Camulos invasion, no one ever heard from Constantine again, thinking he was lost along with Terran.

During the Camulus Pack invasion of Devas, when the separation ceremony broke apart, several star trails above Antillis fell from the heavens onto one side of the lush planet. The stardust burned up the forest, destroying the protection spell (and Magnus's home), leaving a barren, desolate wasteland on one side of the planet. Once Camulos and his soldiers began to take over the Devas system, they found the bare side of the planet to be a strategic place to station the majority of the Camulus forces (since Antillis itself was in the center of the galaxy). They set up a massive military base, making it easy for the Camulus forces to send soldiers and weapons to other planets across the galaxy much more quickly than any other location.

Although the Camulus forces were able to occupy one side of Antillis, the protection spell still lasted on the opposite side of the planet, making it impossible for them to enter and take over the whole planet. Since Callais had originally set up his training for protectors on Antillis, once Callais found the protection spell still lasted on half of the planet, he continued his plans. He created the city of Mari and began his teaching and training once again. He had hope that one day he could figure out how to take back Antillis. Callais thought if he could get back Antillis, he believed it would be easier to take back the other planets as well (with or without Magnus or Magnus's heir). So, Callais was now the head keeper of Antillis, despite his original rank of lower keeper. Antillis is currently the only planet with some hope and chance of defeating the Camulus forces and getting the planet back. However, they have been fighting for years, and hope is fading.

Alderbard is located on the third outer ring of the Devas galaxy, right under the planet Alpharman. Alderbard has a small white star similar to Canopiuis, but unlike Canopiuis, (which has no moon but several orbs that rotate around the planet), Alderbard has one large moon that helps control the flow and movement of the surface. Alderbard is mainly covered with water and land bridges, making water the main element on this planet. Like air, earth, light, and fire… water is also used to enhance spells.

The water is also special in the Devas system. Magnus ensured that when he took charge of the galaxy, the training included how to use water to enhance the connection of the star trails (the star trails were also part of the mother's gift of connection she gave her children). The head keeper here, Lincoln, trained other keepers on how to manipulate water to enhance the connection and travel among the star trails in the Devas system. Lincoln and Magnus also helped Callais train the protectors to use water spells to help aid in star travel with the Devas ships. The training also included using fluid within the being's bodies to create light orbs to shine whenever they found themselves in darkness.

Once the Camulus invasion occurred, Lincoln returned after the separation ceremony to fight against the Camulus Pack assault and occupation of Alderbard. However, Lincoln was unsuccessful in saving Alderbard and never returned for fear of being found out by the Camulus forces stationed across the planet.

The protection spell broke apart over Alderbard as well. But at least ten towns remained under the protection, making it impossible for the Camulus forces to completely take over the planet. The protected cities were safe, but this still didn't stop the Camulus forces from endlessly trying to penetrate the protected areas. Unlike Antillis, the protected towns were scattered across the planet, making it hard for Devas beings to travel between cities, thus, leaving many of the people separated from each other and their loved ones.

If this wasn't difficult enough for the people of Alderbard, a faction of people called the dealers set up several of their operations on Alderbard to provide fake extraction marks to the people. If a person received a fake extraction mark and couldn't pay their debt to the dealer, there was no place for them to hide. If they were brave enough to flee to another city, there was the risk of being caught by the Camulus soldiers. So, most were faced with finding a way to pay off the dealers or risk their lives to make it somewhere else. There was a story of one young girl who was able to flee the dealers and escape the Camulus soldiers' clutches (barely making her escape). However, this was only a story since no one had seen or heard from this young girl, and many believed she was dead. So Alderbard was mostly controlled by either the Camulus soldiers or the dealers—safety and peace weren't options for the people on Alderbard.

Despite the situation on both planets, Callais knew these two planets were the ones that the resistance needed control of first if they were to have a chance against defeating Camulos and his forces—and hopefully, his plans to get them back would work.

Part One

◆—————•—————◆

The New Resistance

Chapter 1
FIRST ORDER

Evie was dreaming again. As always, her dreams would start off as they usually did. Dreams with thick fog and vibrant lights that flickered, split apart, changed shape, and then merged with the surrounding fog and darkness, swirling endlessly around in her mind. However, the lights and fog that had once made her feel sick now didn't have that effect. Like everything else she had come across so far, they seemed to be a pattern, organizing themselves to what she assumed her mind was searching for. The sickening chaos that once was the nightmares was now something she could almost grasp, something she was beginning to understand. Since Evie had discovered who she was and the responsibilities she had to take on, she also found herself dreaming more often about Magnus.

As the dream fog rolled away, Evie was surprised this time to see Magnus's face clearly in her dream—looking straight at her. As he stared deeply at her, she felt tense and nervous, even a little scared, but before she could say or do anything, Magnus flashed her a broad smile and began to speak. *"The darkness began its spread over the universe as Camulos slowly began to destroy and take over each system… piece by piece. At the center of the Darthus galaxy, the senate crowd fell silent throughout the room. The senate had been created by the head keepers from across the universe, comprised of several keepers from several different galaxies, with a united goal to stop Camulos. Darthus is a galaxy central to all the known galaxies in the universe, as to why the senate was held here. As the first ordered meeting of the intergalactic senate convened… I took center stage."*

After Magnus spoke these words, his face drifted away into the fog. When the dream fog cleared again, Evie saw that Magnus was standing in a massive room, seats leading upwards towards a ceiling she couldn't even see. The seats were filled with hundreds of people of different colors, shapes, and sizes, completely surrounding him. Evie realized Magnus was somehow showing her his memory of this meeting in her dream. So, she believed this must be important to know.

Evie continued to focus on the dream, trying remember every detail. Magnus then turned and looked deeply into Evie's eyes again. Before he spoke, Magnus cleared his throat and shuffled in his oversized gown. Somehow, she knew (like a secret voice was whispering this knowledge deep in her mind) that Magnus's gown, since his obsessions began with the ancient text and scrolls (to find a way to defeat Camulos), no longer fit his once-towering frame. She knew that in his younger years, Magnus was a large man in stature. He had broad shoulders, was barrel-chested, and had thick forearms and calves. Magnus had dark curly red hair and a long thick beard with a mustache to match. He also had big red cheeks and nose, lightly freckled skin, and sparkling green eyes. He looked very much like Ellis and her father; however, Magnus was even more prominent in stature than either of them. She also seemed to know that when Magnus was younger, he was vibrant, full of life, wisdom, compassion, and joy—something she now also knew had faded from his soul. As she analyzed him in this current dream state, she noticed that his red, curly hair was all streaked with silvery-white and gray. His once-sparkling, bright eyes now had very deep bags and a slight hollow look. Evie felt a deep sadness looking at his eyes now and wondered about the pain he must have gone through for his demeanor to change so drastically.

Evie was then snapped from her thoughts as she watched Magnus look down at his shuffling hands before he slowly raised his head, stood with absolute confidence, and began to address the surrounding masses. "*Dear keepers of our beloved universe, we are here today because we now have to come to terms that there is no clear answer, no clear path, no clear faith or direction, and there never was …*

"*… There is also no clear right and wrong, nor is there a clear light or dark. We do not live in a universe of just light and dark, but a universe of variety, change, and color…*

"*…Someone once told me the only guaranteed thing in this universe is death—but I disagree. I know there is an absolute guarantee in truth and in love. A guaranteed truth in these varieties and differences that surround us. There is also a guaranteed truth that there will always be hurt and pain. There is also absolute truth in understanding. Understanding that there will always be love as much as there is hate…*

"*… There is also a guarantee that we are unique in every way, adding to the color and variety of the universe. However, we are all ruled by the same absolute forces. These forces are the guarantee we all fall the same direction… down.*"

Evie watched as Magnus took a moment of silence, slowly circling himself around the floor, taking in as many senate members' faces as he could, looking deeply into each of their eyes. Magnus then cleared his throat and continued. "*Snow falls from the sky, and each flake is more unique than the last. Nevertheless, they all still fall to the ground…*

"…what we all forget is that not only did we all fall from the same place, we also landed in the same place. And we all eventually melt into the ground, as our lives give the ground new life, new growth, new love, and new hope…

"…this cycle feeds back into our lives when once again, it becomes so strong, it feeds back to the sky, feeds back to the beyond. This is where we all become one again and where we find our own uniqueness before we fall back down the same way we came …"

Magnus then stood a little taller as his voice became louder. "Our cycle has become toxic, and we no longer have a direction but are moving and surrounded by a chaotic flurry of what Camulos has created. The only way to confront what we have lost is to break this cycle and make a change. I also believe that change is a guaranteed constant. We have to change to grow and move forward to become better than who we were and better than who we are now. We must break this cycle…

"…breaking the cycle can be frightening because there is also no guarantee that our actions will not make things worse, but there is also hope for our actions to make things better. So, I believe we must take this leap together to move forward, to the unknown… but I guarantee we must do this together."

After Magnus finished his speech, he nodded again to the senate crowd as they sat in silence. Then, one by one, Evie watched as each member slowly rose to their feet and began clapping and roaring with such extreme enthusiasm that the senate room walls shook…shaking so hard that it woke her from the dream.

***

After Evie woke from this dream, she felt honored to be Magnus's heir but even more nervous now of the large role she had to fill in his absence. He was so elegant and graceful, yet also powerful and commanding. She began to wonder if she really could handle everything she needed to do. Evie was too anxious to go back to sleep, so she went in search of Callais, hoping he would be in the council room (where he spent almost all of his time now). As she made her way across the winding rope bridge, Bella following at her heels, she passed Regina's dwelling, continuing towards the council room. Suddenly, Evie felt an odd shiver go up her spine and flood her head, almost like she remembered something. But whatever the thought was, it eluded her, so she shook it off and entered the council chambers.

Once she entered, she was surprised to see the old woman, Josephine, was the only one in the room. Evie took a moment to analyze Josephine. She was very old and had features that didn't look like others in the Devas system, and Evie wondered what galaxy she came from. Although Josephine's features had a semblance of humanity (like other beings Evie had noticed from other galaxies), Josephine's features were different. Her eyes were set closer together than human eyes and almost looked like cat eyes in their shape with a hint of a golden-yellow color. Josephine's skin was light but with random brown patches scattered across her fair skin. Evie had been told there were other galaxies Camulos had conquered. Josephine wasn't the only one in Mari that didn't look like other humans Evie was familiar with.

Josephine was intently looking over a scroll and hadn't noticed Evie yet. So, Evie stayed silent, thinking about whether or not she should interrupt her since she wasn't sure what she wanted to say yet. As Evie thought over what she wanted to tell Josephine, she drifted over what she had learned while in Mari. This way, she could clearly explain to Josephine what was bothering her. Evie assumed Josephine, like the rest of the elders she had met, would be patient with her, but also, if she could clearly express her thoughts, she might get clear answers.

As Evie went over different ideas, she remembered Callais and Newton had explained Josephine's history to her when Evie had asked them about keepers. They told her a brief but detailed history of what keepers were, what they did, and the keepers that were part of the resistance (which were not many). Evie learned that each keeper had an interesting past. Still, when they told her of Josephine's history, Evie found her story very intriguing.

Callais and Newton told her that Josephine was a powerful keeper, but before she came to Devas, she had first been Camulos's student. This had baffled Evie, and she wondered why a great resistance leader once worked with Camulos. Callais and Newton answered this by telling her that Josephine was found by Camulos when she was young (before the wars started), so he was the one to first train her. During her training, many keepers realized Josephine was very powerful in her abilities as to why she eventually became a head keeper. Callais and Newton didn't go into detail about what had happened between Camulos and Josephine for Josephine to join the resistance, and Evie never asked for a further explanation. She felt that either Josephine never really told anybody else, or there was a reason they were keeping it a secret. Evie had also learned that Josephine was one of the oldest keepers still alive. It was unknown what bloodline she came from because Evie had learned Josephine was an orphan like herself. This was why Evie found Josephine's past so interesting since she felt like they had a shared experience. Evie thought how lucky she was to be found by Marina and the resistance. She shuddered to think what might have happened if Camulos had found her instead. Her heart then went out to Josephine as she thought about how awful it was for her to be under Camulos.

After thinking over everything Callais and Newton had told her, Evie remembered Josephine was also the one who had compared Evie's confidence to Magnus when she first came to Antillis. So, Evie assumed Josephine must've known Magnus well.

Evie decided she had been thinking long enough and finally built up the courage to speak. She cleared her throat before she spoke, but Evie was surprised the noise didn't seem to startle Josephine. Before Evie could say anything, Josephine looked up casually and smiled. "I was wondering how long you were going to stand there before you said something."

Evie shuffled awkwardly before saying, "Sorry, I didn't want to bother you, but I had a dream and felt I needed to tell someone."

Josephine smiled again and patted the seat next to her. "Come, sit and tell me."

Evie made her way over to the chair and sat down as Josephine placed her wrinkled, frail hand on Evie's shoulder and nodded for her to go on. Evie instantly felt comforted by her touch, and even though she didn't know Josephine well, she felt an instant rush of trust and love. So, she told Josephine about her dream. After she was finished, Josephine was silent for a moment before saying, "I was there at that senate gathering. This is very interesting, Evie. Somehow, I think you might be dreaming Magnus's memories."

"I know," Evie said excitedly. "That's what I thought too. Even before I knew who Magnus was, I felt like I had been dreaming his or others' memories for such a long time now. How can this be?"

Josephine rubbed her hands together and tilted her head as a distant look entered her eyes. After a few seconds of silence, she refocused her gaze on Evie. Then, with a heavy sigh, she said, "I am not sure. I think Magnus somehow found a spell for his heir to find his memories, maybe even others' memories as well. I am not sure how he did this, but he was a very powerful man. I am sure if anyone could find a way to do this, it would be him."

Evie thought about this for a moment, thinking of the right way to express her thoughts. Once she gathered her ideas, she went on to say, "The memories, or dreams, only seem to come in pieces. Do you think we can find a way to see how I can make meaning out of them? I'm guessing there is something important I need to know, but I can't control when they come. Maybe there is a spell or something that could help?"

"Maybe," Josephine replied and then said, "I will talk with the others and see what we can find."

Evie smiled and nodded, hoping they would find an answer soon. But before she could say anything else, Callais and Newton (followed by Apollo and Darwin) entered the room. As soon as Bella saw her friends, she immediately bounced over and recruited them to play. The three companions then ran happily out of the council room, barking and wiggling their tails with delight. Callais chuckled as he affectionately watched the dogs run out. He then turned and saw that Evie was in the room.

"Good, you are already here." He gave Evie a wink before announcing to the others, "We will be starting the council meeting soon."

Callais then turned to Josephine. Evie saw them exchange a secretive glance and was curious about what that meant. But before she could ask, Callais stated, "Josephine, I think I will have you take the lead today."

Josephine smiled, then nodded. "I think I know just what I will say."

Evie just shrugged her shoulders and didn't ask any more questions. She assumed that whatever they had planned, she figured she'd find out soon enough.

***

Shortly after Callais and Newton sat down (joining Evie and Josephine), the rest of the council members began to come in until the room was completely full. Once everyone was seated and quiet, Josephine stood up and gave a respectful nod to the council. She then started addressing them by recounting her own memory of Magnus's speech from the first intergalactic senate meeting—the one Evie had just described from her own dream. After Josephine finished telling her story, she stood a little taller and looked at each member around the room (as Magnus had done during his speech). Then, when she got to Evie, she winked before she continued to say, "With these words from Magnus, we must remember what we are truly fighting for."

Josephine took a deep breath before she went on, "As I look around the room, at each of us here, all scattered from different parts of the Devas galaxy, and some from other galaxies, I see our differences, but I also see our shared love, pain, and hope."

She took a long, thoughtful pause before she continued. "This fight is not just for those of us in this room, but for all of those we have lost in this darkness. For all those who still have hope, and for all of us who believe we can defeat evil."

Evie saw tears began to fill Josephine's eyes as she took another deep breath and went on. "We have all lost so much already, and what we face now could possibly make us lose more, but we have to remember what Magnus said, '*We must take this leap together, for there is hope that one day, this will make the change we need.*'"

Josephine then took her seat. The council room was silent for an extended time; many seemed lost in deep thought. After a long period of silence, with no one saying anything, Evie caught Josephine's eye when she nodded at Evie. Evie shuffled in her seat, realizing it was her turn to speak, struggling to find the right words to say. Evie then felt Callais gently place his hand on her shoulder. Evie turned to look at him as he gave her a little wink. So, she slowly rose to her feet. She felt reluctant to speak since she still didn't understand her role or what to say. But she sucked in a deep breath, pulled herself together, gave Josephine a nod of respect, and turned to face the council members. "I know that I haven't earned my place yet in this battle," Evie said nervously, as she twisted her hands together before she went on, "and I'm not in a place to ask you to fight for me. However, I promise I'll do everything in my power to learn what I need to be able to gain your respect and show you that I'm worthy of being Magnus's heir."

Evie took a long nervous pause. She realized she needed to be confident. So, she stopped twisting her hands and stood up taller. She sucked in another deep breath and boldly went on to say, "I see the pain and suffering that all of you have endured, and I promise to help in whatever way I can to end this agony and sorrow. Not only for the people who surround me today but for all those who need the darkness to end."

Evie then looked towards Callais and Josephine, hoping she said the right things. They both gave her a reassuring nod. Their reassurance gave her some comfort, so she respectfully nodded to the council members as Josephine had done. She was surprised to see many of them give her a courteous nod back as she took her seat. Callais then rose slowly to his feet (still recovering from wounds from the battle with the black ship) as he began to address the members. "What we need more than ever is all of us to unify. We need all of us to believe, once again, that this fight will come to an end. We have been battling for as long as we can remember, and we are only at the beginning."

Callais paused, looked around the room at each member, giving them a reassuring smile, and then added, "What we will face next is unknown. I want everyone here to know that there will be times when this will seem like it will never end. Where the darkness will feel

24

so powerful that you will feel like losing faith. I ask you all here today to not lose hope, to not lose love, and to believe that we CAN and WILL do this."

The council room remained silent as Callais took his seat, with several members giving him a nod of respect. Otto and Atlas then got up and moved some maps and pieces of parchment to the center of the table. Once they finished placing the items down, Otto took his turn to speak. "The first step we believe is necessary is for us is to take back Antillis. We're aware that on the other side of this planet is where the majority of the Camulus forces are stationed."

He paused for a moment. Evie wondered if Otto felt as nervous as she did when addressing the council members. He then pushed his shoulders up, held his head a little higher, and stood a little taller, looking more confident. Evie smiled to herself, realizing that she might be right; he was probably nervous too. She was instantly proud of him for keeping his composure as Otto continued. "This will be a daunting task, and we're outnumbered for sure. Before we can do this, we need to go out into the Devas system and recruit more members in our resistance, so we have a fighting chance."

Otto looked around the room, obviously taking a note from Josephine and Callais. He then added,

"Atlas, Abe, and Ellis will be joining me in recruiting more members. During this time, it will also allow the opportunity for Callais to train those we recruit as well as training Evie in understanding her role and powers in this endeavor." The members all nodded in agreement. So, with no objections, Otto went on, "This will also allow time for those here on Antillis to find weaknesses in the Camulus forces and make plans for our attack when we are ready."

Otto took a deep breath and then finished by saying, "Atlas, Abe, Ellis, and I will need a few other council members who will be willing to help us in finding small resistance factions still in existence and making sure we can get enough new members here safely to train. Is there anyone who will help us?"

Several members of the council raised their hands. After Otto wrote down each member's name, Atlas said, "For those of you who raised their hand, we will be meeting tomorrow inside the waterfall cave to go over our plans and next steps."

Atlas nodded at Otto after he finished as the two took their seats. Callais stood again and said, "Lincoln, Josephine, Newton, Simone, and Declan will be joining me in looking over information we gather and help in not only in training the new recruits who come in but training Evie in what she needs to know. Who here will help me with this?"

Again, several council members raised their hands as Newton counted who would join Callais's team. Callais then added, "I will need as much help as possible since I will be spending much of my time helping Evie."

A few more members then raised their hands as Newton counted once more. Regina then stood up and took her turn to address the members. "I, Emmeline, Amelia, Marina, and Collin will be gathering resources and helping me in aiding others who need us. So, I will need a few members to help me relay messages to Otto and Callais's teams and aid me in my tasks. Who will be willing to help?"

The remaining council members raised their hands as Regina counted who would be her aides. Otto then stood up again and directed everyone's attention to the maps and parchment he and Atlas had previously spread out on the table. The largest map was of the entire Devas galaxy. Evie glanced down at it and recognized it as the map once on the table from Marina's castle back in "the stacks." Now the map was clearer and wasn't swirling around like it had done in the past. Otto then pointed to a small planet on the lower end of the map. "The first place that we believe we should go to find those for recruitment is on Alderbard. We know of several small areas where people are hiding, despite Balor's attempt to eliminate them. We also know that there are several dealer factions. However, we believe that it's possible to persuade some of the dealers to help us." He took a long pause before adding, "We'll be going over this in more detail tomorrow when we meet. However, if there is anyone here in the council that might have some useful information for us before we start, please let us know."

Otto looked around the room as a young woman (a little younger than Otto) raised her hand. Otto nodded for her to speak, and when she stood up, Evie noticed a clear, distinct mark on her left forearm as the woman began to say, "I came from Alderbard and received my fake extraction mark from one of the dealers." She paused while trying to cover her left forearm with her right hand. "The dealer I received it from wasn't a nice man, and I couldn't pay off the debt I owed him. However, another man helped me escape Alderbard when I couldn't pay off the debt. His name is Leo, and I believe I can help you find him."

Otto nodded at the young woman before asking, "I apologize, but what's your name?"

The woman looked awkwardly around the room before answering, "Elizabeth Abebis."

Otto thanked her as Elizabeth took her seat. Otto cleared his throat before he added on to the plan. "The other reason we will be going to Alderbard, besides recruiting members, is we believe that there are not only Devas ships there on Alderbard that weren't found or destroyed by Balor, but we have reason to believe that someone there was aiding Evie to the Devas system. Callais and Newton have told us she arrived by a Devas ship in her first travels before she found her inner power."

Otto paused again as some of the council members gasped. He then looked at Evie and asked, "Do you have any idea who this could've been?"

"No," Evie answered, shaking her head, completely baffled like several others in the room who were now staring at her. "I assumed Callais sent the ship, or somehow it found me."

There were a few chuckles and a few more gasps around the room as Callais leaned in and whispered to Evie, "I believe you might have a friend we do not know of yet."

Evie was stunned and shook her head once more, wondering who was this mystery person helping her that the others wouldn't know about. The council room was also a blur of shocked whispers about this secret person who sent a Devas ship. Eventually, the room settled down and was quiet again. So, Otto went on, "We also have one other reason to go to Alderbard. If we can take Antillis back, Alderbard will be our next objective in this war. Going to Alderbard may restore lost faith and give people on Alderbard new hope. So, when we can return there with the resistance, we may have more allies then."

After Otto finished, the room buzzed with conversations about the new mission. Soon, the council members all agreed with this plan and began to quiet down again as Newton stood up, looked around the room, and nodded at Declan (who sat up taller in his chair). Newton then began his address to the members. "We have some information that we believe is important to share with all of you. We have reason to believe that Clara, who was helping us on Canopiuis, was a spy for the Camulus Pack. So, we all must be very cautious of who we trust since we now believe that many of the people we once thought were on our side could be working for Camulos."

The members murmured again, bouncing thoughts off each other about the possibilities of who might be working with Camulos. Newton then took his seat next to Declan when Evie saw Declan turn his head and wipe a tear from his eye. Evie instantly felt awful for him and wished she could think of something to say to help. However, she always ended up blushing and getting flustered around Declan, so she decided she would think of what to say later to make sure she didn't mess up her words. Evie was then distracted from her thoughts as Callais stood up and began to speak. "We have a plan, and that is a start. Remember that all of us are here for a reason, whatever that may be. All of us must remember those reasons for our fight… We are all in this together."

With those closing words, the council members began to slowly file out of the room. Once the room was clear, Callais looked at Evie and stated, "We will begin tomorrow."

Chapter 2
SOPHIA

David, Ruby, Beth, and Steven landed in Washington. They drove to the ferry, making it across Puget Sound to Whidbey Island. The island wasn't as desolate as the places in Egypt and Russia where they met Amam and Nadia, but still, it was quite a bit out of the way. Once they got off the ferry, Amam was waiting and drove them to the island's far west side. After driving for a bit, they came to a small cabin surrounded by massive trees overlooking the water. Again, it was still a fairly secluded area since David could see no other homes in sight. As he stretched his legs before walking up to the cabin, he looked across the bay and watched the fog over the water begin to lift. David could see, far in the distance, the majestic Olympic Peninsula covered by more massive trees. He took a deep breath and admired the beautiful view for a while before walking over to

Ruby's side as he grabbed her hand and gave it a tight squeeze before approaching the cabin door.

David had noticed that Ruby seemed to be trapped in her thoughts and barely spoke the whole flight. Ruby never kept any secrets from David, and he wondered why his beautiful wife was so lost in her thoughts. David knew that the adventure they had been on so far to help Evie had been full of mystery and questions. Ruby had also never been away from home for so long. So, he figured she was just processing everything and adjusting to their crazy mission. David squeezed Ruby's hand even tighter as they knocked on the front door, and Nadia answered.

Nadia led the group to a small living room, where everyone took a seat. Before long, a woman entered the room, making Ruby gasp loudly. David knew exactly why Ruby gasped. Although the woman was probably about forty years old, her resemblance to Evie was shocking. David thought, *If Evie was forty, that's exactly what she would look like*! The woman had deep red, long, and curly hair, vibrant green eyes, and a multitude of freckles across her nose and cheeks—just like Evie. As the woman took her seat across from David and Ruby, she cleared her throat and (in a thick Irish accent) said, "Me name is Sophia Murphy. I'm very pleased to meet all of yeh."

David and Ruby remained silent, still shocked by

how much this woman looked like Evie. David looked over at Steven and Beth, and he could tell that they were thinking the same thing. Finally, Steven shook his head, saying, "We are pleased to meet you, too." He paused and added, "It's incredible. You look so much like her."

Sophia tilted her head and gave Steven a curious look before asking, "Like who?"

Steven cleared his throat again and answered, "Like our Evie."

Sophia gave them a weak smile. "I believe I may know the reason fer this."

Everyone was waiting for her to finish, but instead, she got up, grabbed something off the shelf, and handed a photo frame to David. David looked at the frame, but instead of a picture inside it, there was an oil painting of three children. David shook his head in disbelief as Ruby looked over at the image and gasped again. Ruby then asked Sophia, "Is that you?" Ruby pointed to the girl in the painting. Sophia nodded. Ruby gasped again. "You look exactly like Evie here!"

Sophia took a seat next to the others and let out a deep sigh before saying, "This is a paintin' of meself an' me brothers when we were younger... before we began to drift apart."

Sophia shifted anxiously in her seat when she added,

"The paintin' was done 'bout a 'undred years ago before we found out 'bout our true past an' our true powers."

Everyone remained quiet, thinking over what Sophia had just said. David rubbed his head again about the time frame. Although Marina had told them that people in Magnus's bloodline lived long lives (assuming Sophia was also one of Magnus's heirs), he was still having difficulty processing this. The others in the room were still silent, not knowing what to say. Sophia finally broke the silence and explained her past.

Sophia told them that she and her brothers were triplets, born and raised in Ireland. They had a very normal life. Then, one day, before they turned thirteen, Marina came to them and told them that they were descendants of a very powerful man named Magnus. She then told them she needed their help. Sophia and her brothers agreed to help. So, Marina began to train them to use their powers and instructed them to help her find a lost item Magnus left behind. Ruby squirmed in her seat, and before Sophia could continue, Ruby said, "Marina is the woman who found Evie and sent us on our mission."

"I know," Sophia answered and gave a weak smile.

Ruby fidgeted in her seat again and nervously said, "I left Evie with her. Please tell me Marina isn't a bad person."

"No," Sophia answered, smiled, and went on, "She

isn't a bad person at all. It was just what 'appened between me an' me brothers that made us drift apart. It 'ad nothin' to do with Marina."

Sophia then explained that while Marina was working with them, she and one of her brothers began to compete for power. They eventually became greedy, thinking that the item that Marina spoke of was a treasure they thought they deserved. Sophia told them she and her brother, Ellis, became so combative and selfish that it destroyed their relationship. Marina then gave up on Sophia and Ellis because they became too corrupt to help any longer. Before Sophia could continue, David interjected, "Evie is also with a man named Ellis right now. Please tell me he is a good man, too."

Sophia gently smiled again before answering, "Yes, he's also everythin' a good man should be. Ellis, well… he can be a little stubborn sometimes, but he's a good man."

David and Ruby took a sigh of relief, realizing that Evie was in safe hands with Marina and Ellis. Sophia continued to tell her story, saying that since she and Ellis began to fight, Marina gave up on them and focused her attention on their other brother, Callum. Sophia explained that Callum told Marina he didn't want anything to do with Marina or his siblings anymore. He stated that he didn't want anything to do with something that would pull his loved ones apart. So, he ran away and hid. This devastated Marina. She thought Callum was the one person in Magnus's bloodline that was pure of heart and would be the one to help solve the mystery behind what Magnus had left them. Sophia continued to explain that with Callum gone, she, Marina, and Ellis reached out to The Keeper's Order to help find him. However, Dermot told them that he couldn't find Callum. All three lost hope, gave up their searching and training, and eventually drifted apart. Sophia then took a deep breath before saying, "I thought I 'ad lost me brothers forever an' decided that it wasn't worth it anymore an' did me best to try an' find Callum an' rebuild me relationship with Ellis... but I couldn't do either."

Sophia said that she eventually joined The Keeper's Order in the hopes that she could help in any way she could and that maybe she would find Callum. Sophia told them as the years went by, she eventually rebuilt her relationship with Ellis; however, it was never as strong as before. She then told them she and Ellis collaborated to try and find Callum. Still, both could never find out where he was, so they gave up once more, and years had gone by since she had worked with or seen Ellis. Sophia then said, "When Callum left, he took a ring with him that was passed down through our family that Marina had told us was important to uncovering Magnus's secrets. I believe he took it 'cause he thought it would continue to destroy me an' Ellis's relationship. Without the ring or Marina trainin' us, again, I believe Callum thought this would save us from our greed and corruption. So, we not only lost our brother, but we also lost the ring."

Sophia let out a long sigh and shifted in her seat. David then asked, "What does this have to do with Evie? Her father's name was Collin."

Sophia forced a smile and plainly stated, "I'm sure he changed his name if he went into hidin'. Wouldn't yeh change yer name if yeh didn't want to be found?" David nodded in agreement.

Sophia's expression then changed. She became somber, and with a strangled whisper, she explained more. "One day, The Order reached out to me and told me Callum 'ad died." Her voice then lowered slightly above a whisper, and her eyes were now filled with tears as she continued. "I was completely devastated. However, they also told me they were searchin' fer a lost child, a lost girl. I began to believe the lost child was me brother's child and, again, tried fer years to search fer the girl." She took a long pause before saying, "This is probably why I look like yer Evie. I believe the lost child is me niece…Callum's daughter."

The room remained silent as each thought deeply about Sophia's story. At the same time, Sophia sniffed back her tears and tried to compose herself. After a few moments of sad silence, Ruby slowly got up, went to the bag they brought, and pulled something out. She then came back and handed a picture frame to Sophia, the picture frame containing the photo of Evie's parents. Ruby then asked, "Is this Callum?"

Sophia looked at the picture in the frame as new tears replaced the old ones. She then choked back a sob. "Yes… This is me brother."

The room remained silent for a long time as Sophia traced her fingers over the photo, letting tears fall freely down her cheeks. She then wiped the last tear away from her eye, looked back up at the others, and wistfully said, "I wish I got to tell him how sorry I am fer what I did an' to tell him I loved him."

David nodded his head and reassuringly. "I'm sure he knew you loved him."

Sophia gave him a grateful smile and looked back down at the photo for a little longer while the others let her have this quiet moment. After a few more minutes, Nadia finally interrupted the silence and asked, "What does the ring have to do with all of this?"

Sophia took a deep sigh before looking up from

the picture and answered, "There are five sacred circles, inscribed with ancient texts, that Magnus gave to five different families 'cross the world. These were families he trusted to hold onto the secrets of Earth's past. Magnus then created The Order to protect the knowledge an' everythin' that he stored 'ere on Earth." She paused and then added, "The Order was told that Magnus hid several ancient texts, among other things, in a hidden city an' that when the time was right, these five sacred circles, if taken to certain sacred places around the planet, would unlock the location of this lost city so we might be able to find the knowledge an' everthin' he stored."

"You said that this was the lost city of Atlantis?" Steven asked, sounding a little confused.

Sophia chuckled. "The city 'as gone by many names, but yes. To the best of our knowledge, the lost city is most likely the ancient city of Atlantis."

David rubbed his head. Again, he was just baffled by the idea and asked, "Amam told us that the rings, or sacred circles, are lost. How do we go about finding them?"

Before Sophia could answer, Ruby interjected. "If we do find these circles, they will help us… help Evie, right?"

"Well, I don't know fer sure what the outcome will be once we find the circles. Not all of them are rings either, and I'm not really sure how they work or what they will do," Sophia replied and went on, "An' also, I don't want to give yeh false hope, but I know that knowledge is power. These circles will connect us to knowledge, so if the knowledge is used fer good, then yes, it should help."

Nadia then added, "I agree with Sophia about us needing to find the circles to find the knowledge that has been lost. However, because The Order members have been destroyed or killed throughout history for what they knew, I believe we will have to be very careful about how we go about moving forward."

Amam then interjected. "Throughout all of Earth's known history, whenever someone had presented knowledge to the public that could change the world for the better, people in power had always found a way to eliminate them and what they knew. Those in power are scared of us... scared of knowledge that they don't understand. This is why so many order members are in hiding... if they haven't already been killed."

Nadia and Sophia nodded in agreement when Steven asked, "How do we protect ourselves then?"

Nadia, Amam, and Sophia all gave each other a hesitant glance when Amam finally answered, "We just have to be careful. Hopefully, in our search through ancient knowledge, we can find a way to stay protected."

Nadia then added, "I have brought several of my texts

with me, and so has Amam. We believe with Sophia's texts we might be able to find answers to help. Hopefully, our search through these texts will not only help us find the circles but protect us and other order members willing to join."

"What if we don't have to search for all five circles?" Ruby asked.

"We will need all five circles to find the city… that I know fer sure," Sophia answered.

Ruby fidgeted in her seat and gave David a worried look before she got back up and went to the bag again. Ruby grabbed a small box from the bag, walked slowly over to Sophia, and handed her the box. "We only need three circles now," Ruby said, looking uneasy.

Sophia opened the box and gasped. David watched as she pulled out two golden objects and held them in front of her. Amam and Nadia also gasped when they saw that Sophia was holding two rings. Ruby took her seat next to David and gave him a guilty look. David just smiled at her and whispered, "You did the right thing, not telling anyone until you knew Evie would be safe, my love."

David then gave Ruby a wink as she gave him a weak smile back. David reached his hand over and placed it on top of Ruby's hand, giving it a quick squeeze when

Amam got up, walked over to Sophia, and asked, "May I see the rings?"

Sophia handed them over to Amam. Amam held up the rings and began to tear up when he said, "This is the ring I lost." As he held the smaller ring up, he added, "This is the ring I almost died for."

Amam then handed the rings back to Sophia and took a seat, wiping a tear away. Nadia turned to Ruby and asked, "Where did you find these?"

"They were Evie's parents' wedding bands," Ruby replied, "But I wasn't sure if they were the rings we were looking for. However, after you told me that they are the only way we may be able to help Evie… I decided to show them to you."

Sophia smiled and nodded. "I would've done the same thin'… I would do anythin' to protect those I love, too."

Ruby smiled and let out a sigh of relief for not having to carry such a heavy burden and secret any longer. Sophia then turned to Amam and gave him a sorrowful look before asking, "Why did yeh almost die for this ring?"

Amam took a deep breath and began his story. "The ring was in my family's possession for many years. When I was a small boy, my mother, the keeper of the ring, became scared. I didn't understand why, but she told me that she had to give the ring to another family who she knew could protect it better than her."

He took another deep breath and then went on, "On our way to meet with the person my mother was going to give the ring to, we were attacked by masked men. We ran from them and hid, but they eventually found us." He paused again before he went on to explain, "We were hiding in a basement of another close friend when we heard the men enter and began to kill those who were hiding us. There was no way out except for a small window. Since I was a child, I was the only one small enough to get through. I didn't want to leave, but my mother told me that this ring was important and needed to be saved no matter what."

Amam wavered before adding, "My mother said it was our family's duty to protect the ring so that all humanity could one day be saved. I didn't want to go, but my mother forced me out the window and told me where to meet this person I needed to give the ring to. So, I reluctantly crawled out the window and ran as fast as I could. However, I could hear my mother's screams as I ran."

Amam began to cry but still continued. "After I ran for a while, and as her screams faded, I couldn't bring myself to run any longer and hid again. I ran and hid for several days and was almost caught a few times by these masked men before a woman caught me in the streets and took the ring from me." Amam wiped away a few tears, now rolling down his cheeks, before continuing. "Before she ran, the woman gave me a concerned look and told me to run away as far as I could and remain hidden for as long as I could. This is why I stayed hidden or lived so far away from others, even after I joined The Order."

Amam sucked in another deep breath and then added, "After she told me this, the woman then ran herself, and I never saw her again despite my efforts to search for her. So, I assumed the ring was stolen and lost forever, and, as a child at the time, there was nothing I could do." He paused once more before he went on, "When I was older and enlisted into The Order, I met Nadia, and she tried to help me find the ring or the woman, but we never could."

Amam then tilted his head in deep thought. "Now, if I think back on it, I believe the woman who took it might have been the person I was supposed to give it to, and she found me before I found her."

Amam shook his head, wiped away the remaining tears on his cheek, and took a deep breath. Sophia looked at him and sympathetically shook her head. "I'm so sorry yeh 'ad to go through all of that... I'm so sorry yeh lost yer mother, Amam."

Amam nodded and wiped the last tear away when Nadia said, "Now that I think about Amam's story, I believe he is right. The woman must have been the person that the ring was intended to go to. This must be how it came to be in Evie's mother's possession, but I am not sure how."

Ruby then nervously spoke up. "I know that I gave you these rings thinking that they would help us and help Evie. However, now I'm scared after hearing Amam's story. I should've kept them a secret. I don't want any of us to die for this mission."

Sophia and Nadia gave Ruby a concerned look when Sophia said, "Unfortunately, Ruby, if we don't 'ave these rings or the other sacred circles an' don't find the answers we need, I'm afraid we will all die anyway. I believe this is the point of our dangerous mission… to find the answers to save us all."

Ruby weakly nodded in agreement, leaned her head on David's shoulder, and began to quietly weep. David kissed the top of her head and whispered something only they could hear. After a few minutes, Ruby had collected herself and boldly stated, "If this is something we must do to save all of us, I guess I'm fine with giving you the rings."

Beth (who had been quiet the whole conversation)

finally spoke up. "Well, it seems we have limited time to accomplish our goals to help Evie. We should get started as soon as possible."

The group nodded in agreement as Sophia and Nadia began to analyze the rings some more while the rest discussed what they would do next. For the next few days, they pored over all the text they had to try and find where the other sacred circles might be located and decipher the inscriptions on the rings. Once again, they all decided they had figured out enough information and began their plans for their next search.

Chapter 3
EVIE'S FIRST ATTEMPT

I t was early morning as Amelia bounced with excitement on the edge of Evie's bed. Evie rubbed her eyes to see Bella running around the room in circles, just as excited as Amelia. Evie smiled at the happy pair, whose joy was so contagious, she joined them in bouncing around the room. The three of them finished getting ready and made their way out to the center room to join Otto, Emmeline, and Atlas, already eating breakfast. As Evie sat down to eat, she really looked at Atlas this time. Although she had been around him a few times, she had been so busy with everything else she hadn't paid him much attention. As she analyzed him, she noticed that Atlas, like Otto, was well-built and muscular but had dark wavy hair (also braided across his head like Otto and Callais). He also had deep gray eyes and was slightly taller than Otto. Evie also noticed he had some features different than a human (like spiked ears and spiked fingers), and she assumed it was because he was from another galaxy. Before she had time to think on this any longer, Evie was quickly interrupted from her thoughts when Otto turned to her and stated, "Callais told me that he would like for you to join him at Regina's when you are ready."

Evie gave a quick nod of agreement as Otto turned to Amelia and told her, "You're responsible for Collin today. You'll be helping him relay messages back and forth between the council members, Callais, and myself."

Amelia gave a slight pout as she touched Evie's arm. Otto understood what her pouting protest meant. "No, Amelia. Today Evie needs to work with Callais alone. I'm sure that when they need your help, they'll let you know."

Amelia hung her head down and slowly nodded in agreement as Evie returned her touch and quietly said, "I'm almost positive I'll need you soon." Evie then gave her a little wink.

Amelia smiled and returned the wink as the group finished their meals and headed off in different directions.

Evie and Bella made their way across the bridge to Regina's dwelling, and Evie was still astounded while looking around at how big the underground city of Mari actually was. Again, she marveled at how big the tree roots were that cascaded and honeycombed throughout the massive cave moving downwards to a bottom she had yet to discover. To Evie, it seemed the cave was endless and went straight through to the other side of the planet. She thought about asking Callais about this but decided to wait for another time when she didn't already have so many other things to figure out and discover.

She was soon distracted from her thoughts when she finally reached Regina's home as Ellis and Aphrodite came bulldozing out and almost knocked Evie to the ground. Ellis grabbed her arm before she could fall backward and pulled her into him, giving her a classic Ellis bear hug. Aphrodite smiled her big slobbery grin at the pair and pressed her body against them, attempting to give her version of a hug. Evie noticed this and lovingly rubbed the top of her massive head, making Aphrodite bark with delight. Bella seemed to want to join in on the action, and she, too, pressed her body up against Ellis and Evie as the happy Aphrodite slobbered all over Bella's tiny head. Evie laughed at this and wiped the sticky drool off Bella's head when Bella barked, wagged her behind, and did a happy little jump. Ellis then released Evie (while bouncing up and down like Bella and Amelia were that morning) and enthusiastically said, "Oh, Evie, this is so excitin'! Don't yeh think?"

Evie lovingly smiled up at him and then bluntly stated, "I'm actually a little nervous."

Ellis smiled even bigger. "Aw, hell, girl. Yeh got this!"

He embraced her once more to where she almost lost her breath, and then Ellis and his enormous dog took off in the direction of the waterfall cave. Before he was entirely out of sight, he hollered, "Show 'em what ye're made of, kid!"

Evie smiled as she watched the giant man and giant dog cross the bridge and out of sight. She then turned around and walked into Regina's home to find Callais, Newton, Regina, and Marina all talking around the small table. Evie cleared her throat to get their attention. They turned towards her and gave her smiling nods. Marina then shuffled over and gave Evie a hug. Bella again saw Apollo and Darwin and quickly enlisted her furry friends to play. Soon, the dogs happily fled out the door, barking and wagging their tails. Callais chuckled again as he lovingly watched the dogs dart out of the dwelling and out of sight, which made Evie smile as well. She then thought, *Callais and other keepers must love their companions as much as I love my Bella.* Callais interrupted her thoughts as he motioned for Evie to sit. As she took her seat, Callais began to tell her, "Today, you and I are going to work on building up your strength and focusing on some of the powers you have already displayed. However, I am curious to know if there is something else you would like to focus on?"

Evie thought for a moment, and then, with some excitement, she answered, "Yes. I've seen several people make light orbs from their hands. I'd really like to know how to do that. It's so cool."

The elders at that table all laughed as Callais happily responded, "Well, that should be an easy goal since you have already surpassed that with the powers you have already demonstrated."

Callais then turned to the rest of the table and said to Regina, "Will you show Marina and Newton the ropes today? And please be sure that Marina meets up with Simone and Josephine. I would like Marina to work more on her powers as well."

Regina nodded in agreement and began quietly talking with Marina about their plans. Callais then turned to Evie as he slowly got up, motioned with his hand, and stated, "To the forest."

Evie got up and followed Callais up the root stairs and out the opening she had first entered when she came to Mari. Once outside the hidden city, she looked around the thick forest and wondered, *How am I going to even have enough room to train?* Callais seemed to have read her thoughts and said, "We will work on the light orbs later, but for the first part of your training, I want to see if you can find the objects I have hidden in the forest."

Evie gave him an inquiring look but just shrugged her shoulders and began to walk into the thick, close-leaning trees that seemed capable of hiding anything. Callais then gently pulled her arm back. "No, Evie, with your mind," he said and gave her a wink.

Evie looked back at him, slightly baffled, and went to open her mouth to ask how, as Callais added, "I need you to find these objects I hid by going into your mind and finding my memories of where I placed them."

Evie, again, gave Callais a confused look before asking, "How?"

Callais then explained that it was similar to traveling the star trails and the dreams, but this time she would be focusing on a specific memory to find what was lost and not a place or a person. Evie shook her head, thinking she wouldn't be able to do what Callais had asked, but shrugged her shoulders and decided to try anyway. She then closed her eyes and began to focus on Callais as she fell further into the depths of her mind. Her mind was foggy at first, but soon, she began to see a shadow moving around in the hazy mist. She concentrated on the shadow, and as it came into view, she saw that it was indeed Callais walking slowly through the forest.

She continued to watch Callais in her mind as he placed a small item under a tree root. Evie was standing behind Callais, and when he moved away, she saw the item was a small figurine of a soldier. Callais then moved forward into the forest and placed another item in another tree knot. As Evie watched, she saw the second item was another small toy soldier. Evie followed Callais once more to see him place a third small toy soldier in a little creek that was rushing and twisting rapidly through the forest and moss-covered rocks. Callais then turned to her and smiled. Evie took this as an indication that all the items were hidden. Evie then opened her eyes to see Callais staring intently at her when he asked, "Did you find them?"

"Yes," Evie replied, absolutely shocked that she was able to actually find them in her mind.

"Now, I need you to bring them here," Callais said with a small smile lingering on his lips.

Evie looked around the deep woods, shrugged again, and took a step into the forest to find these items. Callais touched her arm once more. "No, Evie. Bring them here with your mind."

Evie gave him a dumbfounded look. "What? Bring them here? How?"

Callais, once again, patiently explained, "Magnus was one of the few who could do this... bring an item to him that he thought of. So, do not be upset if you cannot achieve this goal. I want to test how much of your innate power you actually possess. This will give me a good idea of what to train you on."

"You have too much faith in me, I think," Evie said as she gave him a worried look.

Callais chuckled. "Again, this is not a test to see whether you can do it or not, but to see what your powers truly are so I know where to start."

He paused for a moment and then added, "From what Magnus had told me, it is the same as traveling through the stars and dreams. However, instead of taking yourself to the item, you make it come to you. Like I said, this is something that only Magnus could do, and I, only once, was able to do. So, I am only curious at this point if you can do it."

Evie didn't know what to say. So, she just shrugged again, decided to give it a try, and closed her eyes (this time with a bit more trepidation). Soon, she began to see the fog drifting in her mind before it slowly lifted and her surroundings became clear. When she found the location of the first soldier, she focused as hard as she could on the small figurine. She then tried to move it;

however, it was much heavier than Evie anticipated. Evie concentrated even harder, but her head began to hurt. So, she pushed through the pain like she had done in the past. After a few minutes of struggling to move the soldier, she found herself lifting the soldier from under the root and into the air in front of her. In her mind, Evie began to pull the tiny figure with her, back the way she came, back into the swirling fog. Just as Evie started to get the soldier into the fog, she felt her mind begin to spin, like it did when she first looked at the scrolls and maps. Evie tried even harder, but her mind began to spin wildly around in the thick fog. Evie gasped for air—unable to hold the figure in her mind any longer—then opened her eyes and fell to the ground at Callais's feet. It took her a minute to collect herself before she stood up and apologetically shook her head. "I'm so sorry. I tried, I really did, but it was just too much."

Evie raised her head to match Callais's gaze and saw he was standing there with a look of shock on his face. He then held out his hand, and to her amazement, the small toy soldier was in his palm.

The stunned Callais shook his head, turned, and started walking back into Mari in complete silence. Evie, too nervous about disrupting his thoughts, just tailed Callais quietly back into Regina's home to find it empty. Callais sat heavily in a chair by the table, still looking with disbelief at the small figure in his hand. He eventually broke the silence, still shaking his head. "Evie, this is amazing… This is something I have not seen done effectively since Magnus."

He paused again for a long time and then continued. "You have so much more power than I originally thought. I need time to think and reassess how to continue your training."

Callais gave Evie a gentle smile and placed his hand on hers. "You really are who we need, and I am so glad to have you by my side."

Chapter 4

FIRST ENCOUNTERS

◆•————————●————————•◆

After her day in the forest with Callais, Evie dreamt that night of a place she had never seen before. It was a beautiful place, permeated by a distant golden glow, full of vibrantly colored plants and flowers covering a large rolling sea of meadows surrounded by towering mountains. At the foot of the mountains, a small waterfall poured into a river that cascaded across the valley, feeding into a sparkling lake at the meadow's edge. Evie saw three small children, two boys and one girl, playing by the lake, so she slowly walked over to them. As Evie approached the children, she realized they couldn't see her (or at least didn't acknowledge her presence), so Evie decided to just watch them play.

The three children played chase with each other, laughing and giggling as they gleefully ran around. At one point, the little girl picked up a bright yellow flower and whispered something into her hands. The flower then floated out of her palm, dancing and gliding around gracefully in the air before landing on one of the small boys. The boy looked at the flower that had landed on his shoulder and turned to the girl, saying, "Rosalina, they said to not use your powers yet."

The girl giggled. "Oh, Camulos. It is just a flower."

The young Camulos then balled his fist in playful jest when the other young boy came behind him and grabbed Camulos in his arms. "Got you. Now you are the king."

Camulos laughed, then turned and chased him through the fields while yelling, "I will get you, Magnus. You will be the king."

As the boys merrily chased each other, the young girl (Rosalina) turned towards Evie's direction and seemed to actually be looking right at Evie. Evie was frozen, realizing she was seeing Magnus and Camulos as children. Soon, Rosalina slowly approached her and wistfully said, "See, there was once love."

Rosalina suddenly became a blur, and the young girl faded into an old woman standing in the meadow. The ancient woman—who Evie assumed was still Rosalina— reached her hand out to Evie. "You will know where to find me soon, but do not speak of this until then."

Evie was still shocked and didn't know what to think,

but before she could say anything, the meadow and mountains soon began to swirl rapidly around her. Evie was pulled back into the thick stars, foggy dream mist, and then slowly back to her bed in Amelia's room.

***

Evie slowly sat up and shook her head, wanting to desperately wake Amelia and tell her what she had seen in her dream. She then remembered the woman's words, *to not speak of this yet.* Evie shook her head and realized that Magnus and Camulos must have had a sister that no one knew of—Rosalina. Evie thought, *Oh my gosh, she must still be alive*! Evie had an overpowering feeling to wake her friend and tell her everything, but she suppressed the urge as Bella jumped in her lap. Evie decided to whisper to Bella her dream to at least have someone know what she knew. Bella seemed to enjoy the secret and nibbled Evie's ear as the two of them snuggled back into bed.

***

Evie must have overslept. She woke to find Otto and Amelia's home empty and a note on the table from Otto, telling her to meet Callais in the council room when she got up. Evie smiled when she saw a small drawing of Bella at the bottom of the note (which she assumed was from Amelia). Evie ate, got herself ready, and made her way to the council room. As she passed Regina's house, she saw Marina, Simone, Emmeline, and Regina sitting around the table. So, Evie popped in, gave a quick hug to Marina, and headed back out.

As Evie entered the council room, she saw that Callais was already there with several council members, including Otto and Ellis. Once Ellis saw Evie, he gave her a giant bear hug before heading out of the room. As always, Bella drafted Darwin and Apollo to go play with her. Before the happy dogs left the council room, Apollo did something he hadn't done before. He came to Evie's side and nuzzled his nose against her hand. Evie then bent down and gave Apollo a hug and kiss. This made Apollo wiggle his butt with delight as he gave her a wet kiss back and bolted out the door to join his friends. Although Evie had been around Apollo many times, she wondered why he did this, but pushed the thought aside and assumed he was just trying to reassure her and give her comfort (like he knew she had to go through so many new challenges). Evie was just happy again to have so many people and animals around her that she loved and that loved her back. She also thought again about asking Callais or Newton how their dogs always seemed to appear when they needed them. Still, once again, she pushed this thought aside as well—since she already had so much on her plate.

After a few more minutes of waiting, the rest of the council members left, and Evie was left in the room with just Callais, Newton, and Lincoln. As Evie took a seat and waited for the men in the room to tell her the plan, she began to analyze Lincoln for a bit as the others talked. She noticed he was much taller and leaner than Callais and had deep brown skin, hair, and eyes. Evie assumed he was close to Callais's age since Lincoln also had some gray streaks in his hair. Still, he had no distinct features like Josephine, Simone, Atlas, or others she had noticed. So, she assumed Lincoln was from the Devas galaxy.

Evie's thoughts were soon interrupted when Declan came bumbling in, doing a balancing act with his arms full of scrolls, papers, and a platter of food. He placed some things down on the table and looked up at Evie. Evie realized she hadn't had much interaction with Declan since their return to Antillis and was glad to see him. Declan then winked at her once he set a few more things down and gave her a big smile, which Evie quickly returned with flushed cheeks—so she swiftly turned her head so he wouldn't see her blushing. Declan eventually took a seat at the table after putting the rest of his supplies down, which surprised Evie. Before she could say anything, Callais looked directly at Evie and told her, "Lincoln and Newton will be training Declan today, and then they will be joining us later."

Evie looked at Callais with questioning eyes, but again, Callais seemed to read her thoughts and explained, "I still have not figured out how best to train you, but I think that having a team of trainers will be helpful." Callais took a short pause. "I also think it is important that you have a person by your side wherever you go."

He rubbed his chin as if he was trying to think of the right words to say before he went on, "We believe that training Declan to be your 'right-hand man' will be beneficial in moving forward. You will need someone to ground you besides Bella and the elders."

Newton then interjected, "We also think training Amelia will be important, too. Your friendship is obviously strong, but she does not come from a bloodline of keepers. However, Declan does, as to why we also think this will be a good partnership."

Evie glanced at Declan again, who was beaming with pride. She then turned to the other men in the room and nodded in agreement while trying to suppress her blushing with this news that Declan would be working closely with her. Callais then spoke to the others, saying, "Before we head our separate ways to train, I believe that we should look over some of these scrolls we have with Evie to see if there is anything she can see that we have not been able to."

Again, they all nodded in agreement as Lincoln began to unroll the scrolls in the middle of the table. Lincoln then told Evie that although he was the head keeper of Alderbard once, he had left so long ago that many things had changed. He then said that whatever help Evie could give would be beneficial in helping Otto's team (since there were many things about Alderbard he didn't know anymore).

Evie nodded her head in agreement, then positioned herself in the center of the table and looked at the open scrolls. As before, the words, symbols, and drawings on the scrolls began to move. This time they didn't move as rapidly as they had in the past. Again, they seemed to be arranging themselves in a particular order. Evie gave the scrolls a curious gaze (which she had learned was helpful in preventing her head from hurting when analyzing something new). Once the scrolls stopped moving, Evie saw several objects light up and appear across the Devas galaxy map on the table next to the scrolls. The map then made a rapid movement. Soon, a small, blueish planet was levitating off the map as objects began to light up across the surface. Evie then realized she wasn't sure what she should be looking for. So, she turned to Callais and said, "There are a few items on the map that are lighting up…Can you see those?"

Callais gently shook his head when Evie continued. "Well, I'm not sure what we are supposed to be looking for, but there are four objects across this map that are focused on a single planet. However, I'm also not sure what this planet is or what I should be showing you."

Callais leaned over Evie in an attempt to see what she was seeing but couldn't. Evie described once again what she was seeing. After she finished, he put the pieces together and said, "This is the planet Alderbard that you are seeing," Callais paused for a moment and then stated, "We are trying to find anything relevant for Otto's team before they leave. So, if you see anything that would be useful, or that would help aid Otto, that is what we want for now."

Evie looked down again and focused more on the objects that were lit up across the planet. She pointed at one area on the map and said to the men in the room, "This area here has a home or settlement of some sort on it."

Evie reached out and touched the lit-up home as two more objects, similar to the first one, also lit up. Evie pointed these out as well. Callais then turned to

Declan and asked, "Can you please go get Elizabeth? I would like to see if she can confirm if these are areas of people in hiding on Alderbard."

Declan nodded and ran out of the room to fetch Elizabeth. Evie glanced back at the map once Declan left and pointed to another object on the map. "This seems to be some kind of staff. However, it keeps spinning around, pointing to different directions."

Evie pointed at the different directions that staff would stop on when Newton stated, "Maybe there are protector staffs still on Alderbard we are not aware of."

Callais and Lincoln nodded in agreement as Evie focused on the map and pointed out another object. "This right here... must be the ship that Otto mentioned in the council meeting, but it also seems to be surrounded by a few smaller ships as well."

Callais, Lincoln, and Newton all seem to beam with excitement with this detail. Lincoln enthusiastically rubbed his hands together, saying, "This is great news! There must be more than one ship."

Evie smiled, happy she was able to give them some good news. She then turned her focus back to the map when another object lit up that wasn't there before. Evie went to point it out but then hesitated. As she looked closer, it was the face of the woman, Rosalina, from her dream that night. Evie remembered Rosalina's words, and although she felt guilty for not letting Callais and the others know this, something inside her told her that it was important for this to remain a secret. Evie made a mental note of where she saw Rosalina on the map, looked back at the men in the room, and shrugged. "That's all I can find for now."

The others seemed happy with this news as Newton gave Evie a loving pat on the back, and Lincoln spread out another scroll over the map. Evie went to look at the new scroll, expecting it to be much easier to read because she had gained more focus and strength since she first began reading the scrolls. However, to her surprise, this scroll began spinning out of control. Evie was a little shocked by this but decided to lightly focus on the scroll like she had done in the past. However, this time, it didn't stop spinning around. Again, Evie's head began to hurt as she tried to concentrate harder, but to no avail. The scroll would just not stop swirling around. Evie looked up at the men and shook her head in disappointment. "I'm sorry, but I can't seem to focus on this one for some reason."

Callais slightly nodded, and Evie could tell he was just as disappointed as she was about this. But before Callais or Evie could say anything, Declan returned to the room with Elizabeth. Lincoln removed the unreadable scroll from the table to reveal the map of Alderbard again as Elizabeth approached the table. Evie smiled at her, but Elizabeth turned her head down and asked, "What did you need me for?"

Callais told Elizabeth that Evie had spotted some places on the map and wanted confirmation if these were settlements where survivors were hiding on Alderbard. Callais then turned his head to Evie and nodded. Evie, once more, pointed out the settlements to Elizabeth.

Elizabeth looked at the areas Evie pointed out. As Elizabeth was focused on the map, Evie took in her features. Elizabeth was small in stature and very petite like Evie. She had dark, wavy black hair, and although her skin was not as dark as her hair, it was a deep brown. Elizabeth had hazel eyes, and even though it wasn't as noticeable as Evie's freckles, she did have a light covering of freckles across her cheeks. Again, Evie noticed that Elizabeth had features like an average human and decided Elizabeth was also from Devas. Evie also noticed a sadness in Elizabeth's eyes, and she didn't smile (which made Evie wonder why and what had happened to her). After looking over the map, Elizabeth interrupted Evie's thoughts. She confirmed two of the four locations Evie had previously pointed out. Elizabeth then said to Evie, "The other two areas you pointed out, I'm not sure of." She turned to the others in the room, saying, "However, I left Alderbard quite some time ago, so there may be new areas of people in hiding."

Elizabeth then pointed at an area of the map that was not lit up. "This is where we can find Leo. I already told Otto about this area." She paused, looked at the map once more, turned to Evie again, and asked, "Where was one of the other areas you pointed out?"

Evie looked at the map and pointed at one area Elizabeth hadn't confirmed, and Elizabeth shook her head. So, Evie pointed to the last area. Elizabeth screwed her face up a bit and said, "This area, I believe, is a protected area from the fourth-day spells. However, everyone who has gone there said there was nothing there, just a giant lake."

She paused for a brief moment and then finished, "There is a legend that there is an underwater city on Alderbard, but no one knows how to get there. So, I'm unsure if it really exists or not."

Evie glanced down at the map one last time. For a brief moment, Evie saw Rosalina's face again, right over the legendary underwater city. Evie gasped. The others all turned to her with questioning eyes. Evie remembered her secret and quickly said, "Sorry. It's nothing. I just thought it was cool that there might be an underwater city."

Callais and Newton chuckled a bit as they thanked Elizabeth for her time, and she headed out of the council room. Once she was gone, Newton turned to Declan and asked, "Is it okay if we share one last thing with Evie about Clara?"

Declan nodded his head. "Well, if we're going to be partners, she might as well know everything I know." He gave Evie a wink, which (of course) made her blush.

Newton then pulled out the book on Clara (the one Evie had found back on Terran). Newton opened the book and began to speak. "This is a very fascinating piece, and even more interesting that you found it on Terran. We have reason to believe this was a book Magnus wrote himself because it recounts some of Magnus's visits to the Devas galaxy after the break and Camulos's invasion."

Newton paused and then continued. "It seems that at one point, Clara was one of the keepers that Magnus highly trusted on his visits back, and he divulged information to Clara about his plans and intentions."

He took a deep breath and went on, "To make a long story short, it seems that towards the end of Magnus's travels, he began keeping notes of behavioral changes in Clara; however, some of the notes are unclear about what Magnus knew. Although much of it is not clear to us yet, we believe this might be useful in determining who might be spies for the Camulus forces. We may be able to identify behavioral changes or patterns in these spies due to the torture they endured. It might also be useful for us in helping us figure out how Magnus was able to find Terran once it was cast out of the Devas system and how he traveled back and forth undetected by the Camulus forces. If we can figure this out, we may be able to travel to Terran when the time is right... or at least keep it hidden from Camulos if we are to fail."

Evie forced a smile, thinking about the last time she traveled with Callais to Terran, and the weird star vortex appeared out of nowhere. She also thought about how she and Callais almost got caught on their way back into Devas and hoped Newton was right (that they could figure out a way to get to and from Terran without being caught). She also wanted to figure this out so she could see David, Ruby, and her family again, or at least make sure they would stay protected if they couldn't find a way to defeat Camulos. Evie then caught a glimpse of Declan out of the corner of her eye. His head was hanging down a bit, and she could see the pain in his eyes. Evie couldn't tell if he was upset or disappointed about the news of his mother possibly being a spy. She wanted to reach out and hug him but resisted the urge since she wasn't really sure if this would make him feel better. Evie had been quiet for a while as she thought about all of this information. She turned and noticed Newton was giving her a curious look. Evie gave him another small smile and nodded but didn't say anything. Newton realized she needed time to process everything and smiled back before saying, "I will be working with Lincoln and Declan today on researching key characteristics we need to identify in spies as well as training Declan on his powers. Once we meet later, I will have myself or Declan teach you what we have learned."

Evie again nodded in agreement, and with that, Newton gathered the book and waved his hand at Lincoln and Declan. Then the three of them headed out of the council room, leaving Callais and Evie alone. Once they were gone, Evie looked over at Callais, who was now smiling from ear to ear. Evie had never seen him smile this big, and come to think of it, she couldn't remember if she had seen Callais smile at all, only chuckle a bit. Evie admired Callais's smile (which made him much more handsome), and then she curiously asked, "What?"

Callais continued his smile and happily motioned his hand. "Come... I have thought of something to train you on today... I think you will like it." Evie smiled back, and with some nervous excitement, she followed Callais back out to the forest.

This time, when they reached the forest's edge, they didn't stop but went further in. Evie assumed that the previous day's task wasn't on the agenda and followed Callais. After walking through the thick forest (Evie taking a few missteps), they came to a tiny clearing under the massive trees. Callais then turned to Evie with his big grin and asked, "Do you want to learn to fly?"

Evie gasped, jumped up and down, and loudly shouted out, "YES!"

Callais chuckled again before saying, "We have a lot to work on, but I think teaching you how to use the element of air will be very useful."

Evie gave him another curious look and was ready to ask him a question, but he seemed to read her thoughts again and began to tell her, "There are many elements in the Devas galaxy that can be manipulated by a keeper to enhance their powers. It seems that you have an innate knack for the use of light and possibly water since you can use the chain effectively in navigating the star trails." He paused for a moment before continuing. "And since you were able to move the toy soldier with your mind through the fog, I believe you might also have strength in the element of air. So today, I would like to test your abilities with air."

Evie smiled. She was excited about this but then

became nervous and asked, "What if I get in the air and fall?"

Callais gave her a reassuring smile before replying, "Fortunately, I have been lucky enough to be trained by Newton when I was younger in the use of air. Newton is the absolute best keeper in the manipulation of air. So, if you begin to fall, do not worry. I will be here."

Evie smiled again as Callais added one last note. "Also, Newton will be here later, and you will be lucky enough to be trained by him as well."

Evie's smile broadened as she thought about how Newton saved her from falling out of the window back on Canopiuis. She instantly felt comforted to have both of these brave and powerful men helping her through all of this. Evie then turned her focus back on Callais. She watched as he closed his eyes and began making slow, intricate movements with his body. It was like a slow dance—to Evie, it kind of looked like he was doing Tai Chi. Evie could feel the air begin to flow and circulate around Callais's body as he continued to gracefully move his body around. As Evie watched him, in one swift and precise movement, he slowly levitated off the ground. She was amazed as Callais floated further up, above the tree line, and almost out of sight. Then, with a sudden bright crack of sparkling blue light, Callais was back on the ground next to her. Evie gleefully clapped her hands together. Callais smiled again and nodded at her. "Now your turn."

Evie was about to ask how when he added, "Again, it is like traveling the star trails, but this time, you have no destination… just think of floating."

Evie closed her eyes and began to see the fog roll in when Callais interjected one last time. "Concentrate on the flow of air around you. Move your body in the direction the element leads you. It doesn't matter where you feel the air, but whenever you feel it, just move whatever body part it is touching." He paused and then added, "It also helps to think of something you have seen float."

Evie closed her eyes again, followed Callais's instructions, and began to think of things that could float in the air. She remembered the flower that Rosalina had lifted into the air before it softly landed on Camulos. Evie soon became lost in her thoughts of Rosalina's flower and how it gently floated up out of her hands and danced in the air. As Evie began to focus on the flower, she began to feel the air swirl around her. A light breeze touched her arm, so she moved her arm in the direction of the flow. She then felt a stronger gust of air pass across her left leg, so she moved her leg in the direction of the current. The air then began to thicken and swirl around her entire body, so she just let herself follow whatever direction the energy led her. After a few minutes of moving around with the air, she began to feel like she was one with the element—she felt peaceful and powerful all at once.

Before long, she heard from a distance Callais call out her name. She quickly opened her eyes, and to her amazement, she found that she was several yards off the ground. Instantly, Evie became scared, lost her concentration, and began to rapidly plummet downwards. Before she hit the forest floor, her body stopped, and she found herself levitating a few feet off the ground. She was utterly baffled and looked towards Callais to see that he was holding his arms outwards in her direction. Evie immediately realized he was the one who was preventing her from crashing to the ground. Once again, she was amazed by his abilities. Callais slowly lowered his hand as Evie gently landed on the soft, crunchy leaves and damp earth. He then came over to Evie, laughing and clapping. "Fantastic, Evie. Once again, you have strong powers to get that on your first try… Shall we try once more? This time without you falling?"

Evie was still shaken up a bit but nodded at Callais, gathered herself, and closed her eyes again. As before, she thought of Rosalina's flower and concentrated on the flow of the air around her. Evie soon felt herself lifting up into the air and opened her eyes to see she was several yards off the ground again. This time, she maintained her composure and continued thoughts of the floating flower and the currents around her. As she got higher into the air, she found herself above the tree line over the massive forest. Evie smiled, feeling very proud of herself, and continued her thoughts of the flower. As her mind began to wander, she found herself thinking of the flower landing on Camulos. In her mind's eye, she watched the flower gently land on Camulos's shoulder. Then something happened that hadn't happened before. The young Camulos turned his gaze to Evie as a fierce glint entered his eye, and then an evil smile turned on the young boy's lips. Evie then heard in her mind, "*Ah, yes... There you are. So, you are real, girl.*"

Instantly, Evie felt a burning sensation in the back of her neck, sending daggers of pain through her skull, leaving black spots drifting in her vision. She then felt her body freeze in midair, and she couldn't move. Evie felt the element and power slowly drain from her body and mind. She then became scared and thought she would begin to tumble to the ground. However, instead of falling to the ground this time, Evie began to spin wildly around in the air. Her whole body soon began to throb with pain. She felt nauseous as she desperately tried to fight against the sickening force that was throwing her body and mind into frenzied chaos. Evie felt frantic as she attempted to regain control but couldn't. Her head then started to hurt so badly she felt as though she would soon pass out.

Before the intense pain could completely consume her, she suddenly felt a strong jolt pull on her body and a force that seemed to be dragging her downwards. Whatever force was pulling her down then stopped, and she started falling again, tumbling below the tree line. As Evie spun downwards, she felt another strong energy push on her body. She could feel it slowing down her descent, and the horrible pain that was cascading throughout her whole body began to subside as well. Just as she thought she was safe, Evie started to rapidly spiral downwards again, so she closed her eyes and weakly cried out for help. She heard panicked voices all around her crying out for help, and just before she hit the ground, she felt her body collapse into someone's arms. She slowly opened her eyes to see that Declan had caught her just in time. Before she could say anything, she felt her body and mind slip into a deep agonizing pain, and as it filled her soul, everything went dark, and she passed out.

Chapter 5
CAMULOS AND MAGNUS BATTLE

As Evie's mind spiraled into the darkness, she tried to fight through the pain that consumed her body and mind. But no matter how hard she fought, the immense pain continued to increase. So, she decided to just let her body submit to the agony and hoped there would be an end. She felt as though she would continue to fall through the darkness for the rest of time. But then she felt the pain begin to subside, and her body and mind began to move towards something. Before long, the blackness around her faded, and faint lights and shadows replaced the endless dark space. Again, the shadows and lights flickered in her mind for some time. Soon, she found the lights and haze begin to lift, and her body stopped.

It took a moment for everything to clear up around her. When the space around her became visible, Evie found herself standing on a cliff, overlooking a massive battle that was taking place in the valley below. There were warriors of every shape, color, and size, swinging or firing weapons, delivering heavy blows at anything they could hit. Flashes of light streaked across the field, hitting warriors and catching them on fire or turning them into plumes of dust. Fireballs were cascading across the sky, hitting groups of warriors and burning them where they stood. There were giant boulders caught up in dust tornados, barreling through the valley, catching warriors up in its force, flinging and crashing their bodies on the ground or against the cliff walls. It was a complete massacre, and Evie was absolutely horrified. Before she could scream out for all of this to stop, she heard a voice behind her say, "So Magnus, have you finally come to your senses and decided to join me?"

Evie instantly realized she must be dreaming as Magnus, dreaming one of his memories again. Magnus (or Evie) slowly turned around to see a tall, skinny, hooded figure standing behind him. Evie couldn't see the hooded figure's face, but she assumed this must be Camulos. Evie could feel a deep rage building inside Magnus as he answered, "Brother, why would I join you in such madness and destruction? Is this the universe you desire?"

Camulos scornfully laughed, and then, with a growl in his voice, he said, "These wars would end, brother, if you would join me. There would be no reason for us to continue to fight if you could just see I am right… if you could just see how wrong the mother and father are."

Evie, again, could feel the rage increasing inside Magnus. However, underneath all the anger, there was deep sorrow and pain. Magnus then shook his head. "My dear brother, what you are searching for, what you think you will find, or what you think you will accomplish will only lead to more death and destruction. Following this dark path will not save us… it will destroy us."

Camulos then manically laughed and pulled his hood back. Evie gasped. Camulos looked bloodless with dark blue bags under his eyes, and his flesh was so thin he almost looked hollow. Evie could feel Magnus's pain as he looked at his brother, and Evie knew that Magnus was just as shocked to see his brother this way. Camulos looked like the death and destruction he was causing was taking a terrible toll on his body. Camulos then snarled, "So, Magnus, are you telling me you will not be joining my mission?"

Magnus mournfully shook his head. "No, brother. I will not be joining you." He paused before sadly saying, "I will be ending you."

Camulos let out an insane cackle. "Have it your way, brother. I will enjoy destroying you."

Camulos then moved his hands up from his sides, placed his palms towards the sky, and lifted his head upwards. Red light and dark smoke began to swirl around his body, and the air began to thicken around him. The ground started to rumble and shake under Magnus's feet, and as Magnus looked up, Evie could see the sky starting to fill with dark clouds as more red flashing lights streaked across the sky. As Camulos continued to command the energies and elements around him, Evie started to feel the energies increasing inside her (or inside Magnus). It was an overwhelming feeling, and she began to feel scared. As the power inside Magnus started to flow through every atom of his body, Evie felt consumed by the awesomeness of the elements Magnus was commanding. She felt every inch of her body and mind fill up with absolutely indescribable energies—it was pure power. Evie then watched as Camulos began to move his hands together, but before he could release his powers on Magnus… Magnus released first.

Everything Magnus had been holding inside him was freed from his body all at once. Flashes of every color of light, accompanied by forceful wind gusts, water walls, and electric streams of blue energy, completely surrounded Camulos. His body then levitated into the air as Magnus's powers wildly thrashed Camulos around.

Evie thought Camulos was done for, when somehow, Camulos regained control and released a powerful blast of scarlet energy back at Magnus. Magnus then dropped to the ground, and Evie could feel the blow from Camulos sucking the life away from Magnus. Now Evie was terrified. The pain in Magnus's body was complete agony as Magnus struggled to fight back with every breath, and Evie believed he was within an inch of crossing death's door. But before she thought Magnus would die, he summoned what remaining energy he had and bellowed, "Illudis Consummaris!"

All the energy Magnus had conjured then went billowing in Camulos's direction and hit him. Evie watched the power Magnus had released fling Camulos into the air as more flashes of light and energy relentlessly crashed across Camulos's body. Camulos then screamed out in agony, trying to fight back. Once again, Evie thought this was the end for Camulos when another bright flash of red light and dark smoke expelled from Camulos's hands and hit Magnus again. Magnus was soon surrounded by crimson flames, and with every breath he took, he inhaled putrid fumes of black smoke. Evie could feel another bout of excruciating and maddening pain cascade throughout Magnus's body. Evie could tell Magnus was struggling to regain energy and fight back this time. However, Magnus reached to the core of his body and pulled on the last bit of life he had left. He then barely mumbled, "Domuis."

A blinding light then flashed and surrounded Evie, Magnus, and Camulos. Before she could process anything, Evie found her body quickly whisked upwards, whisked into the sky, and back into the stars. She then found herself floating again in deep space, and she felt herself begin to cry. However, she knew she was crying Magnus's tears.

***

Evie woke after the nightmarish memory to find herself in Regina's home laid out across the table. She went to move her body but quickly realized she couldn't. She then tried to speak but also found this to be a challenge. She discovered the agony Magnus had suffered in the dream (memory) was anguish that was now inside her body as well. Finally, with a tremendous amount of pain, she managed to slowly turn her head to see Amelia standing close by. However, before she could attempt to do or say anything, Amelia saw Evie was awake and began to frantically gesture her hands. Regina noticed this and immediately rushed over to Evie's side and began to rub potions across Evie's forehead. She then gently cooed, "You are okay. Just stay still for now."

Evie, realizing she was safe, closed her eyes as everything quickly became black. Not long after her eyes were closed, the thick, hazy dream fog came rolling swiftly into her mind. She desperately tried to fight it. She didn't want to fall into another horrible dream... another horrible memory. But she couldn't fight it, and the dream fog continued to take her away.

Chapter 6

ROSALINA ENCOUNTER

❖•────────●────────•❖

Although Evie's physical body was weak from her last dream, as the misty fog tumbled around in her mind, she felt some force behind the haze that began to strengthen her. As she became stronger, Evie began to wander through the cloudy dream vapors as if she was searching for something she had lost but couldn't remember what it was. She wasn't sure what she was looking for but had an overwhelming feeling to keep moving in the direction she was headed. After a few more minutes of navigating through the flickering shadows and swirling fog, the shadowy gray haze lifted, and she found herself in a small cave that was dripping with sparkling water. As Evie looked around the damp cave, still unsure what she was looking for, she heard a muffled bark coming from a large opening on the far side of the cave wall. Evie weakly hollered out, "Bella?"

The muffled bark immediately returned Evie's call, and she quickly scurried down the opening towards her beloved dog. As Evie navigated through the dark, twisting path, she could smell the wet dirt and felt the slippery rocks slide under her hands as she braced herself against the walls. She struggled through the path for a few more minutes. Soon, she saw a small light at the end and made her way as fast as possible to where the light was shining while calling out for Bella. When she reached the lit opening, Evie found Bella patiently waiting for her. Bella quickly came to Evie's side as Evie scooped her up, and Bella happily gave her a wet kiss on the nose. Evie sighed in relief and snuggled Bella up into her arms, burying her face in Bella's soft, wiry fur.

As she pulled her face away and looked around, she found herself in a much larger cave that was lit up with bright, sparkling purple orbs. The room was obviously someone's living space because it looked similar to a living room. Then Evie nervously thought, *But whose living space?* Evie stood there for a bit longer, too scared to move forward. Before she could think any longer, a door on the far side of the room creaked open. Evie took a step back and thought of going back the way she came, but she felt the overwhelming force come back, giving her more strength. As the door slowly inched open, a small, old woman shuffled across the floor towards Evie—which she immediately recognized as Rosalina.

Evie analyzed Rosalina and thought, *Rosalina must be ancient; she looks much older than anyone I have met so far.* Rosalina's hair was completely white, and there wasn't much there. She was so wrinkled it was hard to make out where her eyes began and her chin ended. As Rosalina glanced up at Evie, Evie realized she had the eye color of a cat. They were sparkly golden in color and even in the shape of a cat's—like Josephine's eyes. With a harder look, Evie realized that between the wrinkles on Rosalina's neck, there was a red scar that went from one side of her neck to the other side—like her throat had been slit. Rosalina then approached Evie and looked her directly in the eyes, saying, "You have found yourself a very good companion." Rosalina smiled at Bella and went on, "We do not have much time. You need to know that Camulos now knows you exist, and it will not be long before he figures out where you are."

Rosalina paused, then slowly walked over to Evie. Once she reached Evie's side, Rosalina moved Evie's hair over and touched the back of her neck. Evie instantly felt a burning pain in the spot where Rosalina was touching. But before she could say anything, Rosalina said, "It seems Camulos may have marked you. I know that he has not mastered his mark, but I am sure it will not be long before he figures out how to use this spell to find you. You need to learn to strengthen your powers to hide."

Evie touched the painful spot on the back of her neck and instantly became frightened, thinking about how she was now marked by this evil man. Before she could ask anything, Rosalina then held out her shaking hand to Evie. "Even though you are in the protected forest, if you do not learn how to protect yourself, he *will* find you. Like I said, Camulos's mark is not something that has been perfected. But once you are marked, he will be able to find you when he completes his spell. It is vital now that you go back and have your people train you on protection spells before you can move forward… it may be the only way to save you from his control once he figures out how to work his tracking spell."

Evie shook her head in vigorous agreement. She had so many questions for this woman, but before she could ask anything, Rosalina went on, "This will not be the last time we see each other. Remember, do not let anyone know about me yet. It is crucial for yours and the others' safety that you do not reveal I am alive."

Evie once again nodded in agreement, but before she could ask any questions, she felt a sharp, sudden pull from outside of her mind. Evie quickly fell back into the swirling fog as Rosalina slowly fell out of sight.

***

Evie woke up to find herself still on the table in Regina's home, but this time she could move. She slowly pulled herself upright, so she was sitting on the table. She tried to look around the room but realized her eyes were fuzzy and rubbed them. Evie then felt Bella give her a wet kiss on the nose, and Apollo let out a bark. When she moved her hands away and was able to focus clearly, she saw Declan standing right in front of her with his back turned. Bella then wagged her tail as Apollo let out a happy whine to get the others' attention. Declan turned his head, saw that Evie was awake, and immediately grabbed her up in a firm embrace, making Evie wince in pain. He quickly pulled away and apologized, but Evie gently smiled, looked at Declan's worried face, and reassuringly told him, "I'm fine. I promise… just a little sore." She then wearily shook her head and asked, "What happened?"

As Evie spoke, Amelia, Regina, and Callais heard her voice and came rushing from across the room, all with worried looks across their face. As they approached the table, Evie held her hand up and, once again, stated, "I promise I'm fine."

Everyone took a big sigh of relief as Callais came closer to the table and asked her, "What happened up there, Evie?"

Evie gave him a baffled look and shook her head in confusion before replying, "I was hoping you would tell me what happened."

Callais then began to explain to her that she was doing well, when suddenly, she began to swing violently around the air. He then told her, "Newton must have been training Declan nearby because he saw you spinning in the air and had to use much of his own powers to bring you down to the ground... It was like your body was fighting Newton's powers." Callais paused, shaking his head, and then added, "Once Newton got you down, you began to fall so fast, I could not even catch you... Luckily, Declan is a fast runner and was able to catch you before you hit the ground."

Evie shook her head in disbelief and then looked at Declan. But unlike all the other times she looked at him and blushed, this time she saw him with new eyes and instantly felt comforted by the idea that Declan would be by her side through all of this. Evie then smiled at Declan as he placed his hand on her thigh and gave it a squeeze. "I promise, Evie, I will never let anything bad happen to you... ever!"

Evie then placed her hand over his and squeezed it back. "I know you will never leave my side... thank you so much!"

Declan gave her a loving smile back as the two held their hands in place for a bit longer. Newton then came towards the table using a cane, and Darwin stood next to his other side to support him. Evie's heart sank when she realized that Newton was injured as tears filled her eyes, and she regretfully shook her head. "Oh, god, Newton. I'm so sorry."

Newton placed his hand on her shoulder and gave it a loving squeeze. "No tears, girl. I am fine. Just need to regain some energy." He paused for a moment, tilted his head, gave Evie a curious look, and then asked, "What were you fighting up there? Can you remember?"

Evie rubbed her head as she slowly began to remember what happened. She explained everything to them— remembering to leave Rosalina out of the details. She also decided not to tell them of the dream she had of Magnus either. Something about the dream made her realize she had to think more about the meaning behind it. So, she just decided to tell them that before she began to lose control, she believed she heard Camulos's voice inside her head, which she also believed caused her to fall and pass out. When Evie finished her story, she looked around the room as each person's face became more sullen and worried. Newton then cleared his throat. "Well, you put up a good fight, and that is good news ... as for the rest, we have a lot to work on. It seems we may have less time than we thought."

Evie then saw Newton and Callais exchange worried glances. Before she could ask about this, she suddenly remembered what Rosalina told her and blurted out, "What about protection spells? Would they be useful to learn?"

Both Callais and Newton exchanged another glance that Evie couldn't interpret. But again, before Evie could say anything else, Callais answered, "Yes, I believe that would be an excellent idea." He then paused, and in a tone a father would use, he told Evie, "Now get some rest and let Regina finish her work."

Evie nodded in compliance as Callais, Newton, and their two faithful companions headed out of the room. Regina tried to shove Declan and Amelia out, but the two refused to leave. So, Regina shrugged her shoulders and let out an exasperated sigh, "Fine. Then you two need to make yourself useful and help me."

Amelia and Declan agreed as the three of them began

to pull items from the shelf. Knowing she was in good hands, Evie pulled Bella into her chest, laid back down, and fell asleep.

Chapter 7
DREAM CONTACT

◆━━━━━●━━━━━◆

After a few more days of sleeping, Evie woke one night to see that she and Regina were alone in the room. Evie slowly raised her head and mumbled Regina's name. Regina immediately came rushing to her side as Evie asked, "Where's everyone?"

Regina gently rubbed Evie's forehead, saying, "I sent them to the cave to find some more flowers for you. They did not want to leave your side, but I needed their help so I could stay on watch."

"I'm so glad to have so many people who care about me," Evie said with a grateful smile.

Evie then thought of David and Ruby and how much she missed them and asked Regina, "Can you help me tell my parents I'm okay again?"

Regina looked at the tired girl and wanted to tell her to wait until she had more strength, but shook her head in agreement because she knew how important it was to Evie. So, Regina slowly placed her hands on Evie's head and closed her eyes. Evie followed suit, touched Bella's head, and closed her eyes as well. She soon saw Regina walking through the dream fog, so Evie followed her. After a long time wandering through the swampy haze, the fog cleared, and Evie could see herself and Regina standing in front of David and Rudy. Evie bounced with excitement and ran towards them as Regina pulled her arm back. "They cannot see you as you are now. However, we can try and go further into the dream state to let them know you are okay."

Evie nodded and watched Regina place her arms outward as a small shimmering light extended from Regina's hands, landing on David and Ruby. Soon, the older couple lowered to the ground and closed their eyes. Regina then nodded to Evie, and Evie took this as her signal to start.

Even though Evie was in the dream fog with Regina, she closed her eyes again. Once her eyes were closed, she was surprised to see David and Ruby standing right in front of her. Evie didn't even think about how this was happening (she was just so excited to see them) and quickly ran over to them. David and Ruby seemed shocked to see Evie as well but didn't think twice about it, as they stretched their arms out, and the threesome were soon embracing each other. Happy tears were streaming down all of their faces, and when they finally let go and pulled back, David said, "Oh, sweetheart, we're so glad to see you." He then looked around his surroundings, trying to figure out what was happening, and asked, "Are we dreaming?"

Evie nodded yes and began to tell them she was using the dream state to find them with a woman named Regina. Evie then went on to tell them about everything that had been happening to her. However, she didn't want them to worry too much—so she left out some details. Although Evie hated lying to them, she knew that it would be too much to explain or for them to understand. After she finished telling as much as she could about what was happening, Evie also told them, "Regina says she can help me reach you in the dream state, but she also told me something about a watcher glass that could help us stay in communication without dreams. Do you think you may be able to ask someone in The Keeper's Order about this?"

Ruby gave Evie a quick smile and hug before she told Evie, "A woman we met named Nadia mentioned something about this, but she said she lost her glass… I'll ask her again to see if that is something we can find."

Evie smiled and gave Ruby another hug before saying, "I hope you find one. I miss you guys so much. I'd like to see you whenever I want and not just through dreams."

David and Ruby then wrapped their arms around her as David kissed her forehead, saying, "We will do everything we can to find a watcher glass. We miss you so much, sweetheart…We love you more than you'll ever know, our beautiful, brave girl!"

Evie smiled broadly, knowing that they loved her deeply, and they wanted her back just as much as she wanted to be back with them—and she desperately hoped that she would be soon.

David then began to tell Evie a little more about their own journey. After they finished telling Evie about everything they had been through—which also baffled Evie—David and Ruby told her that they found a woman named Sophia, Evie's aunt. Evie stood there completely shocked, shook herself, and excitedly blurted out, "What? I have an aunt?"

Ruby and David then told her everything Sophia had told them. When they finished, Evie was overwhelmed by all the information they had found out about her father. She began to cry, then shook her head in sudden realization. "Oh my God… Ellis is my uncle!"

Ruby gave her a hesitant look before she asked, "Is he a nice man?"

Evie smiled and wiped a tear away before she happily replied, "He's the greatest… and he takes really good care of me. I can't wait for you guys to meet him."

Ruby and David smiled as Ruby let out a sigh of relief and let her worries go with the news that Ellis was a good person taking care of Evie.

After talking a while longer, Evie heard Regina gently calling her name in her mind. She knew it was time to go. Evie embraced David and Ruby once more and said goodbye. She then drifted back into the fog. When she opened her eyes, she saw David and Ruby get up from the ground and walk away, holding onto one another. Regina then placed her hand on Evie's hand as they floated back into the hazy fog and sparkling stars again. It wasn't long before Evie found herself back in Regina's dwelling as tears began to well up in Evie's eyes, thinking of David and Ruby. Regina wiped a tear away and gently said, "Do not worry, child. Hopefully, you will be with them soon." She paused for a moment and, in a motherly tone, told Evie, "Now close your eyes and get some rest."

Evie nodded her head once more and slowly lowered herself on the table as Bella jumped up next to her, and the pair fell asleep.

Chapter 8
NEWTON AND DECLAN

ewton watched Declan from across the room as the boy scurried about collecting scrolls for the next council meeting. Newton smiled to himself, thinking about the young man he was so very proud of and how much he had grown since the moment Declan came into his life. As Newton continued to watch Declan, his thoughts wandered to those early years and how Declan became like a son to him.

When she was younger, Newton was Clara's trainer, and they, too, developed a very close relationship. Since Clara's parents had died when she was a child, Newton became like a father to her as well. After her training was completed with Newton, she went out into the Devas galaxy, and a few years had passed without Newton having any contact with Clara. Then, one day, Clara came to him, clearly pregnant. However, instead of being happy about her pregnancy, she was frightened and scared. She told Newton the reason for her fear was that her unborn child's father was a soldier in the Camulus forces. She explained that she had a quick and toxic love affair with the soldier, but the affair soon ended when he became violent and aggressive towards her. Clara had escaped him but learned shortly after that she was pregnant and had nowhere to go. After hearing her story, Newton didn't even hesitate to take her in, helped hide her, and was overjoyed to help her raise her child. Newton never pressed Clara about her relationship with the soldier or who he was. At that time, Newton never even considered that she might be a spy (since she was so scared). All Newton needed to know was that Clara was terrified, and he wanted to make sure she and her child were safe.

So, Newton watched Declan grow and enjoyed every moment of it. Declan was rambunctious and curious about everything and always collected insects and frogs that he would bring home until Clara found them and scolded him for bringing them into the house. Although both Clara and Newton were keepers, Clara was hesitant to train Declan as a keeper for fear he would try and leave the underground city of Kali and join the resistance. Newton respected her decision but would tell Declan bedtime stories every night about how good must defeat evil, stories of the resistance, Magnus, and the hope of a savior.

As Newton watched Declan scurry about, Callais entered the room, snapping Newton out of his thoughts. Then—out of earshot from Declan—Callais asked what Newton thought about training Declan as a keeper and becoming Evie's right-hand man. Newton smiled and looked across the room at the young man, beaming with pride. "I believe that would be a perfect partnership."

After Callais left the room, Newton approached Declan, placed his hand on his shoulder, and asked, "How would you feel about being trained as a keeper and helping Evie in her journey?"

"YES, YES, YES!" Declan shouted while he jumped up and down.

Newton laughed at Declan's reaction and, again, was proud to have helped raise such a brave young man. A few days later, Newton and Declan met with the others in the council room. Once the meeting was over, they told Evie the news…Declan would be her right-hand man!

***

After Newton and Declan left the meeting (where they told Evie she and Declan would be partners), Newton and Declan retreated to the forest to begin working on Declan's training and powers. Because Newton was highly skilled in the element of air (and he knew that Callais was also training Evie that day on the manipulation of air), Newton figured that would be a great place to start Declan's training as well. They wandered into the forest for some time when they found a small clearing and began.

Newton explained to Declan how to use his mind to concentrate on the flow of air in his body, mind, and surroundings. He also provided the same advice to Declan that Callais had provided to Evie—to picture something Declan had seen float before. After Newton finished telling Declan the instructions, Declan closed his eyes and pictured his mother. He thought about when he was a small boy, how Clara would take him into the city of Candor (the city above Kali) to heal others. Declan concentrated on how Clara would float from window to window, building to building, to provide healing and care for those in need. As he watched his mother float in his mind's eye, he began to feel the flow of air and energy surrounding him. He followed Newton's instructions and allowed his body and mind to move with the flow of the element. After a while, he heard Newton clap and shout from below, "Fantastic job, boy!"

Declan opened his eyes and found that he was floating in the air, several feet above Newton's position. Declan smiled and began to float around more. Newton watched in awe as he saw how easy it was for Declan to master this new skill, and he became full of pride again. Newton continued to watch Declan rise into the air as Declan floated to the top of the tree line. Newton then saw Declan frantically motion his hands to get Newton's attention. Newton followed the direction in which Declan was pointing and saw that Evie was spinning wildly in the air… completely out of control.

Newton immediately went to action, placed his arms up, and directed his powers to pull Evie down. As he began to pull Evie down, Newton suddenly felt a stabbing pain shoot down his arms, making him instantly drop his arms down to his sides. Newton quickly put his arms back up, fought through the pain, and began to pull Evie down once more. Newton could feel the violent force Evie was fighting in the air and quickly chanted a protection spell over the young girl as he continued his attempt to pull Evie down. Just as he reached his threshold for pain, he started to lose control, and Evie began to tumble rapidly to the ground again. Newton became terrified as he tried to bring his arms up once more to help her but found the pain was too intense, and he was beginning to lose consciousness. Right before Newton felt he would pass out from the pain, he saw a flash of light crack across the sky and watched as Declan came out of the bright light, hit the ground below, and ran faster than Newton had ever seen anyone run before (almost as if there was some kind of unseen force pushing Declan across the forest floor). Newton watched as Declan reached Evie just in time to catch her, and when Newton realized she was safe, he finally passed out from the pain.

***

Newton woke from his fainting episode to find that Atlas (who had been scouting the forest that day) was carrying him back to Mari. The two entered Regina's dwelling to find her quickly at work healing Evie. Declan then came running across the room to Newton when Declan realized that Newton was hurt as well. He frantically shouted out for someone to help, and soon, Marina was by Newton's side and began to work on his injuries. Newton winced in pain as she rubbed some potion on his arms but took a deep breath and asked Marina, "Is Evie okay?"

"I am not sure," Marina answered with a worried expression.

Newton then nodded back in Evie's direction. "Please go to her. I will be fine."

Marina paused and was going to say no, but Newton could see the pain and fear in her eyes. "Please. Go help her." He nodded once more in Evie's direction.

She gave him a grateful smile as Marina rushed back to Evie's side and helped Regina. Then, Atlas and Emmeline came to Newton's and began to take care of his injuries. Newton felt relieved that Evie was being taken care of, and so was he... so he slowly fell asleep.

***

Newton woke the next day, feeling much better but still very sore. He slowly got up but found it was hard to move. Emmeline saw him get up and helped him to his feet. Newton could see that Regina was still working tirelessly on Evie as Amelia brought him a cane so he could walk across the room. Once Newton reached Evie's side, he could see that Declan was perched on the floor next to her, gently stroking Evie's hand. Newton could see Declan was weeping and kept repeating, "Please be okay, please."

Newton placed his hand on top of the young man's head. Declan looked up and stood to his feet to give Newton a tight embrace. When Declan released the old man, Newton said, "Come…Let us give Regina room to work."

Declan stood firm where he was. "No, I'm not going to leave her side. You told me that I needed to be there for her no matter what. So, I'm not leaving."

Newton gave him a sympathetic look, knowing nothing he could do or say that would change Declan's mind. So, he gently patted Declan on the shoulder and slowly made his way back to the other side of the room, where Emmeline once again began to work on healing his injuries.

***

Once Evie was healed and back up on her feet (and Newton began to feel better), he started his training with Declan again. When it was Newton's turn to train Evie, Declan was either being taught by Callais or Lincoln or joined Otto in working on protector training. It was soon apparent to everyone who worked with Declan that he was, like Evie, quick to learn his new powers, spells, and the manipulation of elements. The Antillis resistance elders were glad of their choice to pair the two together. Soon, they planned on joining Evie and Declan to work on their powers together.

Chapter 9
To Alderbard

After a few days of rest from her scary fall, the Camulos encounter in the forest, and her dreams, Evie finally felt like herself again—and just in time. The council had called a meeting before Otto's team was to head to Alderbard on their mission. After Evie finished her breakfast, she and Amelia made their way to Regina's for a quick check-in on Evie's health, who soon gave the girls the go-ahead to join the council meeting. As the girls entered, the council room was swarming, filled with nervous energy, members talking among themselves about the task at hand. Evie scanned the packed room and found Ellis in the far corner, proudly wearing some kind of armor, with Aphrodite right by his side. Evie made her way over to Ellis as he picked her up off her feet and swung her around (almost knocking a few nearby council members over), saying, "Oh, Evie,

I'm so glad to see yeh up an' 'bout. I came in a few times to visit yeh, but yeh were sound asleep."

He placed Evie on the ground, with his giant hairy arms wrapped around her. Aphrodite laid her head on their arms as Evie leaned down and gave Aphrodite a big hug—which she returned with a slobbery kiss. Evie looked up to see tears streaming down Ellis's cheeks. Ellis didn't even bother to wipe them away as he gently kissed the top of Evie's head. "I'm goin' to miss yeh, girl. So, yeh keep yerself outta trouble until I get back, an' then we can wreck some hell together."

He gave her another tight squeeze and a wink as Evie wrapped her arms tightly around his barrel chest and began to sob. It just hit Evie that Ellis was leaving off to some dangerous place, and Evie became scared. Ellis returned the embrace and gently swayed her back and forth. "Don't worry, girl. There's nothin' in this world that will stop me from comin' back to yeh… I promise that."

For a moment, it seemed like there was only Ellis and Evie in the room as they continued their long embrace. Ellis then cleared his throat, pulled Evie back, and gave her one last look as he wiped a tear from her cheek. Evie then lovingly looked at Ellis and told him, "I figured out how we are related."

"How?" Ellis asked, giving her a curious look.

"You're my Uncle Ellis. Your brother, Callum, is my father," Evie answered, smiling from ear to ear.

Ellis began to actually cry as he swept Evie up into his arms again. "Oh, Evie, this is the best news I ever received. Now nothin' will stop us."

Ellis swung her around some more, kissed the top of her head again as he set her down, and said, "I'm just so sorry I never got to see Callum an' tell him how much I loved him an' apologize for what I did."

Evie saw that Ellis was trying to choke back his tears, so she wrapped her arms around him again, "Well, we have each other now, and I couldn't be happier... I love you, Ellis."

Ellis pulled her back again and looked lovingly at her (this time letting the tears fall freely down his face). "I love yeh so much, too, kiddo."

Ellis pulled her into him again and wrapped his arms tightly around Evie right as Callais and Newton entered the room with Otto and Atlas behind them wearing armor similar to Ellis's. The council members slowly took their seats as Callais approached the table, nodding his head to all the members in the room before he spoke. "Today, we send off our brave warriors on a dangerous mission to Alderbard. I know that this is hard for us, but it must be done. To those of you who leave us today, I must say that you are all so heroic for taking on this endeavor. I hope to all see you soon, returned safely to the loving arms of your family and friends. We all thank you all for your service to the resistance and wish you a safe journey there and back."

Callais moved from the table, and Evie saw tears well up in his eyes as he patted Otto on the shoulder. Otto placed his hand on Callais's hand and whispered something in his ear as the two embraced. Otto released Callais, approached the table, and cleared his throat. "Council members, we know what lies ahead will be challenging, and there will be times we may not be able to communicate. But hold steady and never give up hope of the fight. I know that for those of us who go to Alderbard today, we'll never give up."

The council members all stood up and placed their hands over their hearts, which Evie believed to be a sign of respect for warriors going to battle in the Devas galaxy. Otto's team slowly filed out of the room as the council members shook hands with the soldiers leaving. As the warriors made their exit, Evie ran out of the room and grabbed Ellis in a massive hug once more. She could also see that Emmeline and Amelia were crying, their arms firmly wrapped around Otto. Ellis then gave Evie the biggest hug, taking the air out of her. But she didn't care and squeezed him back as hard as she could. Aphrodite soon joined the hug, pressing her large body against the two, quietly whimpering. As Ellis released, he said one last thing before he walked away. "I love yeh, kid."

Evie began to sob uncontrollably as she watched her Ellis and the Antillis warriors walk out of Mari towards their dangerous destination. Evie continued to cry when she felt someone wrap their arms around her as she buried her face in whoever was holding her. She assumed it was Amelia holding her; however, she found herself in Declan's embrace when she pulled back. Evie didn't pull back or blush like she always did around him. Instead, she just held him tighter, continuing to sob harder. Declan just held her, gently stroking her hair. After Evie stopped crying and pulled herself together, Declan placed his hand on her lower back and escorted her into the council room.

There, Evie could see a red-eyed Amelia and Emmeline, both who quickly came to Evie's side as the threesome embraced each other. Once again, the girls cried some more before they finally collected themselves and faced the council room. To their surprise, many of the members in the room seem to be wiping tears from their eyes as well. Evie realized that many people here today just watched a loved one go to war—Evie's heart hurt more than it ever had. After a long moment of silence in the room, Callais cleared his throat and, with a shaky voice, said, "We will reconvene tomorrow. For now, I believe that it is best we all have time to process before we continue."

The members all agreed and left the council room, leaving Callais, Emmeline, Newton, Amelia, Declan, Abe, and Lincoln in the room. (It had been noted that Abe would stay behind and help train others while Otto and the others went to Alderbard.) Evie hadn't paid much attention to Abe since they hadn't had much interaction. She had learned Abe's last name was Alexopolis and noticed that Abe was about the same size as Otto and Atlas but had sharp-pointed ears, long fingers, very light skin, and grayish eyes. He also was much thinner than Otto and Atlas but still muscular compared to his height. Evie stared a bit longer and wondered where he came from. Before thinking about this any longer, she quickly realized she hadn't seen Marina in days. She then turned to Newton and asked, "Where's Marina?"

Newton looked up, and Evie could see he also had red, watery eyes. Before she could start crying again (thinking of Ellis), Newton answered, "She has been training with Simone. She came to visit you when you were asleep, and I promised her that I would send you to her when you woke."

Evie felt relieved and asked, "Did she know Ellis was leaving?"

"Do not worry. They had a chance to say their goodbyes," Newton answered with a gentle smile.

Evie felt much better about this and settled down into a chair when Callais said, "Actually, Evie, today you will be going with Newton to see Marina and Simone to be trained in protection spells. I will be joining you later, but I think it is time for me to spend a little time training Amelia and Declan."

Just as he finished, Collin came rushing in, out of breath, carrying an armful of scrolls. Evie realized that Collin must've taken over Declan's duties running around doing errands for others now that Declan was taking on a more significant role. Collin saw Evie, smiled his toothless grin, dropped the scrolls, ran over to Evie, and gave her a big hug. Evie smiled as she pulled Collin up and swung him around like Ellis had done with her. Collin giggled as Evie set him down, and Newton lightly scolded him for dropping the scrolls on the ground. Collin hung his head down, picked up scrolls, and set them gently on the table. Evie flashed him another smile before Collin ran out of the room. As Evie watched Collin run out, following just behind him, coming from somewhere, Bella, Apollo, and Darwin chased after him. After Collin left, Newton began to shuffle through the scrolls and selected a few as he turned to Evie and stated, "Shall we go find Marina and Simone?"

Evie smiled and nodded, but before she left the room, she gave Amelia a hug and whispered good luck to her. Just as she was about to follow Newton out of the room, Declan grabbed her arm and embraced her one last time as well. Evie felt warm all over and held Declan a little longer than a usual hug. As she pulled away to leave, Declan gently leaned over and kissed her on the cheek. Evie stood there shocked for a minute, with her hand across the place where he had kissed her, and then smiled at him before she continued to follow Newton.

Chapter 10
PROTECTIONS TRAINING

As Evie followed Newton down the stairs and across the winding bridges, she became lost in her thoughts as she tried to figure out what her feelings for Declan meant. She had never been in love with someone before, and she was starting to wonder if this was what falling in love felt like. She was disrupted from her thoughts as she followed Newton into a root dwelling (far below any of the dwellings she had been in before). There, sitting at a table, was Marina. Evie ran over to her and hugged her. Marina returned the hug as Evie began to well up with tears again, thinking of Ellis. Marina seemed to read her thoughts. "There, there, girl. He will be back soon. Once that man makes up his mind about something, there is no stopping him. I promise!"

Evie grinned as she pulled away from Marina, thinking of Ellis and how bold and brave he was. Evie noticed that Marina also had a few tears in her eyes before Evie took a seat between the two elders. Simone then approached the table, saying, "Newton described to me what happened to you the other day, and I think I know why Camulos was able to get in your mind." She paused and continued. "Although this side of Antillis is covered by the fourth-day protection spell, it seems that the protection of the spell only extends to slightly above the tree line. Once above the tree line, there is no protection, so I think it was a wise choice you made to be trained in protection spells."

Evie analyzed Simone's features for a minute as she was talking. Simone was much different than any other being she had seen so far. All the other people that weren't from the Devas galaxy looked similar to humans. Although Simone looked human enough, she had light green skin, dark purple hair and eyes, and was much taller than anyone else (even taller than Otto). Simone was also very lean and muscular, and with every movement Simone made, Evie could see the muscles flex under her body. However, Evie also thought Simone seemed very graceful, almost like every move she made was a well-organized dance. Otto had told Evie that Simone was a great Denidis warrior. Still, Evie never got the chance to ask further questions about Simone because she had been so busy while on Antillis. Evie was then distracted from her thoughts when she noticed that she had been quiet for a while and everyone was staring at her, so she quickly asked, "What's the protection spell?"

Newton gave her a quick wink and then replied, "When we learned that Camulos had conquered all the other galaxies, the keepers of Devas decided it would be best to separate from the rest of the universe and hide until we could find a way to defeat him. The ceremony was to last for six days. On the fourth day, we created a protection spell to protect us from Camulos finding us once we separated." Newton then took a deep breath before he went on, "Unfortunately, we never made it to the sixth day, and Camulos invaded the Devas galaxy on the fifth day, disrupting the separation ceremony."

Simone then began adding on to Newton's story. "However, the fourth-day protection spell did not break completely, and many of the planets in the Devas system still have areas where the protection covers them. This is why it has been hard for Camulos to completely take over the Devas galaxy since we can still hide from him, and he has not been able to find a way to break the protection spell… yet." Simone took another deep breath and finished by saying, "This is also why we have been able to fight him off for a thousand years now."

"That's a powerful spell to be able to protect a whole galaxy for that long," Evie stated with a gasp. "I still can't believe that you have been fighting for that long. Now I understand why everyone is so tired from having to endure that pain for such a lengthy time... but I don't think I'm strong enough to learn protection spells and use them to fight Camulos any better than anyone else could. Are you sure I can do this?"

Newton smiled at Evie and patted her hand. "Callais will most likely train you not only in keeper powers but as a protector as well. However, you are right. Protection spells go beyond that of what a protector is trained in. Fortunately for us, Simone and Josephine were some of the original creators of the protection spells that were used in the separation ceremony, so we are blessed to have Simone with us today." He then gave her a broad smile. "Also, please do not doubt yourself, Evie. You are much stronger than you give yourself credit for, and you have all of us on your side as well."

Evie smiled and took a deep breath. Newton's words gave her some reassurance, but she was still worried. Newton winked at Evie as if he understood her thoughts and then nodded at Simone. Simone nodded back, saying, "We have recovered several scrolls that will help guide you in using protection. These spells will not only help you hide from Camulos but to fight him or others when the time comes."

Evie became a little nervous at the thought of fighting. She had never really been in a fight. The closest she ever came to fighting someone was when she was in elementary school. A bully pushed her to the ground before Evie stood up and took a swing—completely missing the bully. Marina placed her hand on Evie's hand, which Evie hadn't realized was shaking until Marina's touch stopped it. Marina gave Evie a gentle smile, saying, "I know that this is a lot to take on, but I believe in you. I know, without a doubt, like Newton said, and all of us believe, you have the strength to do this, love."

Evie smiled at Marina and was overwhelmed by the love she felt for her and was glad to have Marina by her side. Simone then began to unroll a scroll and place it on the table for Evie to look at as Simone explained what was on the scroll. Evie was glad for this because much of the scroll seemed to be in a language, although somewhat familiar, she couldn't quite make out. Simone then explained that when first practicing any spell, it was wise to chant words until the user was comfortable without the words. She then elaborated that chanting the spell helped guide the direction or purpose for its intended use. Simone then placed a glass of the Virdis on the center of the table and said to Evie, "I want you to hide this glass from me."

Evie gave her a confused look when Simone pushed the scroll in front of Evie and pointed out a passage on the top of the scroll. Evie stared at it, but she still couldn't read it when Marina reassuringly nodded. "Take your time...I know you can do this."

Evie again looked down at the scroll and began to lightly focus on the passage. Slowly, after the words moved for a brief period, they became clearer. Soon, Evie could read the passage and began to speak the words out loud when Simone interjected, "One last thing. It is helpful to direct your focus through your hands to guide the spell where it needs to go. Like with any element, you must feel the flow of power around you."

Evie nodded, then reached her hand out towards the glass and concentrated on the flow of energy around her. Once she felt the power inside her increase and she had a good hold on the energies inside her body, she looked back down at the passage and read out loud, "*Through the cover of light, fade your soul. Through covered sight, be with light no more.*"

Evie looked up from the scroll to see the green drink slowly fade from sight. She was shocked to see an empty spot where the glass once was and dropped her hand.

The moment she dropped her hand, the glass reappeared. Simone proudly smiled, saying, "Callais told me you were good at using your powers, but this was amazing to see on a first try."

Evie beamed with pride but then, with slight disappointment, shook her head, saying, "But it only disappeared for a minute. Why?"

"That, dear, will be mostly what we train on," Simone answered as she continued to explain. "Controlling a power, any power, for a long time takes many years to practice. I know we do not have long to train you, but I believe the same thing as Callais and others. Your powers are strong enough that the little time we have may be on our side."

Evie smiled with pride again as she looked at Marina and Newton, who also seemed to share in her joy as they both smiled proudly back at her. Newton clapped, rubbed his hands together, and excitedly asked, "Shall we practice some more?" Evie nodded as Simone, Newton, and Marina began to unroll more scrolls.

Over the next few hours, Evie began to practice over and over again, making things disappear and then reappear, with each disappearance lasting a little longer. Finally, Evie began to feel fatigued, and the group decided to call it a day when Callais entered the room, with Amelia, Declan,

Collin, and a group of rowdy dogs behind him. Evie was glad to see them all as Collin came running to her side, jumping up and down, excitedly shouting, "Look what I found, Evie!"

Evie looked in the direction Collin was pointing and saw a new dog in the group. Collin then said, "I was playing in the forest with the dogs, and this dog came running over to me. She chose me, Evie!"

Collin lowered himself to the ground and wrapped his arms around this new dog. Although the dog was covered in mud, Evie recognized it as a type of cattle dog. Evie got down on her knees next to Collin and noticed the dog had one blue eye and one brown eye as Collin proudly said, "I named her River, and she really did choose me, Evie, honest."

Evie ruffled the top of Collin's head and said to the new dog, "Nice to meet you, River."

River then extended her paw out to Evie as Evie shook it like a handshake. Collin laughed, "I taught her that. She's really smart!"

Evie smiled at Collin as the elders talked for a bit before everyone began to head off to their separate dwellings when Evie overheard Callais ask Newton, "Where did you find Collin?"

Newton shook his head and quietly whispered

something to Callais that Evie couldn't hear. Newton then headed off in a separate direction. Callais made his way up the stairs, opposite where Evie and Amelia were headed. Evie reminded herself to ask Callais or Newton more about Collin later. She hollered for Bella and made her way home. *Home*, Evie thought, *I guess this is home now.*

Chapter 11
FINDING THE WATCHER GLASS

After David and Ruby's dream where Evie visited them, Ruby decided to ask Nadia about the watcher glass. Nadia, again, told Ruby she had lost hers and didn't know where another one might be. However, she told Ruby she would search the texts again to see if anything in them would help find a watcher glass. Ruby was upset. She wanted to reach Evie whenever she wanted and was tired of sporadic dreams visits where Ruby had limited time with Evie. Ruby also knew that Evie had told her she was in another galaxy, so obviously, phone calls were out of the question.

Ruby was huffing around the room, thinking about how frustrating everything had been so far when she grabbed their bag and Evie's jewelry box fell out, crashing to the floor. Ruby looked down at the jewelry box and began to cry. She knew this was one of Evie's only possessions she had left of her parents. Ruby bent down to pick up the shattered pieces and saw that the piece with the inscription Evie's mother had etched into the top had fallen out. Ruby picked it up and went to put it back in its place when she saw a small green mirror behind where the inscription had been. Ruby took out the green mirror and saw that she couldn't see her reflection, but what looked like a fog moving across the surface. Ruby looked closer at it when, suddenly, a woman's face appeared in it. Ruby shook her head and looked harder as the woman's face seemed to be looking right back at her. Ruby then heard the woman say, "Hello, Ruby, I am Regina. I see you have found a watcher's glass?"

Ruby almost dropped the mirror, completely shocked that this woman was talking to her through a mirror. Ruby then remembered that Evie had mentioned a woman named Regina who was helping her. Although Ruby had never seen Regina before, Regina somehow seemed to know who she was. Before Ruby had time to think about this, she thought of Evie, got excited, and almost shouted at the mirror, "Is Evie with you?"

"She is here on Antillis, but she is not with me currently," Regina replied with a smile and went on to say, "I have been searching for you. I am glad you found a watcher glass."

Ruby was even more baffled but didn't ask any questions about the mirror. She desperately wanted to see Evie, so she just asked, "Can I talk to Evie?"

"Yes. Please give me a minute," Regina replied and faded from sight.

Ruby watched as the fog covered the surface again. Ruby wanted to go find David very badly, but she was so excited to see Evie that she didn't want to place the mirror down. Soon, the fog began to move around when, again, a hazy face appeared in the mirror. Ruby then saw a fluff of red hair and shouted, "Evie, is that you?"

The image in the mirror then cleared, and Ruby could see Evie perfectly as Evie excitedly said, "Ruby. Oh my god, you found the glass. I can't believe it!"

Ruby was ecstatic to see Evie and immediately told Evie how much she missed her and loved her. She then told Evie about the accident with her mother's jewelry box; however, she found the watcher glass behind the inscription. Ruby then promised she would find a way to fix the box. Evie smiled at Ruby. "It's okay, Ruby. I'm just so glad we can talk whenever we want now."

Ruby smiled back, and the two began to talk more about everything they were doing when David walked into the room, began laughing, and jokingly said, "Oh, my lovely wife. Has this journey made you lose your mind to where you are talking to yourself now?"

Ruby swung around and held the glass up to David's face, saying, "It's our Evie…I found a watcher glass."

David looked at Ruby, completely stunned, and then back at the mirror to see Evie's smiling face. Evie then happily waved. "Hi, David."

David jumped across the room and grabbed the mirror. "Evie, is it really you? It's so good to see you, sweetheart."

David then turned his head and hollered out Steven and Beth's names when Steven and Beth came running into the room, looking worried. David then held up the mirror up to Steven and Beth when Evie waved again, saying, "Hi, Steven. Hi, Beth. It's good to see the both of you."

Steven took a step back and shook his head as Ruby explained to them about finding the watcher glass. Beth wasn't as shocked and just excited to see that they had finally made contact with Evie. After Steven's shock wore off, they all talked for a couple hours, sharing stories, and sharing love.

Nadia entered the room and saw that they were talking into something shiny when she finally realized that they had a watcher glass. She was shocked by this, wondering how they found it, but she didn't interrupt their conversation—she knew how important it was for them to talk to Evie. After a while longer of intense and animated conversation, Evie finally told them she had to leave, but she would ask Regina about keeping the glass, or at least ask Regina if she could use it whenever she wanted. They then all said tear-filled goodbyes before Evie faded out of sight, and they were left staring at a foggy mirror. After a few more minutes of silence and Ruby wiping her tears away, Nadia finally spoke. "I see you have found a watcher glass."

Ruby nodded and then explained where she found it. Nadia thoughtfully rubbed her chin. "I think Evie's mother might have an interesting story as well."

Nadia then smiled before saying, "I am glad you have been able to contact Evie, but I would also like to use it as well if you allow me. I believe I may be able to make some contact with others we might need on our mission in finding out some more answers."

"Of course," David answered, smiled, and added, "You just let us know when our girl reaches out to us again."

Nadia nodded in agreement as David handed her the glass, saying, "I hope we can find out some more answers so we can bring our girl home."

Nadia took the glass and nodded. "I promise we will do everything we can so that happens."

Chapter 12
DECLAN AND EVIE UNITE

It was early in the morning when Evie woke and heard a commotion outside her room. She slowly got up and made her way into the kitchen to see Emmeline, Amelia, and, to her surprise, Declan, all nosily talking about their plans for the day. When Declan saw Evie enter the room, he quickly ran over and shared the exciting news that they would be working together that day. Evie smiled and lightly blushed—as she always did around Declan. They all devoured breakfast quickly. Then Evie and Declan said their goodbyes to the others and made their way to the council room where Newton, Lincoln, and Callais were already waiting for them. Before they could all start the plans for the day, Collin came rushing into the room with scrolls and maps as he set them on the table. Collin was ready to make his way out the door when Callais told him to wait. Collin impatiently wiggled where he stood as the rest of the group began talking. After a few minutes, Collin felt he couldn't stand still any longer when he finally interjected, "Can I go now? I want to go play with the dogs in the forest before someone else makes me do something for them."

Evie giggled as Callais gently replied, "Actually, Collin, you will be joining us today and helping Evie and Declan."

Collin's smile widened as he bolted across the room and happily wrapped his arms around Evie. "Did you hear that? I get to help you today!"

Evie bent down and wrapped Collin up in a hug. "I'm so excited that you get to help me!"

As she released him, Collin was still beaming with pride as the group made their way out into the forest when the group of rowdy dogs rushed by them to go play. Collin watched longingly as the dogs ran around the forest playing chase. He then hollered at them, "I'll play with you tomorrow."

Collin shrugged his tiny shoulders and followed the rest of the group further into the forest, where they came to a stopping place next to a small river, running rapidly through the thick trees. Evie caught herself gazing at Declan while they waited, trying to determine how she felt about him. She noticed that his curly, long blond hair was braided down the sides over his ears as many of the other warriors (like Atlas, Callais, and Otto) wore their hair. Evie realized that Declan was now wearing his hair like many of the resistance fighters, and she felt herself blush again, thinking of how brave and handsome he looked.

As Declan, Evie, and Collin stood patiently by as the three elders conversed, Evie's thoughts of Declan were soon interrupted when a rustling noise cracked behind them. Evie quickly turned to see a large paw emerge from behind a giant bush. Suddenly, a large dog came dashing out from the bushes and jumped up, placing her paws across Declan's chest. The dog almost knocked Declan down, but he was strong enough to hold up the dog's mighty push. The dog dropped her paws off Declan and began to lick his hand as she rubbed her body against his leg. Evie and Collin smiled when Collin enthusiastically said, "Hey, she picked you like River picked me."

The three of them smiled at each other as the big dog continued to rub her giant body across Declan's leg when the elders turned and saw the new addition. Newton saw that the dog was rubbing up on Declan as he clapped his hands together, saying, "I was hoping you would find a companion soon. I believe she is perfect for you."

Declan smiled a proud grin and rubbed the top of his new companion's head. She was a blueish-gray color and had short hair and a stubby nose. Evie wasn't sure what kind of breed she was, but like Aphrodite, she was definitely a large breed. Declan continued to rub his new friend's head when Collin asked, "What are you going to name her?"

Declan looked down, deeply analyzing the beautiful, giant beast. After a few moments, he proudly said, "I think she looks like an Artemis. Don't you?" Collin shook his head in agreement as the group continued their plan for the day.

Callais then told Evie and Declan that he wanted them to work more on water, air, and protection spells that they had already learned. The goal was not to use their powers individually but to unite them as one. Evie and Declan exchanged nervous glances as Callais continued to explain the task they must accomplish together. Callais told them that he wanted them to stop the flow of the small river and raise the water into the air as they cast a protection spell around the water. Again, Evie and Declan looked at each other, and you could see the trepidation in each of their eyes. Newton then placed his hands on Declan's shoulders, and Lincoln placed his hands on Evie's shoulders. Callais then continued. "Newton and Lincoln will help you in guiding your spells. Lincoln will help Evie control the water while Newton will help Declan control the air."

Callais paused and then went on, "Before they can help you, the two of you must find each other in your minds and see what the other will do before you can combine your strengths."

Callais again paused and rubbed his bearded chin before adding, "Once you find each other, and you have stopped the water and raised it into the air, you can then cast the final protection spell over the water and make it disappear."

Evie and Declan both gulped, took a big sigh as they glanced at each other once more, and slowly closed their eyes. Once her eyes were closed, Evie found herself in the fog as usual and began to think of Declan. She thought it was weird to think of him even though he was standing right next to her. As the fog started to move, Evie focused on Declan's beautiful blue eyes, and even then, she could feel herself blush. Soon, Evie saw Declan standing in front of her, flashing his big, beautiful smile.

Declan reached for Evie's hand as she slowly took it. She then heard a quiet voice in the distance, telling her to open her eyes and stop the river. Evie recognized it as Lincoln's voice. So, she slowly opened her eyes, placed her hands in front of her, allowed herself to feel the flow of the water through her body, and began to slow the current of the river. As the river began to slow down, she felt a push in her mind. Evie then saw the river rise in the air as it slowly spun into the tree branches above. She stood there amazed for a moment when she felt another push inside her mind. She closed her eyes once more and saw Declan in front of her, with his arms stretched out. She realized he was controlling the air elements while she had been controlling the water. She then approached Declan in her mind again, and once she was by his side, he turned and looked at her as the pair placed their arms outwards in unison. Evie could feel not only her own powers but also Declan's power throughout her entire body. She was surprised how much stronger she felt with Declan standing next to her and how much easier it was for her to control the element she was holding onto. She then heard Declan whisper inside her mind, '*Ready,*' and the pair cast the final protection spell. Evie then opened her eyes to see the water stream floating in the air slowly fade out of sight.

As Evie and Declan dropped their hands, the water reappeared and then crashed back down to the ground, finding its way back to the forest floor, continuing its journey through the trees. Collin was clapping his hands and jumping up and down, saying, "That was so great, guys! Do it again!"

Evie and Declan laughed at the excited young boy. Declan then came over to Evie's side and embraced her from behind. "Wow, Evie. I could really feel how strong you are," he said, smiling from ear to ear.

Instead of blushing this time, Evie turned into Declan's arms and smiled. "I know. It was so amazing. I felt so much stronger with you by my side."

The pair locked eyes for a moment, then released each other to see the elders looking at them with pride. Collin, who had been watching Declan and Evie do this amazing trick, soon became impatient and loudly asked, "When is it my turn to do something neat?"

Callais and Newton exchanged a secretive glance when Newton turned to Collin and asked, "Collin, do you remember where I found you?"

Collin shook his head no as Newton went on, "I found you on the streets of Candor when you were a little younger than you are now."

Newton paused as a sorrowful look came across his face before continuing. "When I found you, you were badly injured and barely alive. And when I went to pick you up, even though you were passed out, a powerful force blocked me from grabbing you and blew me back to the ground." He paused and sadly shook his head, "I figured out you had a strong protection spell placed over you, and I was eventually able to break it before I brought you back to Kali with me."

Collin scrunched his nose. "I don't remember any of that. I just remember waking up in Clara's house."

Newton gently lowered to one knee, so he was eye level with the young boy, and asked, "Do you remember where you came from before I found you or how you lost your arm?"

Collin lowered his head, placed his right hand across his lower left elbow where his forearm and hand used to be, and sadly answered, "I don't remember anything really… just fire and pain." He paused and apologetically added, "I'm sorry."

Newton gently patted the young boy on the shoulder. "That is okay, Collin. I am just glad I found you."

Collin began to weep as he went to Evie's side and wiped his tears on her sleeve. She bent down and held Collin in her arms as he began to cry more. Evie thought about how much the poor child must have suffered before he was found, and she, too, began to cry with him. After a brief period of silence, as the two held each other, Callais then cleared his throat. Evie and Collin released each other and collected themselves as Callais stated, "Well, Collin… The reason we brought you here today is we think you might have powers like Evie and Declan."

Collin's demeanor quickly changed as he again became excited and bounced back, saying, "Really? That's great!"

Callais then added, "Evie told me that she wanted to learn how to make light orbs. So, I thought that we could show both you and Evie how to do that today."

Both Evie and Collin were now bouncing around with joy. Even though Evie had been working on much more powerful spells, she was glad that she finally got the opportunity to learn how to make light orbs. Callais then explained to the pair how to make a light orb. He told them that the first time a person did it, it had to start in the mind. He then said that once a person got really good at the spell, it became effortless to make an orb without going into the mind. Callais then instructed Evie to take Collin's hand, and before they both closed their eyes, Callais told Collin he was to wait until Evie found him in the fog.

Soon, the pair held hands as Evie closed her eyes and began to focus on Collin. Evie thought that she would see fog like always when she closed her eyes; however, this time, Evie found herself surrounded by darkness and fire instead. Evie began to freak out and was going to open her eyes when she heard Collin's screams through the shadows and flames. Evie frantically searched for the direction of the screams when she finally saw Collin standing a few yards in front of her. She dashed in Collin's direction when suddenly, a giant fire wall appeared between the two. Evie stumbled backward from the raging flames but could still hear Collin screaming. She advanced towards the fire again, but the flames coiled like a viper and struck out with licks of fire going in all directions. Evie jumped back again but then focused, using all of her mind and energy as she held her hands out to the flames, cast an air spell, and watched as the fire wall split apart. She quickly sprinted through the separated inferno and scooped Collin in her arms. As soon as she had Collin in her arms, Evie quickly opened her eyes. Once her eyes were open, Evie saw that she was holding Collin in the forest as his body fell limp in her arms, and the rest of the group was staring at them, horror stretched across their faces.

Everyone was stunned and frozen in their place, unsure what had happened or what to do. But Declan jumped to action, quickly picked up Collin, and ran across the forest, again, faster than any of them had ever seen before. The rest of the group chased after Declan as fast as they could. When they finally reached the opening to Mari and raced down the steps towards Regina's, Declan had already placed Collin on the healing table, where Regina was working on him. Declan stood there, looking desperate and scared. Evie reached Declan's side as they watched Regina and the elders begin their work on Collin.

***

Evie and Declan stayed at Regina's for the next few days, helping her heal Collin. As Evie took her turn to watch him, she would look at the slender-limbed, sweaty, and disheveled little boy with deathly pale skin and would cry, wishing she could take away his pain and save him somehow. She felt desperate and hollow, knowing there was nothing she could do. There was doubt that Collin would pull through, but they never gave up hope and worked endlessly on the small boy. River never left the boy's side and lay next to his tiny body while the others did their work. After a few days, to everyone's relief, Collin opened his eyes, slowly turned his head towards his dog, wrapped his arms around River's neck, and softly whispered, "I'm back."

***

Once Collin returned to his normal playful self, Evie began to wonder what had happened to him. So, she decided to approach Callais and figure out why this occurred. She found Callais in the council room late one evening, poring over some scrolls. Evie cleared her throat as Callais looked up, and Evie asked, "Why did that happen to Collin? Why was there fire instead of fog?"

Callais solemnly shook his head. "I think there might be more to Collin's story than we know." He then moved his head in the directions of the scrolls. "I am trying to figure out what happened, Evie, I promise. For now, I think it is best Collin goes back to playing with the dogs and running errands, so he stays safe."

Evie nodded in agreement when she saw a tear run down Callais's cheek. Evie then asked, "Why is Collin missing an arm?"

Callais took a deep sigh. "Balor Kronius, Camulos's right-hand man, and Agronas Fotias, Camulos's wife, created a machine that could extract memory, thoughts, and dreams from the Devas people."

"I remember Otto saying something about this, but I don't understand what it has to do with missing arms," Evie said, shaking her head.

Callais nodded and went on, "During the separation ceremony, we created a spell that would help preserve people's memories of our true past once we separated. However, when Camulos invaded and the ceremony fell apart, many people's memories were lost. This is probably why no one on Terran remembers their true past either." He paused and then added, "Josephine then created a spell so people would remember and stay connected to each other through dreams."

Callais took another deep breath. "When Camulos found out that this dream spell was cast, he enlisted Balor and Agronas to create what is called the extraction machine. When it was first created, it was unsure who had received extraction and who had not, so once they were done extracting thoughts, memories, and dreams from a person, they marked them with a tattoo on their lower left arm."

Callais took another long pause, wearily rubbed his head, and went on, "To fool the Camulus forces, a group of people called the dealers started to give people fake extraction marks so that if they were captured, the Camulus forces would think they already had been tortured. The dealers charged people a high price, and if they could not repay that debt, they were often turned over to the Camulus forces, or the dealers would capture their friends and family and threaten them."

"That's horrible," Evie gasped. "But it still doesn't explain the missing arm."

Callais held up his hand as he went on to explain, "Many people who myself or others rescued had the marks already on their arms from Balor and Agronas. We found that the mark allowed the Camulus pack to know who received extraction and who did not and as a way to monitor them once they were released. We tried our hardest to break Agronas's tracking spell entwined within the mark, but we could not."

Callais lowered his chin to his chest before looking back up. "The only way we could ensure those we saved could remain safe was to amputate their arm."

"That's just awful." Evie gasped again. "I can't believe Camulos and his people would do such horrible things."

Callais then began to tear up as Evie went to his side and wrapped her arms around his shoulders. Callais then said, "I am not sure who took Collin's arm, but they must have known to do this so Camulos, Balor, and Agronas couldn't find him." Callais took another deep breath as tears began to fall down his face before saying, "I do not know what happened to Collin, and I do not understand the evil that would hurt a child. Besides every other reason to stop Camulos and his darkness, the torture of children is our greatest reason."

Evie kept her arms around Callais as the both of them thought deeply about the horrors of Camulos and his powers. Evie then promised she would do everything she could to stop him, especially from ever hurting her beautiful Collin again.

Chapter 13
AMELIA'S DREAMS

◆•————————•————————•◆

F or weeks, since Evie was working with Callais and Declan, Amelia ran around between Regina and Simone helping where she could. One day, while at Simone's dwelling, Marina was looking over some scrolls when Amelia dropped a drawing in front of her. Marina grabbed the drawing and said thank you but didn't think much of it—she just thought it was the young girl's way of showing appreciation towards her. Marina turned her head up and smiled at Amelia when Amelia began to wave her hand back at the drawing for Marina to look at. Marina complied, looked at the picture, and was instantly shocked by what she saw. She turned her head back up at Amelia and asked, "Did you draw this?"

Amelia nodded gleefully as Marina looked back down at the drawing again. As she analyzed it further, her initial shock became even more awed. She realized this was a picture of her and Ellis back in Ireland—at Marina's home. It was a drawing of Marina training Ellis when he was a young boy, soon after finding him. Marina looked back up at the girl and asked, "How could you know this?"

Like she had done with Evie, Amelia motioned her hands to indicate that she was sleeping and then continued to maneuver her hands so that Marina finally understood what Amelia was saying. Marina then blurted, "You can see the past in your dreams?"

Amelia, again, nodded yes and then placed another drawing down as Marina quickly grabbed it and analyzed it. There, in the picture, she saw Ellis as a grown man in armor fighting with the giant beast, Aphrodite, by his side. Marina was even more shocked and asked Amelia, "Has this happened yet?"

Amelia shook her head no when Marina jumped up and excitedly asked, "You dream about the future too?"

Amelia smiled a big grin and shook her head yes when Marina went on to ask, "Does anyone know of this power you have?"

Amelia shrugged her shoulders and moved her hand side to side to indicate 'maybe' just as Simone entered the room. Marina gave Simone a baffled look and handed her the drawings. "You have to see this," she said, still overwhelmed by what she had just learned.

Simone took the pages as Marina explained the drawings and that the girl could see the past and future in her dreams. Simone also stood there in shock for a minute after the explanation. She then took the drawings and rushed out of the dwelling, leaving Marina and Amelia still standing in complete silence. Amelia just shrugged her shoulders, and Marina plopped back in her seat, still completely baffled. Not much later, Simone returned with Newton and Callais. Callais curiously approached Amelia and asked, "Is this true, Amelia? Can you see the past and future in your dreams?"

Amelia began to gesture her hands as Callais watched her. He had basically helped raise her since he and Otto had rescued her from Sirios, so he was very familiar with how she spoke with her hands. After a few minutes of watching her, Callais turned to the others, saying, "She tells me that she can see the past and future in her dreams, but only in bits and pieces and in short flashes… not enough to know exactly what is going on." He then turned to Amelia and asked, "Why have you never told me?"

Amelia shrugged her shoulders and began to gesture her hands again. When she was done, Callais, once again, turned to the others. "She did not think they were real since many of the people she dreamt about, she did not know." He paused and then finished, "She said that it was not until she saw Evie and those she brought with her that she thought her dreams might be real."

Callais then turned to Amelia and asked, "How long have you had these dreams?"

Amelia hung her head down for a minute and began to gesture her hands once again. When she was finished, tears welled up in her eyes as Callais made his way over to her and embraced her. Once he let her go, he explained again to the others, "She told me when she was captured by Balor, Agronas came in and starting putting thoughts in her head." He paused again before continuing. "Apparently, the spells Agronas used were not working at first, and Amelia began to see things in her head of people she did not know."

Callais paused a little longer, clearly upset over Amelia's torture, and then finished saying, "We rescued her before Balor and Agronas could finish their work, and since then, Amelia says she could dream about the past and future... Somehow, whatever they did to her mind allowed for this to happen."

Callais then placed his hand on Amelia's shoulder as she started to cry again. He pulled her into him as the pair embraced. The others were silent for a while as he comforted the girl. Newton then gently cleared his throat, saying, "Since we cannot train Collin any longer until we figure out how to help him, maybe we could start training Amelia to help Evie and Declan. She seems to have a power that might be useful if we can learn to understand it."

Amelia pulled back from Callais's embrace and began to smile as she bounced up and down, begging Callais to say yes. Callais was worried about her dreams and what they might do to her, but he saw how much she wanted to be a part of Evie's team. So, he reluctantly said, "Okay, Amelia, but as soon as something goes wrong, you are done. Otto would kill me himself if anything happened to you."

Amelia jumped up once more and hugged Callais tightly as she bolted out of the room to tell Evie the news. The elders all stood there quietly thinking over what her dreams might mean when, finally, Marina broke the silence and asked, "How do we figure out how to interpret her dreams?"

The others all looked at each other and shook their heads, not really knowing what to think. Newton then sighed and got up. "I will go tell Josephine. Maybe there is something in the scrolls that can help us."

The elders agreed with the plan, so Newton left to find Josephine and see if she would know what to do.

**

The next day, Callais called Evie, Declan, and Amelia to the council room, where he told them that he wanted to begin working with all three of them. This made Evie happy, but she felt a little scared after what happened to Collin and asked, "Will anything hurt her?"

"I am not really sure, Evie," Callais shook his head, "But I promise, I will do everything I can to not let that happen."

Evie gave Callais a worried look when Amelia began to gesture her hands. Evie watched until she understood what Amelia was saying—that she was brave enough to handle anything. She wasn't going to let anyone stop her. Evie smiled after Amelia finished and embraced her friend, saying, "I know. You're the bravest person I know!"

Amelia flashed a toothy grin as Callais instructed the three to hold hands and go into the dream state. He explained that Amelia was to take the lead once they found each other, and Evie and Declan were to follow. Evie curiously asked, "What are we looking for?"

"I am not sure, " Callais answered. "I just want to see if you can see what Amelia sees and come back and tell me."

The three then closed their eyes as they slowly rolled into the misty dream fog. Soon, the fog cleared, and Evie saw Amelia and Declan standing in front of her. They stood there for a while in the hazy surroundings when Declan looked at Amelia and asked, "Where to?"

Amelia scanned the surroundings, and once she gathered her bearings, she motioned her hands for them to follow. After walking for a brief period in the haze, the fog began to lift, and soon, the three of them found that they were standing on the edge of a giant lake. Evie had never seen this place before, but she felt there was something familiar about it. But she couldn't figure out why and just decided to follow Amelia's lead.

As the three stood at the edge of the lake, taking in the view, a dark shadow passed over them. When they looked up, Evie saw a massive Devas ship (even bigger than the one that brought her to Canopiuis) fly above them. The three of them were astounded by the ship's size. Then, all of a sudden, the massive ship flashed in the air and dove into the lake below the surface, making a giant wave crash across the lake and splash up on their feet. Declan and Evie stood there completely shocked and amazed while Amelia jumped up and down with excitement. She then directed their attention back to the water. The water then parted, and Evie was able to see, at the bottom of the lake, an enormous bubble surrounding a large city.

Amelia excitedly clapped her hands together and then turned to the still-shocked Evie and Declan. Before Evie or Declan could say anything, Amelia shrugged her shoulders as the dream fog rolled, and soon, the threesome found themselves back in the council room on Antillis.

Once their heads cleared and they had collected themselves, Callais asked them what they saw. After another minute of confused silence, Declan excitedly explained what they witnessed. When he had finished, Callais turned to Amelia and asked, "Have you seen this before in your dreams?"

Amelia nodded and began to maneuver her hands again as Callais watched. When she was done, he sat there in silence for a while before saying, "Well, I guess it is true. There does seem to be an underwater city on Alderbard." He paused, rubbed his forehead (obviously trying to process the information), and asked Amelia, "Are there people there?"

Amelia gestured her hands again, and when she finished, Callais told Evie and Declan, "She thinks there are people there. She also says she has dreams of a woman who lives there who has contacted her before. She also believes this woman has helped her in dreams."

Evie stood there even more shocked than before and

thought, *Could Rosalina also be contacting Amelia?* Evie was so excited about this and wanted to say something, but she knew she must keep Rosalina a secret. Evie remembered Rosalina told her that the others could be in danger if her existence was known. So, regretfully, Evie quickly pushed the thought aside about telling the others. She then caught Callais giving her a curious look as he asked, "Do you know anything about this, Evie?"

She paused, desperately wanting to tell them everything, and she hated lying, but instead, she shrugged, saying, "I'm not sure."

Luckily, the answer seemed to satisfy Callais, and she didn't have to explain any further. Callais then turned back to Amelia, "Good job, Amelia. We will keep working on this to find out what it means. In the meantime, the three of you go take a day off and enjoy yourself."

The threesome were happy about this. They all needed a break! They then left Callais in the council room, deep in his thoughts, and made their way to the forest to play with Collin and the dogs.

Part Two

RESISTANCE OF ALDERBARD

Chapter 14
FIRST TO ALDERBARD

———•———•———

It was dark as the Antillis resistance team descended from the star trails and landed on a small island in the center of a giant body of water on Alderbard. Otto motioned his forces towards a small patch of trees, where they took cover, as Atlas took a headcount to ensure that all of the team was present. Once all were accounted for, Otto waved his fist in the air as the team waited at the edge of the small tree forest. They found themselves overlooking a land bridge that connected the small island to a larger landmass. Otto again made another hand signal, in which Elizabeth understood for her to come to his side. Although the team had done extensive training and planning for their secret mission to Alderbard, it was Elizabeth's duty to help the team navigate safely to where there was a known protected town.

The land bridge was long and narrow. Nothing on

the land bridge provided cover for the team, making it wide open for anyone watching. Otto quietly chanted a protector invisibility spell over the team before making their way across the open path. The spell was a temporary spell that was often used by Devas protectors, making the armor they were wearing shimmer and then slowly match the surrounding environment, so the armor was almost completely invisible. The invisibility spell also made it so an enemy couldn't see them, but they could still see each other while under the spell. A few of the team members were also equipped with a large broadsword, which had been cast with spells by Callais, Simone, Newton, and Lincoln before they left. The spells were similar to the spells originally cast on the Devas protector staff but didn't have the powers to levitate objects. However, the swords could protect them like a large shield, defending them from attacks. Lincoln also had trained the team on spells that would help them while on Alderbard in manipulating water (since water was the main element on this planet). Atlas was particularly good with water spells. Although Lincoln was once the head keeper of Alderbard, he thought about going with the team, but he decided against this. Lincoln knew he would be useful, but since he was well known on Alderbard by the Camulus forces, he didn't want to jeopardize their mission… so, he stayed behind.

The team had to make it through a city occupied by Camulus forces to reach the small resistance town on the opposite side. Although they had discussed landing in the protected town itself, there were two reasons they chose to land where they did. They made this decision because of the original protection spell that covered the resistance town. The spell prevented Camulus forces from entering a protected area. Although Devas beings could enter a protected field, Otto decided that without giving the town's people prior notice of their entry, the Alderbard people might see them as a threat and attack. The second reason, with Alderbard being a planet of mostly water and land bridges, the Camulus force's black ships were constantly hovering over the cities on Alderbard. Because of Alderbard's terrain, the black ships always searched and controlled the cities from the skies. The resistance team didn't want to be seen as a threat from above by the Camulus force's dark ships as they descended from the star trails and possibly be attacked. So, they concluded entering on foot might provide them the opportunity to avoid the dark ships and to be recognized as resistance fighters... and hope that someone might also recognize Elizabeth.

Once Elizabeth was by Otto's side, they quietly whispered to each other when Otto, again, motioned with his hand for the team to move forward. The group slowly crossed the land bridge. Before they reached the other side, a black ship began to pass over the far side of the land bridge where they had just been. Although they were camouflaged, Otto made a quick hand motion as the team quickly raced across the remaining stretch. Once they reached the other side, they scattered, hiding among the many barrels and large bins at the water's edge. Just as the last team member took cover, the black ship blasted a bright light down—shining right where they had scattered from. The spotlight then moved rapidly back and forth across the bridge, as if it was searching for something ... or someone. The ship searched for a few minutes, but since they were all well-hidden, the light receded, and the ship slowly moved out of sight. Otto moved from the shadows where he had been hiding and made a bird chirping noise as his team slowly gathered back by his side. Otto again made several hand signals to his team before handing Atlas and Ellis each a piece of parchment with a map drawn on it. As soon as he was done giving instructions, the team split into three different directions into the city, one team following Otto and the other two teams following Ellis and Atlas.

Because Ellis was a novice resistance fighter and new to the Devas galaxy, Elizabeth joined his team to ensure that they could safely navigate the occupied city. The plan was for the three teams to split into different directions to reduce being caught as a large group. The split was also chosen because if one team was to be caught, two other teams had the chance to make it through the occupied city to their destination and complete their mission. Once through the city, the three teams would unite before entering the small resistance town in a protected area outside of the occupied city limits.

Elizabeth and Ellis held their position as they watched Otto's and Atlas's teams enter the city. Once Atlas's and Otto's teams were out of sight, Elizabeth and Ellis gathered their team and entered the city's east side through a small path between large buildings. The route was narrow at first, not allowing any opportunity for escape if they were caught here. Although they knew this was dangerous, Elizabeth knew of an underground tunnel at the end of this path that would take them under the majority of the city... hopefully undetected. This path was chosen because fewer soldiers were stationed on the east side of the city. The other two teams' route was much more perilous and heavily guarded by Camulus forces.

After an hour of navigating through the narrow path, Elizabeth held her hand up in a hold position like Otto had done. She motioned her hand as two team members came behind her. The team was at the end of the narrow path; however, there was a large uncovered opening that they had to cross to get to the tunnel. Elizabeth motioned her hand once more as one member ran to the center of the opening and hid behind a large bush. He then motioned his hands to Elizabeth and Ellis, indicating everything was clear. The rest of Ellis and Elizabeth's team then dashed across the clearing, making it safely to the other side. Once everyone was back together, they saw a black ship appear over the clearing, shining another spotlight down where they had just crossed. The team froze briefly when Ellis quickly motioned to the others, and Elizabeth took the lead. Elizabeth then led the team to a nearby building and down some stairs into a basement. The basement was connected to a large tunnel when Elizabeth quickly motioned for the others to follow and ran into the tunnel. The rest of the team followed, and after a few minutes of running down the tunnel, Elizabeth again held up her hand. The team stopped to catch their breath and collect themselves. Ellis then looked back down the tunnel and quietly whispered, "I think we're safe fer now!"

The team nodded in agreement as Aphrodite nudged Ellis's hand. Ellis seemed to understand what she meant and passed around the Virdis in a canteen he brought. They all took a big swig of the green drink before they began their trek under the occupied city.

After another hour of traveling through the tunnel, the team came to another stairway leading upwards. Ellis and Elizabeth gathered their team again as they went over the map and their plan again. Ellis then directed two team members to the top of the stairway. After a few minutes, the rest of the team heard a chirping noise, indicating the others to follow. Once the rest of the team made their way up the staircase, they saw that they only had about two hundred more yards to go before they were out of the city and at the meeting place. Ellis thought this was a good thing that they didn't have far to go since the spell Otto placed on their armor was wearing off, making them more visible now. They then began their way across the remaining space when they saw Atlas's team come from the center of the city and dash across the open space, safely making it to the meeting spot.

This excited Ellis, and before he knew it, he let out a shout. Ellis quickly tried to subdue himself; however, it was too late. A bright light instantly shined down right on Ellis and his team. Soon, several Camulus soldiers dropped down from the sky on top of them. Instantly, Ellis and his team drew their swords out and began to fight. Aphrodite's protective instincts took over as she began to charge the attacking soldiers with extreme ferocity. At first, it was an even-numbered battle—especially with the large dog at their side—but shortly after, another black ship appeared in the sky when more soldiers began to drop from above. Ellis and his team were soon surrounded. Just as they thought they would be captured or killed, a blast of air came from the city's west side. The explosion of air caught the Camulus soldiers off guard, knocking several of them to the ground. Ellis looked in the direction of the blast and saw Otto and his team begin to charge the Camulus soldiers. Aphrodite took advantage of the air spell and Otto's advance and began to chase and drag fallen soldiers away from Ellis and his team. Ellis's and Otto's teams began to fight when Ellis saw a blast of water knock down several more Camulus soldiers nearby. Ellis turned and saw that Atlas had joined the battle.

Atlas had been waiting to attack since he knew that he and his team were the only ones who had made it to the protected side of the city. Because of this, Atlas knew they had to wait to help Ellis. Their goal was to carry out the original mission if no other resistance members made it to the protected area. Atlas and his team helplessly watched Ellis's team battle. When Atlas saw Otto's attack, he realized it was time for him to engage, so he cast a water spell, creating massive water balls engulfing several Camulus soldiers. Otto saw the water balls around the soldiers. He released another air spell, lifting the Camulus soldiers into the air and spinning them wildly around. Otto then cast more air spells, sending the water balls and soldiers flying across the sky and out of sight. Soon there was so much chaos among the remaining Camulus soldiers that they couldn't hold formation any longer. Otto saw that the ranks of the Camulus forces had been broken and quickly commanded Ellis's team and his own team to run. The rest of the Antillis fighters quickly crossed the remaining few yards together, making their way safely into the protected zone, where the Camulus forces couldn't touch them... for now.

Chapter 15
ALDERBARD'S RESISTANCE

◆•━━━━━━━●━━━━━━━•◆

Although the original plan for the Antillis resistance team was to enter the protected town on Alderbard undetected, the commotion from the battle on the outskirts of the Camulus-occupied city alerted several townspeople to convene. When the Antillis team reached the edges of the protected city, the townspeople were prepared for an attack. The protector invisibility spell they were all wearing had now worn entirely off. Before Otto could cast another spell, he looked in front of him and saw that several people were charging at them in an attack formation. Before Otto could even respond, Ellis grabbed Elizabeth's arm and dragged her to the front line, yelling out, "Tell 'em who yeh 're!"

Elizabeth had no idea what to do. She tried yelling but found that she was so frightened, nothing came out. So, she quickly took off her armor on her left arm and raised it in the air, baring the fake extraction mark for all to see. As Elizabeth did this, Ellis immediately dropped his sword and took off his armor. The rest of the Antillis members quickly followed suit. When the charging forces neared the unarmored and unarmed invaders, the Antillis team heard a man yell out to the charging masses, "HALT!"

Only a few yards now stood between the Antillis members and the attacking townspeople. The man who yelled then approached the Antillis resistance. After a brief moment of uneasiness, the man walked towards Elizabeth as she held her breath. Elizabeth knew who he was, but because it had been several years since she had seen him, she was unsure if he would recognize her. After another few seconds of analysis, the man clapped his hands together, turned toward the crowd of townspeople, and shouted, "She is one of us!"

A blur of whispers and sighs of relief rushed through the crowd. Elizabeth released the held breath from her lungs when the man turned and faced her again. He then asked, "What are you doing back? I thought I'd never see you again after what happened."

Elizabeth motioned her hand behind her, saying loud enough for all to hear, "We are resistance fighters from Antillis... We have come to recruit new fighters against Camulos."

A low hush and light whispers fell over the crowd again. The man then turned to the others and introduced himself. "My name is Leo Kimathis… Come, let's replenish your bodies as we talk."

The townspeople slowly reentered the protected city to their respective homes as the Antillis team followed Leo into the heart of the city.

As they walked through the town, Ellis intently analyzed the surroundings in case there were any traps or tricks. Although Elizabeth knew this man and seemed to trust him, Ellis was still uneasy. As he looked around, the town itself looked like a typical fishing village. Many homes had nets, harpoons, fishing poles, and other miscellaneous fishing gear hanging around. There was also a powerful fish smell throughout the city, making Ellis queasy a few times when he took in a big whiff of air. After walking for a bit, Ellis determined the town was safe. So, he turned his focus to Leo and analyzed the man.

Leo was a large man with thick muscles and broad shoulders. His skin tone was dark black, and he had shaved his hair on his head like the crown of a rooster with facial hair, manicured into a long-pointed braided strip hanging off his chin. Ellis also noticed Leo bore a fake extraction mark on his left forearm like Elizabeth. Unlike Elizabeth, he was covered in multiple scars honeycombed all across his body. One of Leo's eyes was covered by a black patch, and the other eye was a light golden-brown. Ellis wondered what happened to Leo's eye but kept his thoughts to himself. Ellis also noticed Leo wasn't as tall as he was but was almost the same girth. Ellis's thoughts were interrupted when Leo led the group into a small home.

Although Leo's home was small, he led the Antillis members to the back and down a staircase into a much larger underground room. Ellis figured the room was set up as a meeting space for Alderbard's own resistance, as there were many maps and battles plans laid out across tables and hung across the walls. Once inside, Leo then asked the Antillis team, "Who's the keeper with you?"

The whole team looked at Leo with confusion and then around the room at each other, still confused. Leo then gestured his hand towards Aphrodite. Ellis laughed, realizing Aphrodite was why Leo thought this, and said, "Oh yeah. I guess she's mine."

Leo looked at Ellis with questioning eyes as Ellis continued. "Well, she was Magnus's dog, but I'm guessin' since he's not with us anymore, she chose to stick 'round with me."

Leo, once again, looked inquisitively at Ellis and asked, "Why would Magnus leave his beloved with you?"

Ellis huffed a little and shrugged his shoulders. "Well, I'm guessin' it's because I'm one of his descendants, an' she just must like me."

Leo gasped as he looked around the room at the others before asking, "So, it's true… Magnus left us a hero?"

Otto nodded and placed his hand on Leo's shoulder, saying, "We have a lot to tell you."

The members then all sat down as a woman entered the room bringing food and drinks, and Otto filled Leo in on the long journey they had been on so far.

Chapter 16
ELIZABETH'S STORY

s Otto told Leo about the Antillis team's journey and finding Evie (and the others), Elizabeth began to think about the last time she was on Alderbard and what had happened to her to make her leave the planet...

Elizabeth was born and raised on Alderbard and didn't know a time when the Camulus Pack didn't exist on the planet. All she had ever known was to live in a constant state of fear. She lived in a town called Adarais that was completely surrounded by the Camulus Pack. It was far from any other protected villages and cities on Alderbard, making Adarais more secluded from other Devas people on the planet. Not only was the town completely surrounded, but Adarais was the first place the dealers set up their fake extraction mark businesses. So, the town was crawling with seedy dealers and shady people making dark deals and keeping deep secrets.

Her parents and her younger brother, Ben, were constantly moving around trying to avoid the dangers in Adarais. One day, a dealer named Zane came to Elizabeth's home and told them that some of the other dealers had made a pact with the Camulus forces to infiltrate the protected cities and towns to capture and turn people over to the Camulus Pack who hadn't received extraction marks. Elizabeth's father then made a deal with Zane to provide him and his family with fake extraction marks so they wouldn't be turned over. The deal was that Elizabeth and her younger brother were to serve five years under Zane. Although Elizabeth's father didn't want to make this deal, Zane had promised that he would take good care of the children. And, since there was really no other choice to keep their family protected, Elizabeth's father reluctantly made the deal.

Zane kept his word the first year, and Elizabeth and Ben were well treated and mostly did household chores and errands. Zane wasn't necessarily cruel, but he drank a lot, and if Elizabeth and Ben didn't do exactly as he asked, they would often receive light beatings. Still, this was better than what most others received who were in debt to the dealers. Often others who owed debts to the dealers were tortured, and if they didn't abide by the dealer's requests, they were turned over to the Camulus Pack.

Besides drinking a lot, Zane also liked to gamble. Late one night, Zane came home after a night of gambling and had lost a lot of money. He couldn't afford to pay off his debt and made an exchange for Elizabeth and Ben to work for the man he owed instead. Zane told Elizabeth he was sorry but had made a deal with this new man to treat them well. Elizabeth learned that the man's name was Jafari. Although Jafari had promised Zane he would treat Elizabeth and Ben well, he had a nasty reputation for torturing and violating his captives... especially the young girls. Now that Elizabeth had learned who she and Ben were going to be turned over to, she decided to make a plan to escape.

Elizabeth knew that the town of Adarais had several underground tunnels that were dug out when the Camulus Pack first invaded Alderbard. This was true across the whole planet. They were first dug out as a way for people to hide until they learned of the protection spell that still lasted across several towns on Alderbard. The tunnels were also where many dealers first set up their businesses until they became bold enough to come out of the tunnels and openly do their work above-ground. It had been many years since these tunnels were used, and many of them had been blocked off since the dealers moved to the surface. However, when Elizabeth and Ben were younger, they found a few tunnels that had not been blocked off and would play in them. She knew of one in particular that led right to the outskirts of Adarais. She also knew that the next town closest to Adarais was sixty miles away, and she and Ben would have to find a way to get through unprotected areas without being caught by Camulus soldiers. Although this was a dangerous idea, she knew she must try anyway.

Late that night, while Zane was in a drunken slumber, Elizabeth and Ben made their escape. Fortunately, getting to the tunnel wasn't a problem since most of the people in the town were asleep, and those on guard mainly were watching over Adarais borders. They made it through the tunnel with ease and were soon on the outskirts of town. Before they left the city's protection field, Elizabeth scanned the area and saw no one in sight. So, she and Ben slowly moved across the border and into the Camulus-force occupied area.

They were able to get reasonably far the first couple of hours since it was still late at night and completely dark. As the morning hours began to come closer, Elizabeth looked for a place to hide since they were still several miles away from their destination, and she knew that they would be easily spotted in daylight. After an hour of searching, she found a spot next to a giant lake where she believed some large rocks would provide enough shelter to cover them both. However, right before they reached the rocks, a Camulus black ship appeared above them in a plume of dark smoke. They started sprinting towards their hiding spot as Camulus soldiers began to drop from the sky, charging towards them. But before they could reach their destination, a large man came at them, scooped Elizabeth and Ben up in his arms, and ran towards the lake. Elizabeth screamed and kicked and was able to release herself from this man. The man was still holding Ben as Ben tried desperately to escape from this large man as well. Before Elizabeth could do anything, the large man threw Ben in the shallow end of the lake and came back towards her. She was absolutely frantic. Behind her were Camulus soldiers, still charging in her direction, and this large man in front of her. Before she could think of what to do, the man shouted, "They can't get you in the lake."

She then saw Ben wading back out of the water towards her and this large man, when the man turned to Ben and yelled, "Stay, boy."

When he turned back to Elizabeth, it was too late. One of the Camulus soldiers had already caught her. The man then gave her an apologetic look and ran for the lake himself as Elizabeth was dragged off and lifted into the floating black ship.

***

Elizabeth was thrown into a dark cell and shackled to the wall. She then felt the ship lift away, and when it landed again, she was blindfolded and taken to another cell where she was shackled to the wall again. Over several days, the Camulus soldiers would come in and beat her while demanding she answer their questions. They asked her several things, but she didn't know half of the stuff they asked about since she was so young. However, after one horrible beating (that barely left her alive), she did tell them her name. She had no idea how long she had been in the cell or how long this would go on. Then, one night, she heard a loud commotion outside her cell. There were several blasts from weapons being fired and several people yelling and screaming. Before she knew it, her cell door burst open, and there was the large man from the lake standing in her doorway. He was soon by her side, unshackling her, saying, "We must hurry… follow me as quickly as you can."

Elizabeth jumped to her feet and followed this man without a sound. She still had no idea who he was, but he was saving her, and that's all she needed to know. She thought, *Wherever he is taking me or whatever he has in store for me has to be better than this.*

Elizabeth followed the man for a few hours in complete silence, ducking behind barrels and hiding in doorframes until they were finally out of the Camulus-occupied city. The man then turned to her, "We are almost there. Can you run?"

Elizabeth quickly nodded. Although she had been badly beaten, between the adrenaline of the escape and the hope that she would soon be safe, the pain she felt was nothing. She was quickly running as fast as she could behind this large man, running so hard all she could hear was her breathing and panting ringing and pounding inside her head. After what felt like running a marathon, the large man slowed down to a trot and pointed in front of him, "We are here."

He and Elizabeth entered a small fishing village when the man turned to her. "You are safe now." He then gave her a soft smile and introduced himself. "My name is Leo."

Elizabeth gave a weak and exhausted smile back before wearily saying, "I'm Elizabeth... thank you for saving me."

Leo then gave her a wink and motioned for her to follow. Elizabeth followed him to a small home in the center of the town. When they entered the home, she became lost in excitement when she saw that Ben was sleeping soundly on a cot next to the fireplace. Before she could run over to her brother, Leo touched her arm, "Let him sleep for now. I have some things I would like to ask you first."

Elizabeth nodded again, but knowing her brother was safe (and so was she), she decided she would comply with whatever this man asked of her. Elizabeth and Leo then sat down at the table near the fireplace as Leo waved his hand across the table. "Get some food and drink first, and then we can talk."

Elizabeth saw some bread, cheese, and dried fish on the table, along with a jug of red wine. She was starving. She had no idea when she last ate. So, she happily took some food and wine, filling her belly up to the brim. When she was done, Elizabeth looked over at Leo to see him staring at her with a sorrowful look across his face. He then cleared his throat before saying, "I know that you think you are safe right now, but I need to know what you told the Camulus soldiers while you were their captive."

Elizabeth gave him a curious look before she answered, "I don't know anything. All the things they asked me, I knew nothing about, so I couldn't answer them even if I wanted to."

Leo gave her another worried look before asking, "Did you tell them your name?"

Elizabeth then lowered her head and quietly answered, "Yes, I did."

Leo then pushed himself up from the table and paced the room. When he stopped, he turned back to Elizabeth with a more worried expression on his face than before. He once again cleared his throat before saying, "There are many spies in the protected cities and towns across Alderbard that are working for the Camulus Pack." He paused before he went on, "Now that the Camulus soldiers know your name, they will tell these spies to look for you. These spies get a hefty payday for turning over our own to them."

Leo then began to pace the room again before he wearily sat back down, gave Elizabeth an apologetic look, and then said, "Because of this, you are not safe here. Not just in this town, but anywhere on Alderbard." He took a big sigh, shaking his head. "You can't stay here."

Elizabeth began to tear up and shook her head before she sadly asked, "Where can I go then?"

"There is a woman here who has come from another planet in Devas to teach some of us about healing." He then wearily rubbed his head before telling her, "She is planning on leaving soon. I will ask her if you can go with her."

Elizabeth nodded in agreement as Leo motioned towards the cot Ben was on. "Get some rest. I will go talk to her tonight, and hopefully, I will have an answer for you in the morning."

Elizabeth only nodded her head again and went to Ben's side, wrapped him up in her arms, nuzzled her face deep into his hair, and slowly fell asleep.

***

The next morning, Elizabeth woke to someone poking her arm. When she opened her eyes, she saw Ben smiling widely at her. When he saw she was awake, he wrapped his arms around her, saying, "Ahhhh, sissy, I knew Leo would save you. I'm so happy you're here."

Ben then dragged her over to the table, where they ate breakfast. Leo was nowhere in sight, but she didn't care at this point. She was just happy to be with her brother and safe for now.

After they had finished eating and were clearing up the dishes, Leo entered the home with a tall, beautiful woman following behind him. Leo motioned for Elizabeth and Ben to take a seat as Leo and the woman sat down. Leo motioned his hand towards the woman. "This is Clara."

Clara nodded and gently smiled at Elizabeth. "Leo has told me of your predicament. I have agreed with him that it is not safe for you to stay here, and I have agreed to take you with me to someplace you can be safe."

Elizabeth gave a grateful smile and quietly said,

"Thank you." She then looked over at Ben and asked, "Can my brother come too?"

Leo and Clara exchanged a secretive glance before Clara answered, "No… he cannot."

Elizabeth and Ben began to tear up when Elizabeth asked, "Why can't he go?"

Clara gave her a sad glance before replying, "It is dangerous enough for one person to travel and leave this planet, let alone two people. If I was to take the both of you, I am afraid we might not be able to escape unnoticed. Ben must stay behind."

Elizabeth and Ben were both crying now. Leo walked over to Elizabeth's side, patted her shoulder, and reassuringly stated, "I promise I will take good care of your brother. I also promise, when it's safe, I will send for you again, and you will be back together."

Elizabeth wanted desperately to protest and not leave. Still, she knew she could put both herself and Ben in danger if she stayed behind. She then wiped away a tear, leaned into Ben, and whispered, "Ben, I must go with Clara, and you must stay here." Ben began to weep harder. Elizabeth felt hot tears pouring down her face as she continued. "I promise, we will be back together soon."

Ben then sucked up a sob, nodded his head in agreement, and wrapped his arms tightly around his sister. The two held onto each other for a while when Elizabeth sucked in a deep breath, released her brother, and turned to Clara and Leo, saying, "Okay, I'll go with you. Just please promise me you'll take good care of Ben."

Leo patted her shoulder again. "I promise. I'll treat him like he was my own son."

Clara then interjected, "I am sorry, but we do not have much time. We must leave now!"

Elizabeth nodded, wiped away the last tear falling down her cheek, gave Ben another hug, and followed Clara out of the home.

***

Soon, Elizabeth and Clara were traveling the star trails and floating in the dark sky. Elizabeth was astounded by this. Still, she was so overwhelmed she didn't ask any questions. After traveling through the sparkling night, they approached a bright green planet. Clara and Elizabeth landed on the surface and walked through the thick trees for a while when they came to a cave outcropping. Elizabeth followed Clara into a massive underground city. Again, she was astounded by the view but didn't ask any questions. For some reason, Clara intimidated her, but she didn't know why. After walking down some winding rope bridges and giant root steps, Clara took her to a dwelling where an old woman was sitting, looking over several scrolls scattered across a large table. Clara then introduced Elizabeth to the old woman named Josephine, explained the situation, and then turned back to Elizabeth, saying, "You will be safe here. I must go, but I promise I will keep in contact so when it is safe, we can reunite you with your brother."

Elizabeth was only able to mumble out a thank you as she watched Clara leave… and that was how Elizabeth came to be a resident of Antillis and came to be a resistance fighter… so she might be able to see her brother once again.

Chapter 17
DAVI AND SILAS

O tto finished explaining to Leo about the journey of the Antillis team and how they had found Evie (Magnus's true-of-heart heir), Ellis, and Marina, as well as some of the lost relics and texts. After Leo listened to their story, he decided to call a meeting of the available Alderbard resistance members. While they waited for Alderbard resistance members to show up, Leo told them they were in the town of Davi, where he had started his own resistance against the Camulus forces. When the Alderbard members were finally present, Leo and the Antillis team briefed the Davi resistance members about their mission. After the meeting, Leo sent many people out into other protected towns and cities across Alderbard to recruit resistance members to return with the Antillis team. Leo and Otto also created a special team of resistance members, including Atlas, who would head a team to find any ships or staffs that still might have been located on Alderbard.

Over the next few weeks, many people came to Davi willing to join the fight and be trained or with information of the whereabouts of the ship and staffs. Once Otto had several willing people to take back to Antillis, he began to plan a return mission, leaving Atlas, Elizabeth, and Leo in charge of recruiting more resistance members and finding the ship and staffs while he was gone. After a month of recruitment, Otto was prepared to leave with the new members when Atlas came storming into Leo's underground meeting room, out of breath, "We have found..." Atlas paused between gasps of air. "...We have found a ship... and two staffs."

The resistance members in the room all shouted with joy as Atlas gasped for air one more time and added, "That's not all... We had a skirmish with some Camulus soldiers, and two things happened."

Atlas took another deep breath as the room held their breaths, now in anticipation, when Atlas followed up. "The soldiers caught us, and we were cornered. One of the Camulus soldiers, after we thought there was no way out, approached us and said that he was no longer happy with Camulos's rule... he and his soldiers told us they want to defect and join the resistance."

Atlas took another pause and continued. "Elizabeth has the soldiers who want to defect held in the next town over. The leader of these soldiers wants to talk to you."

Otto and Leo exchanged glances. Both were hesitant because they believed this could be a trap or a trick. The two men moved closer to each other and quietly conversed so no one else could hear them. After they stopped, Leo said, "I believe that Otto is too important to go into an unprotected area. I will meet with these men, and Otto will continue his mission to take new recruits back to Antillis."

Once Leo finished, Atlas interjected one last time. "There is one more thing."

He hung his head down and became a little more sullen before saying, "One of the soldiers in this group escaped. The leader and the remaining soldiers that are being held said that this man who escaped didn't share their sentiments in defecting." Atlas paused and rubbed his head before finishing, "They believe he may have escaped to alert Balor. So, we may not have long before Balor comes to Alderbard with more soldiers."

Leo and Otto gave each other worried glances again. Otto also rubbed his head and said, "Well, we must move quickly then."

Otto then turned to the rest of the members, stating, "Since I can travel the star trails on my own with the help of my Antillis team members, I think it will be wise for those of you we leave here on Alderbard to procure the ship and staffs that Atlas has stated were found." He paused a moment and then finished, "This way, you can defend yourselves if Balor does come to Alderbard, and you will also have a way to reach Antillis with other recruits if I'm unable to return."

Leo and the rest of the members agreed to this. The next day, Otto gathered his team, including Ellis and several new recruits, and headed back to Antillis.

***

As Otto drifted off the planet into the star trails with his team, he was surprised to find the trip out of Davi was much easier than their entry. He figured the fourth-day protection spell not only covered the town, but unlike with Antillis's protected area, the spell extended off the planet for several hundred miles. This made their departure undetectable to the Camulus forces and black ships until they were a safe distance away from the planet—which was a huge relief. Now Otto knew entering and leaving Alderbard (or at least Davi) would be much easier than previously thought.

The same day Otto left, Leo and Atlas went to

interrogate the defected soldiers. Because of Alderbard's terrain, the next town was on another small island surrounded by a massive body of open water. Fortunately, Atlas had been trained by Lincoln in water spells, and he was able to cast a spell over the open water. Atlas cast his spell, when soon, a large fog rolled over the top of the water, covering Leo and Atlas so they could move across unseen.

Once across the water, Leo and Atlas entered the small town and approached a home where Elizabeth was detaining the soldiers. They entered the room and found ten soldiers shackled to several chairs and tables across the room. To their surprise, Elizabeth was guarding them, holding a Devas protector staff. Before they could ask questions, a young man approached them, shook Leo's arm, and introduced himself to Atlas. "My name is Ben. I'm Elizabeth's brother. I found this staff and know where we can find another one, as well as a ship."

Atlas and Leo smiled from ear to ear. Leo then proudly slapped Ben on the back. "This is fantastic news. Thanks for your help, son!" Ben proudly smiled back.

Atlas noticed that Ben looked exactly like Elizabeth, with dark skin and hazel eyes but much taller and lankier than she was. He also noticed that Elizabeth's usual sullen demeanor had changed. Even though she was intently guarding the captured soldiers, she looked much happier. Atlas assumed that Elizabeth being reunited with her brother was the reason for the drastic change. Before Atlas could think any longer about Ben and Elizabeth, Leo interjected, "I think it would be wise for us to wait and talk about the locations of the other staff and ship until we aren't in front of enemy soldiers."

Ben nodded in agreement and went and stood proudly by Elizabeth's side. Leo then approached the shackled soldiers and asked, "Which one of you is in charge?"

A young man, who was tall, lean, and muscular, with a greenish skin tone, purple hair, and purple eyes, cleared his throat and mumbled, "I am."

Leo took a step closer to the man and asked, "What's your name?"

The young man proudly held his head up a bit and with more confidence, answered, "My name is Silas. I was born after the wars started, but my family came from Denidis. They were Denidis warriors, captured, tortured, or killed by Camulos and his forces." He paused and finished saying, "I and my soldiers have all come from other galaxies that were taken over by Camulos. We were all forced to become soldiers in his war when we were children… but we no longer want to fight for him."

Leo looked at each of the soldiers in the room. They

were all young, and all of them looked defeated and tired. He looked at Elizabeth and said, "Feed them and let them get some rest. I need some time to think."

Elizabeth nodded as she and Ben gathered some food and fed the soldiers. Atlas and Leo then retreated to another nearby home that Leo knew was safe. That night, Atlas and Leo discussed what they would do.

***

The next morning, the pair returned to the home and saw the soldiers were already eating breakfast. Even though there was less tension in the room from the previous day, Elizabeth still held the Devas protector staff while feeding the captive soldiers. Leo approached the soldiers, saying, "We believe your story and think that you'll be helpful in aiding us in our endeavor." He paused and finished, "We also believe it's unsafe and unwise for you to stay here on Alderbard. For this, we have several reasons, which we'll not tell you at this time. However, because we believe you, we have also decided for Atlas to take you somewhere we know you can be safe and help us."

Silas gave him a worried look and asked, "Where?"

Leo again looked intently at Silas before answering, "Even though we believe your story, we still don't trust you. The plans we have will not be yours to know, but we promise you and your people will be safe."

Silas nodded in agreement (realizing he didn't have much of a choice). "Whatever you have planned for us has to be better than what we have already endured. We'll go wherever you need us to."

The rest of the soldiers all muttered in agreement. Atlas and Leo then pulled Elizabeth and Ben outside of the home—out of earshot—and explained that Atlas would take the soldiers back to Antillis, where Callais, Simone, and the others can determine what to do with them. Elizabeth then nervously asked, "With Atlas, Otto, and Ellis gone, will we be able to continue our plans?"

"Don't worry," Atlas answered. "I'll only be taking them there and then coming straight back to help you finish the mission here."

Leo then added, "We can accomplish much of what we need in the meantime without him or the others. I promise that we are much more prepared than when you left here."

Elizabeth then remembered how hard it was for them to get to Alderbard in the first place, and now, with the threat of Balor coming, she once again stated her fears. Leo then placed his hand on her shoulder. "Have faith. We're all stronger than you think."

Elizabeth shrugged her shoulders and sighed. Ben then placed his hand on her opposite shoulder, saying, "Don't worry. Leo and I have been doing a lot of work here on Alderbard. Our resources and forces are much stronger than they were."

Elizabeth smiled at her brother and pulled him into her. She sighed once more and then pulled back and nodded in agreement.

The next day, before Atlas left with the soldiers, he placed a spell on them that Callais had taught him, allowing them to enter the protected town for a temporary period. He then cast a spell over the water, making fog roll over the top again. Atlas and the soldiers made it across the water safely. When they reached the edges of the protected area, they entered and made their departure to the star trails… to Antillis.

Chapter 18
FINDING OTHERS

N adia had spent days trying to get the watcher glass to work. However, she couldn't get through to anyone like she had done in the past, nor did the glass ever become clear enough to answer any questions she had. She became concerned that maybe all the other watcher glasses had been lost or destroyed and that this glass would only be useful to contact Evie. Evie had made contact almost every day since they found the mirror. Still, Nadia didn't get much information from Evie either. So, the glass was mainly used by Ruby, David, Steven, or Beth, who would use it to talk to Evie. Sophia also used the glass often, having very long conversations with Evie about her father, Ellis, and other questions they had for each other.

One day, Nadia was trying to get the glass to focus when a woman, Regina, came through. Nadia thought she had reached someone in The Order, but Regina told her that she was with Evie and not on Terran. Nadia asked her about finding others on Terran, but it also came to the same end. Regina didn't know much more than Nadia about finding others on Terran. Regina had told Nadia she thought Terran had been lost, so Regina hadn't contacted anyone from Terran besides David and Ruby. Nadia decided that maybe the glass was a lost cause. After several weeks of trying, Nadia finally decided to give up. She went to place the glass down after another endless search, when suddenly, she heard a man's voice say, "Maria?"

Nadia picked the glass up and could see a man with dark hair and light eyes looking right back at her. The man (with a soft Spanish accent) then said, "You are not Maria?"

"No. I am not," Nadia replied and then asked, "Who is Maria?"

The man looked nervously around before answering, "Maria is my sister. I haven't been able to find her for years. However, when my glass began to move around again, I thought she was trying to reach out to me. Is she with you?"

Nadia now realized that Maria was Evie's mother, since it was Evie's mother's jewelry box where the glass was found. Nadia didn't want to tell this man his sister was dead, so she simply said, "No. She is not with me."

Nadia then paused and added, "However, we could use some help. I know you do not know me, but we are part of The Keeper's Order, and we are searching for lost people and knowledge. If you would be willing, I would like to meet with you in person."

The man looked nervous again. "I can meet you if you help me find my sister."

Nadia felt guilty knowing what this man would find out about his sister's fate if he came, but she knew they needed help. So, she just nodded, saying, "I am sure we can give you some answers if you come."

The man also nodded, and Nadia gave him the information of where they were. He then told her that he would be there in three days before he disappeared, and the glass then turned foggy again. Nadia quickly put the glass down and went to tell the others the news.

***

Nadia told the others what had happened with the watcher glass and that this man who reached out to her was asking for Maria. However, she told the others that she hadn't told him that Maria was dead. David and Ruby seemed upset about Nadia not telling the man of his sister's fate but agreed that they needed the help.

David felt even worse over the next three days, thinking of how the man would react once he heard the news.

***

Three days later, a taxi pulled up in Sophia's driveway. Before David could go over to the man, he saw Sophia go out to greet him. David watched as Sophia spoke with him. Sophia then stopped speaking when David saw the man drop to the ground and began to cry. Sophia got down on her knees and wrapped her arms around the man as she tried to console him. David realized that Sophia must've told him about Maria's fate. He felt awful but somewhat relieved that Sophia had the courage to tell this man right away. David watched the man collect himself and stand back up as Sophia escorted him to the cabin. David followed them inside, and once inside, he could see tears in Maria's brother's eyes. So, David went over, held his hand out, and apologetically said, "I'm so sorry."

The man gave David a sad look and gently shook David's hand before saying, "I'm Alvaro Diaitz, Maria's brother. Who are you?"

David introduced himself and then curiously stated, "Maria's last name is Borbón. Are you sure she was your sister?"

Alvaro sadly shook his head before he replied, "I figured she changed her last name when she ran away. That's probably one of the many reasons it was so hard to find her."

Before David could say anything more, Ruby, Steven, Beth, Amam, and Nadia entered the room. Everyone made introductions as they all took seats. Sophia then told the others, "I 'ad to tell him 'bout Maria. I felt it was unfair to bring him 'ere under false pretenses that he could find his sister."

The others nodded in agreement with Sophia's decision as Nadia, in a sorrowful tone, said, "I am sorry that I deceived you, but we need help, and I believe your sister knew things that we need to know. I hope that you will still want to help us, bring your sister peace, and help your niece."

"My niece? I have a niece? Is she here?" Alvaro asked, with a shocked look on his face.

David shook his head no when Alvaro stated, "I didn't know Maria had a child. I would like to meet her. Where is she?"

The room remained silent. Alvaro looked at the others, hoping for an answer, but since no one responded, he went on, "I don't understand. Why is my niece not here, and why do you need my help?"

Steven then cleared his throat and began to tell Alvaro everything they knew and everything they had been doing. After Steven finished telling the story, Alvaro looked around the room, but David noticed he didn't seem shocked by their story. After a brief period of silence, Alvaro finally spoke. "My family has been in The Order for a very long time now. I'm now head of the family and our secrets. Maria was supposed to be the one in my place, but she ran away a long time ago, saying she didn't want the responsibility."

Alvaro took a deep breath. "I spent years trying to find her because she knew certain things that I don't even know. It was our mother who trained her and shared knowledge with Maria to lead our family. I've only been able to learn about my family and their responsibilities through the texts and books we have." He sighed and went on, "After Maria ran away, my mother was devastated and began to seclude herself. I knew our family's mission needed to be carried on, but my mother gave me very little help. So, what I have learned, I have done mostly on my own."

David then asked, "What have you learned?"

Alvaro then explained that his family was enlisted by Magnus a thousand years ago to protect and preserve knowledge. Alvaro told them his family was given knowledge that they stored in a hidden city for Magnus. Alvaro continued to explain, saying, "My family was also in charge of creating sacred circles for Magnus to give to other families around the world to keep the knowledge hidden from corrupt rulers until Magnus's protection of Earth wore off."

Alvaro took a deep breath and began to tell them that the sacred circles were made of gold and cast with spells from Magnus. The circles were encrypted with several different ancient languages so that if they were found by someone who wanted to use them for evil, they would have to know each of these languages to decipher them. Alvaro then explained that his family was enlisted by Magnus because they had special powers connected to powerful beings called keepers. Alvaro then said, "Apparently, keepers can manipulate and control elements, and my family could manipulate the element of gold for Magnus to cast these spells." Alvaro then took another breath and continued. "My family also has the ability to manipulate gold with other elements as well. So, these sacred circles, once they are deciphered, are to be taken to different locations around the world and placed in areas across the planet that hold Earth's greatest secrets."

Everyone was silent for a while when Amam finally spoke up. "So, not only do we need to decipher these sacred circles, but now we need to take them all across the planet.. . and if we find these locations, a spell needs be used to manipulate gold with other elements to find the lost city?" Amam took a deep breath before adding, "This is impossible."

Alvaro shook his head. "No. It's not. Although I don't know as much as Maria did, I've learned how to manipulate elements myself. I've also been trying to learn the spells that we need to combine elements. I've also trained my two brothers on how to do this as well." He paused before adding, "Not only that, but I've learned there are three other people that have this keeper power."

Ruby gasped, shook her head in disbelief, and then asked, "Where do we find these people?"

"That, I do not know," Alvaro replied and went on, "It seems that these people are lost or don't want to be found." He paused and then added, "Although I've found the spells to combine elements, I don't know how to read all of the text to complete these spells. So, I tried to find these people, but to no avail. However, I believe that finding all of you wasn't a coincidence."

He took another pause before telling them, "My mother can read the scripts that I can't, but she refused to help me without Maria. I'm afraid if we tell her of Maria's fate, this will devastate her more. However, I also believe if we tell her that Maria has a daughter, and my niece needs our help, I think I might be able to convince my mother to help us."

Alvaro then looked around the room. "Meeting you, and with all the information we have combined, I believe we can all help each other."

So, once again, over the next few days, they looked over all the texts and books and made more plans to head off on another great adventure.

Chapter 19

SIMONE AND SILAS

◆•————— ● —————•◆

As Atlas made his approach over the protected forest of Antillis, he again cast a spell over the captured soldiers, allowing them temporary entry into the forest. Once they reached the ground, Atlas told the soldiers to rip pieces of their uniforms off and cover their eyes. A young man, who had been on watch, approached Atlas and the blindfolded soldiers. Atlas explained to the young man what was happening, and they both led the soldiers towards the underground city of Mari. Getting the soldiers to Mari was a struggle since the forest floor was hard to navigate not blindfolded, but the group finally made it to Mari's entrance. Once inside the city, Atlas un-blindfolded the soldiers when Simone approached them. Simone was about to lecture Atlas, but she stopped and took one large stride over to Silas. Simone then grabbed Silas and held him in a tight embrace as she began to sob. Silas was stunned as Simone continued her embrace. When she pulled back, tears were running down her face, and she said, "My dear boy. I am sure you do not remember me, but I could never forget your face."

She paused, took a deep breath, and told him, "I thought you were dead... I am so happy to see you alive." Simone then turned to Atlas, her arm still wrapped around Silas's shoulders, and proudly stated, "This is my sister's son!"

Silas took a step back, and then he, too, began to lightly weep with this new knowledge that he had an aunt. Silas quickly wiped the tears from his eyes and stood there looking at Simone for a minute. As a Camulus soldier, he wasn't allowed to show emotion, so he was shocked by his own tears. Simone embraced him once more. This time, Silas hesitantly returned the embrace.

Soon, Simone was shuffling the soldiers down the path and bridges into a large room where Otto and Callais were already waiting. Atlas pulled Callais and Otto aside and debriefed them on the situation. Regina, Emmeline, and Amelia were in the room and had brought food and healing supplies since some of the soldiers had been slightly hurt trying to get through the thick Antillis forest. After they were fed and a few minor repairs to their injuries were made, Calais approached the group of soldiers and earnestly stated, "Welcome. We are glad you are here with us."

The soldiers, who had all been a little tense and shocked from their star travels and entering the city, all let go a sigh of relief. They had been treated so poorly for so long, they were just glad to have kindness shown to them by their captors. Callais then told them, "We are truly glad you are here. However, until we have learned more about your situation and learn to trust you, unfortunately, you will have to be treated as protected prisoners." He paused and then continued. "But have no fear. We do not treat our prisoners as Camulos and his forces have done. You will be kept in locked and guarded rooms, but we will treat you kindly and fairly. So, be sure to let us know what you need… In the meantime, get some rest."

Before Callais left the room, he chanted a spell over the soldiers so that they were able to remain in the protected city. The soldiers seemed to be more relieved than upset by their captive situation. Simone led them out of the room and into another large room, with bars and guards, and bedding, food, and water. Simone chanted a quick spell over the opening to ensure there would be no escape. Simone then looked at Silas with watery eyes and told him, "Do not worry. I promise this is where you belong."

***

As Simone made her way back to the council room, she began to think of her past and her first encounter with Camulos where she lost her beloved sister. Camulos was known as the God of war, darkness, and destruction. He didn't start being known as this but earned his title after one of the first battles ensued between five neighboring galaxies and where Simone first fought him. Although Simone knew the Camulus Pack didn't initiate the battle, she did know they saw an opportunity to influence their power. What Camulos did in this first battle was what earned him the title God of war, darkness, and destruction and what led to the expansion of the wars across the rest of the galaxies.

Simone remembered that Camulos and his forces came into the middle of this small war in the Denaban galaxy. Denaban itself was a galaxy caught in the middle of the other warring galaxies. Although the people of the Denaban system wanted peace, they had to enter the small war, if only to protect themselves. Simone was the head keeper of this galaxy and came from the planet of

Denidis. Denidis was the planet in the Denaban system where great warriors were bred only for the purpose of battle and protection—not only for the protection of their own galaxy but for protection in other galaxies who enlisted their services—and since birth, they were trained to be warriors against darkness. Like Simone, the beings on Denidis were all very tall and lean, had extremely muscular builds, and had greenish skin tones. Simone knew that Denidis warriors attracted Camulos more than anything, mostly because he wanted to either extinguish these warriors or find a way to turn them to his side. So, Camulos took advantage of the war in the Denaban system and decided to invade Denidis. However, Simone was ready when Camulos's dark ships and forces came in under the cover of night and landed across the planet. Once they were on the ground, Camulos made his commands to his troops and, in a powerful voice, said, "Take as many as you can alive… but kill them if they resist."

Simone waited patiently in her position when she saw a malicious flicker in Camulos's eyes as an evil smile inched slowly across his face. The Camulus forces then began to creep up on the quiet sleeping villages across Denidis. Before Camulos's forces could reach the villages across the planet, Simone made her command to all her warriors with one simple word, "FIGHT!"

In an instant, Simone's warriors came out from surrounding forests and trenches across the fields where they had been hiding and charged Camulos's forces as the first great battle ensued.

The battle lasted for days, and it seemed as though no side would win. There were casualities and bloodied fallen bodies on all sides. Laid out across all the battlefields were soldiers screaming and dying—reaching their arms up if they were pulling at some unseen force for help. Simone stood up after taking down another Camulus soldier, completely covered in blood, and looked up from the chaos of the battle. That was when she saw Camulos with his right-hand man, Balor, standing on the far side of the battlefield she was fighting on. They were both unscathed as they laughed while watching the horrific scene unfold. Simone became enraged and charged in their direction, struggling to climb over the injured warriors all around her as they, too, tried to pull her down. As she neared Camulos and Balor, she was prepared to strike when she saw a smile stretch across Camulos's face again, and he said in a voice that seemed to ring inside her head, "KILL THEM ALL."

Simone watched as he placed his palms together, and Balor held some kind of weapon in front of Camulos's hands. Then a great ball of white fire came billowing out from Camulos's closed fists into the weapon Balor was holding. Simone then watched the fireball shoot out of the weapon and land on the far side of the battlefield. Simone looked where the fireball landed and gasped in horror as the fireball expanded and quickly began to cover the battlefield. She watched all warriors, on all sides, burn to the ground... burn to death. The fire spread rapidly across the field with nowhere for anyone to escape as she watched the fire come closer to where she stood. A flicker of madness then consumed her as she turned to look at Camulos and made one last lunge towards him. Then, all of a sudden, a blinding flash of white light appeared out of nowhere, encapsulating Simone in its force, before knocking her to the ground. When the light faded, Simone slowly stood up and found that Camulos was gone. She was alone, left in silence and darkness, standing on top of more than ten thousand corpses, one of which was her sister's corpse... Simone was the only survivor.

Simone knew that Camulos was one of the first keepers the mother and father created, and she knew he had special powers beyond those of the other keepers. When Simone made her report about the battle to others, many keepers weren't willing to go after Camulos because of these special powers. Even once they learned of Camulos's destruction on Denidis, many didn't believe that Camulos was capable of this type of chaos. Some believed Simone, and many saw the aftermath of the battle on Denidis. However, many still thought that this kind of power couldn't exist. The few who believed Simone spread stories of Camulos's power and destruction, earning Camulos his deadly title. Simone being the only survivor made many question if Camulos truly could've done such a horrible thing or if he was even at the Denidis battle. So, with this doubt among the keepers, the power and manipulation of elements done by Camulos and his forces escalated the bickering among the galaxies into further discourse, and, eventually, an intergalactic war ensued across the far reaches of the universe.

After the Denidis battle, Simone tried to find her sister's son but couldn't. The village where Silas was supposed to be was destroyed. All she found was a single black raven cawing out a remorseful song over the dead. The raven, Indy, she took as her companion to remind her of the pain and her promise to continue to fight against the darkness. As Camulos's power spread, Simone vowed to stop him in any way she could. She was eventually enlisted by Callais to join his resistance, and Simone hoped that one day, she could defeat the darkness that now consumed the universe.

Chapter 20
SEND OUT THE SPIES

Over the next few days, the council members discussed their plans. They went over what to do with the captive soldiers and reviewed the news brought back from Alderbard. They also conversed and made plans for training the many new recruits that Otto had brought back. The council agreed that Atlas should return to Alderbard to continue the mission already in place and that Otto should return to Alderbard. Still, Callais wanted to keep him on Antillis for a while to help train Ellis a bit more. This way, Ellis could help train the new recruits with Abe. After making a few more decisions, Atlas headed back to Alderbard, and the rest of the resistance team prepared for their next steps.

Although Otto had brought back many new recruits, it was still not enough to attack the Camulus base on Antillis. Even with the news that Leo and Elizabeth were still getting more recruits and that two staffs and a ship were being searched for, Callais was still uneasy about the resistance's numbers and resources. With this fear in mind, Callais called a private meeting with Simone, Newton, Josephine, and Lincoln. The meeting didn't occur in the council room like usual. This time Callais called the four other elders to a small room, deep in the bowels of the underground city. Once the elders were inside the room, Callais then cast a spell over the entrance, ensuring further privacy. Newton gave Callais a curious look as Callais went on to answer his concerns. "Even though we have made a lot of progress, I am afraid we still do not have enough people or resources to take over the Camulus base on Antillis." He paused and then continued. "It is too dangerous to send another mission to any other planet to get more resistance fighters, and we do not have the people to do so even if we wanted to."

Callais then paced the room for a bit and went on, "I believe it is wise to implement a few other strategies that may help us in taking Antillis back."

Once again, Callais paused and looked directly at Simone. "Simone, I would like to place you in charge of recruiting some spies to infiltrate the Camulus base here on Antillis."

Simone nodded in agreement as Callais held up his

hand. "I know that you have agreed, but I am afraid that what I must ask of you may be something you have to think on." He paused again before saying, "Because we have Silas and the other soldiers, and they know about how the Camulus forces operate better than us, I would like to recruit some of the captive soldiers to pose as Camulus soldiers and spy for us."

Simone looked at Callais and wanted to say no, but she simply said, "I am not sure if they will do this."

Callais nodded. "I know this is hard for you to ask of your nephew and the others, but we need people who know how the soldiers operate. We also now know that there is unrest and conflict in the Camulus forces. So, if we send in spies, we may be able to achieve several things."

Callais explained to the elders that there would be a few spies, each with a specific task. He reiterated that the captured soldier spies knew how the Camulus forces operated, knew who the head officers were, knew their resources, and could report this back to the Antillis team. Callais told them that since the captive soldiers had already been among the Camulus ranks, it would be easier to send them in to relay information instead of trying to train Antillis fighters to infiltrate the Camulus base. Callais then explained that captive soldiers who didn't want to be spies could teach some of the resistance fighters how the Camulus forces operated. Callais then said, "We could then send in more of our resistance fighters as spies to help gather information once they are trained."

Callais then explained that the spies could also spread the news to other unhappy Camulus soldiers about possibly defecting themselves. Callais then told them, "We also know the Camulus forces will expect extreme force from the resistance since the officers of the Camulus force use extreme punishing techniques to command their soldiers. Having the spies spread rumors that our resistance will also use these methods on those who do not defect will hopefully scare some into eventually defecting or at least distract them from our plans."

Callais then went on to say that he had an idea of a few Antillis resistance members that might be willing to spy for the resistance, but having a few of the captured soldiers return with the Antillis spies might be the best chance they had in gathering sufficient information. The group of five elders were quiet for a while after Callais had finished. After a few minutes of deep thought, the elders eventually decided this was needed. Simone then stood up and said, "I will go and get Silas."

Simone left the room, and shortly after, she returned with Silas. Callais once again explained what he needed to Silas. When Callais was done, Silas dropped heavily into a chair nearby. He took in a deep breath before saying, "I know that there are a few of my people I can't ask to do this because they're so defeated and tired." He paused and took another deep breath, before finishing, "I'll do this for you, and I believe two of my people may be willing to spy for the resistance. I also believe my other men will help train the resistance fighters as well."

Callais nodded his head in respect towards Silas as Newton approached the young man. "You are truly a brave man for doing this. I know how hard this must be. Just know that we…" Newton gestured his hand towards the others before finishing, "…will do anything we can to help you and ensure your safety. You belong somewhere you can finally be free."

Silas took a deep breath and wiped an unexpected tear from his cheek again as Simone escorted him out of the room.

***

Over the next few weeks, Otto trained Ellis in protector and watcher spells, strategies, and tactics so Ellis could stay behind and help train the new recruits. Once Otto felt confident in Ellis's abilities, he again made a tear-filled departure from Antillis, promising Amelia, Emmeline, and Evie he would be back soon. Otto then left for Alderbard.

During this time, Simone trained Silas, two of his soldiers, and a few other Antillis resistance members as spies. Simone also taught them spells to communicate with the resistance base while in the field. Callais and the others soon came to trust Silas and his soldiers, and the spies were then sent out to the Camulus base on Antillis. The other captive soldiers joined Ellis, Abe, and the new recruits from Alderbard, teaching them everything they knew of the Camulus forces.

Regina continued her training with her team, while Newton and Lincoln continued to work with Marina and Declan. Like Magnus had done, Josephine secluded herself with the ancient text and scrolls. She hoped she would be able to find anything that could help the others. Callais, once again, focused on Evie and her training. Amelia and the others came to help whenever they were needed. There was new energy among the resistance, and there was hope for the first time in a long time.

Chapter 21
SEARCHING ALDERBARD

❖•——————— ● ——————— •❖

Otto landed safely back on Alderbard and rejoined Leo, Atlas, Elizabeth, and Ben. While Otto was gone, they had accomplished a lot. The Alderbard team had recruited many new members and found the other staff. They also had plans to retrieve the hidden Devas ship. Although Balor hadn't come as anticipated, there was a renewed effort among the Camulus forces across the planet, and more soldiers and ships had been sent to Alderbard. There was still a rumor that Balor was coming, but there had been no confirmation of this so far. Even though the Camulus forces had renewed their efforts, the Alderbard team had effectively extracted most Devas people to the protected towns and cities. The towns and cities were crowded, but the Devas people on Alderbard also had new energy like the Antillis occupants… there was hope again.

The Alderbard resistance team decided the first thing they must do would be to get the Devas ship. They figured this would be the goal they needed to achieve first because if Balor was to come, they would at least have a ship to battle against him. If Balor didn't return, then they would have the ship to take new recruits to Antillis. Even though Atlas and Otto could take people on the star trails, having the ship would allow Leo to bring many others, lightening the load for Atlas and Otto. Since there was a renewed energy and hope among the Alderbard people, many volunteered to stay on Alderbard and continue to hold the planet steady until the Antillis resistance could come back and help free Alderbard once the Antillis mission was complete.

Once the plans had been laid out, Leo held a meeting in his underground room as the resistance team went over the plans to retrieve the Devas ship. The ship was found in a cave near the large protected lake. However, it was trapped behind rocks that had fallen (or had been purposely placed over the cave entrance). Leo told Otto and Atlas he had planned on using explosives to blow the rocks from the cave entrance. Leo then said, "However, with the renewed effort of the Camulus forces, I'm afraid this would alert Camulus soldiers to the cave, and we wouldn't have enough time to retrieve the ship safely."

Leo asked Atlas and Otto (since they were now back with the team) to devise a plan of using spells to gently move the rocks from the entryway. Otto nodded and told the others, "This will take longer than an explosion, and it may weaken mine and Atlas's strength after using spells for such an intense task."

The others nodded in agreement, realizing this was also a challenge. Atlas then suggested that if using the spells weakened them, they should have resistance members trained as protectors and watchers to guard over Otto and Atlas while working on this task. Atlas then went on to say, "This will ensure that if the Camulus forces find us while we are moving the rocks, and if Otto and myself are depleted from the spells, the resistance members we bring with us can protect and defend themselves until we regain our strength."

Everyone agreed to this plan, and over the next few weeks, Otto and Atlas trained many resistance members in protector and watcher spells and strategies until they felt they were all prepared. Otto and Atlas also trained Elizabeth and Ben. Still, they decided it would be best to leave the two of them behind to get more Alderbard beings into protected cities while they were gone. Leaving Elizabeth and Ben behind would also provide protection and help to the Alderbard beings if anything went wrong. Otto also trained Elizabeth specifically in using her dreams to navigate and communicate with Callais in the dream state—in case Otto and his team were not to return. Soon, the Alderbard resistance decided they were ready, and the next day, Otto and his team left for the cave.

***

Fortunately for Otto's team, the route to the cave was mostly through several protected cities and towns. There was very little travel through unprotected areas, and Leo had planned so well that they could quickly get through the unprotected areas. Although the lake itself was under the protection spell, the area where the cave was located wasn't. This was why they had to be careful to avoid the Camulus forces' attention. Once they neared the cave, two scouts were sent forward to ensure the area was clear. The signal was soon given for the rest of the team to approach. They slowly maneuvered around the cave as Atlas and Otto approached the rock-covered entrance.

Otto and Atlas took a few minutes to assess the rocks. Although many of the stones were small, several large boulders, some as big as a small home, also covered the entrance. Otto and Atlas decided it would be best to move as many small rocks as possible. This way, they wouldn't create a rock-slide trying to move the larger ones first. Slowly but surely, the pair began their task. They both had been trained in the use of air, earth, and water elements. However, Otto obviously had more strength with air and earth, while Atlas was better at water spells. They each began to use their spells individually to remove the smaller boulders. Although Leo could use some spells, he wasn't ever classically trained as a resistance fighter/ protector and hadn't used spells very often. So, he and the other Alderbard members watched in awe as Otto and Atlas began to command the energies around them and move their bodies with the flow of the surrounding forces. Otto would use air and earth spells to get under a rock, lift it into the air, and move it away. Atlas did the same but moved the rocks with water balls. For a while, the space around everyone was filled with air, earth, and water, rapidly moving all around them like being caught up in a thunderstorm with heavy rain and forceful wind.

After a few hours, all the smaller rocks were gone, and the larger boulders were all that was left. Otto and Atlas took a quick break (as they were feeling weak from their first task of removing the smaller objects). Again, both were well trained in using spells, but as protectors, they weren't powerful spells like a keeper could command.

They couldn't hold the energies of the elements for as long as a keeper could either. After a brief rest and some Virdis, the pair joined forces and created water, earth, and air spells. With the combined elemental forces, Otto and Atlas were able to move the larger rocks the same way they had with the smaller ones. Once again, the others watched in awe as these large rocks and boulders were lifted into the sky as Otto and Atlas gently moved them through the powerful surrounding winds and energy onto the ground. However, it was much more demanding and took longer to get under the large objects and move them away from the entrance. A few times, they would have a large rock in the air, surrounded by a water ball, when the spells would lose momentum, and the rock would drop back down with a large crash. Removing the large rocks took much longer, and there were a few times they had to take a break.

Finally, as Otto and Atlas began to feel exhausted, they moved one more massive rock. When the large boulder was cleared, several other rocks fell down, creating a plume of dust. When the dust settled from the last rock-slide, Otto and Atlas could see, through the darkness of the cave, a shimmering light reflecting from the sun above on the sails of an enormous Devas ship. Otto gave Atlas a congratulatory slap on the back as the team cheered when they saw the Devas ship. Otto then quickly commanded the team to enter the cave, and they boarded the ship. It had been a long time since any of them had seen a Devas ship and a long time since Otto and Atlas had captained one. It took Otto a few stabs at remembering how to operate the ship. But he figured it out, and soon, the crew slowly made their way out of the cave and began to float in the air.

Just as they got the ship away from the cave entrance, a loud boom and flash of light came screeching across the sky. The crew turned to see a ball of white fire whiz past the deck of the Devas ship. The crew then saw a massive black ship, much larger than any stationed on Alderbard, come billowing out of black smoke, aiming cannons in their direction. The crew became frantic as a voice echoed across the sky from the black ship, saying, "Surrender now or be destroyed." Otto immediately recognized the voice as Balor's.

Otto quickly turned the Devas ship toward the protected lake (only a hundred yards away). At the same time, Leo and Atlas commanded the crew to the cannons. Atlas, although still weak, also chanted a quick spell under his breath of protection… hoping it would help.

The crew quickly took their places across the deck as Leo fired the first shot from his location. A blast of purple-and-yellow fire shot violently from the cannon at the black ship. The black ship was hit hard. Although white fire was very powerful (because it was one of Camulos's creations), the yellow-and-purple fire, called Hepha, was created by several Devas keepers. The keepers' combined spells to create Hepha were much more potent than white fire and took out a good portion of the black ship, creating chaos across the decks. Otto quickly took advantage of this, and with the last remaining strength he had, he cast an air spell into the sails of the Devas ship. In seconds, the Devas ship safely entered the protected area on the lake. The crew could hear Balor bellow across the sky in anger. Balor then bombarded the protected area with relentless blasts of white fire, but to no avail. The protection spell over the lake was too powerful to penetrate. After a few more yards into the protected area, the ship fell out of Balor's sight.

***

As Otto and his crew sailed over the giant lake, they explored the ship. While exploring the decks and lower cabins, they found a room full of several more protector staffs and several Devas swords and armor. In the captain's quarters, they also discovered several maps and scrolls.

They couldn't read many of the scrolls; however, one of the maps seemed to show where a few other smaller Devas ships were located. Surprisingly, they discovered that these smaller ships seemed to be located on the protected lake.

They searched the lake at these locations for the next few days but found no other ships. Feeling a little frustrated, they decided they needed a plan to return to Davi and get the rest of the resistance recruits to Antillis without being caught by Balor. They also needed to figure out how to get back soon because they were beginning to run out of supplies. The crew docked over a small island in the center of the lake as they made their plans. They made several plans over the next couple of days, none of which seemed to be good enough. Feeling defeated again, Otto retreated to his cabin. He fell asleep and slowly began to roll into a fog... and into a dream.

Although Otto had learned to contact Callais and a few others through the dream state, he hadn't done this often. Otto wandered in the fog for a while, thinking he would see Callais and tell him what was happening, when Otto saw a shadowy figure approaching him. As he moved towards the shadow, everything around him began to clear up, and the figure came into full view. Otto was shocked... the figure wasn't Callais, but Evie.

Chapter 22
EVIE'S HELP

It had been a long time since Otto had left Emmeline, Amelia, Evie, and the others, and they were beginning to get worried because there had been no word from him. Evie tried many times to reach out to Otto in her dreams but only found herself in restless dreams and sleep with no answers. After several nights of fitful sleep, Evie finally found herself in a steady dream fog, chasing the sound of Bella's bark in the distance. Evie followed Bella's barks and whines for a while until she found the surrounding hazy mist beginning to clear, and Evie was once again in Rosalina's dwelling, watching Bella bounce around the room. Rosalina entered the room from the back door, slowly shuffled over to a chair, and motioned for Evie to take the one next to her. Evie sat down as Bella jumped in her lap, and Evie stated, "It's so good to see you again. I've been working on protection spells like you asked."

Rosalina gently smiled and nodded. "I am glad to hear that, child, but I am afraid your friends are in dire need of your help."

"Who's in trouble?" Evie asked with a worried look.

Rosalina explained to her Otto's situation and that he was safe for now but that he needed a way out... and quickly. Evie felt the hairs on her neck go up. She was glad Otto was safe but had no idea what she was supposed to do. Evie shook off her nervous feelings and said, "I don't know what I can do to help."

Rosalina gently smiled at her, placed her shaking, wrinkled hand on Evie's hand, and said, "I can help them, but I am afraid there is only very little I can do without being exposed. I need you to help where I cannot."

Evie placed her hand over Rosalina's ancient hand. "I'll do anything. Just tell me what to do."

Rosalina explained that Otto and his team were over the protected lake. She told Evie the lake held four smaller Devas ships they needed to find. However, these ships were at the bottom of the lake, and Otto's team didn't know this. She then told Evie, "You need to visit Otto in your dreams and tell him how to retrieve these sunken ships."

Evie nodded in vigorous agreement as Rosalina continued to explain that Otto had a map of where the ships were located. She told Evie that she must tell Otto the spells he needed to use to get the sunken ships. Evie listened intently, wishing she had a pen and paper to write this down. But because she didn't, she listened and absorbed every last detail she could to be sure to save her friends. Once Evie knew her part in helping Otto, Rosalina told her that because Balor had found Otto and the others, it would be a struggle for Otto and his crew to get back to the rest of the resistance on Alderbard undetected. Rosalina explained she would help once Otto retrieved the sunken ships. She explained how she would cast a powerful spell that would take Otto and his crew safely back to Davi, hopefully, undetected by Balor. Rosalina then explained to Evie the quickest route to get back to Davi and that Evie must relay this message to Otto since the spell wouldn't last long. Evie, once again, listened intently to every detail to ensure she knew exactly what she needed to do. Rosalina then finished the instructions by saying, "Although we can help them get the remaining ships and get back to Davi safely... I am afraid that is where we can no longer help."

Evie looked at her with questioning eyes when Rosalina continued. "Escaping Alderbard will be difficult since the resistance has angered Balor. I am unsure of what Balor may do if he catches Otto and the others while they try to make their escape back to Antillis."

Evie was saddened by this news when Rosalina said, "You must tell Otto of this and that you cannot help. So, he must prepare as best as he can for the escape on his own."

Evie nodded once again and took a deep breath. Soon, the dream fog began to roll in once more, and Rosalina fell out of sight.

***

Evie woke up full of emotions. She wanted desperately to tell Amelia about her dream but knew she couldn't. Evie knew she still had to keep Rosalina a secret, and she also didn't want to worry her beloved friend about Otto's peril. Evie spent the next couple of hours trying to fall back asleep but couldn't because of all her overwhelming feelings. Finally, as the morning hours began to break, Evie began to feel tired and fell back into slumber. Evie focused with all her power on Otto. Soon, Evie was traveling through the starry fog when she found Otto.

Chapter 23
FINDING THE SHIPS

◆•─────●─────•◆

As the dream fog cleared, Evie saw Otto standing in front of her, and she could tell he was shocked to see her. As Evie approached Otto, he said, "Evie, I didn't expect to see you!"

Evie smiled, reached out, and hugged him. He returned the embrace and gently kissed the top of her head when he pulled back and asked, "Why are you here?"

"I've come to help you," Evie replied

Otto chuckled. "Well, I don't think there is much you can do in your dreams to help us."

"I know how you can get those lost ships and how to get you back to Davi safely," Evie replied with a big toothy smile.

Otto jumped up, grabbed Evie, and spun her around. He placed her down and happily said, "You are truly a lifesaver right now!"

Evie bounced up and down a bit to see the joy in Otto's face as she began to explain about the ships. She told him that they had the correct location where the ships were, but they were sunk below the water. Otto slapped his hand to his forehead. "I should've thought of that."

Evie then told Otto that he and Atlas would have to use a combination of air and water spells to retrieve them, but there was also a catch. Otto looked at Evie with questioning eyes and asked, "What's the catch?"

"The ships were sunk on purpose using a spell that can only be broken by another specific spell," Evie replied and went on, "This specific spell, when combined with the water and air elements, will lift the ships to the surface for you."

Otto gave Evie a curious look before asking, "What spell is this?"

Evie took a deep sigh and continued. "I'm not sure how to use the spell exactly. However, the ship you are on has a scroll with a spell that you must use. The spell is called *aoratis*."

Otto shook his head. "Evie, I can't read the scrolls, nor do I think anyone here can."

Evie looked at him and placed her hand lovingly on his arm, saying, "Yes, you can. I know you can."

Otto again shook his head and asked, "How?"

Evie explained to him what Rosalina had told her, of course, leaving out Rosalina's existence. She told Otto he could find the right scroll by placing his hands over the pile of scrolls and then chanting the word *aoratis*. Evie said that this should make the scroll with the spell appear. She then told him once he had the right scroll, he must chant *aoratis anoxis,* and the spell should reveal itself to him. Otto rubbed the top of his head, baffled by all the information. Then a large smile stretched across his face as he said, "Evie, thank you so much, but how do you know this?"

Evie shook her head. "There is no time to explain right now, but once you have all the ships, you will only have a short time to get back to Davi."

Evie then explained to him that once they had the ships, they must take a specific route to get them back safely. She told him the spell wouldn't last long, so they must act quickly. Otto looked at Evie and asked again, "Spell?"

Evie shook her head as if there was no time to explain again and grabbed Otto in another tight embrace. He returned the hug and thanked her. Evie cleared her throat, shook her head, saying, "I'm afraid there's some bad news, too."

Otto looked at her and nodded for her to continue as she went on, "Once you get back to the others on

Alderbard, I don't think I can help you any further in your escape plans so you can make it back to Antillis."

Otto nodded again and wrapped his arms around her. "Evie, you have done more than enough. Don't worry. I'm sure we will figure something out and get back to you safely."

Otto then pulled Evie closer as they embraced one last time before the fog began to roll in, and Evie felt herself back in her bed on Antillis.

***

Evie opened her eyes to see Amelia staring at her wide-eyed and bushy-tailed. Evie quickly sat up and hugged Amelia. Although Evie couldn't tell her about Rosalina or Otto's situation, Evie told Amelia she had a dream of Otto and that he was okay. Amelia became overjoyed as tears poured down her face, and she raced out of the room—which Evie assumed was to tell Emmeline and the others about Evie's good news.

Chapter 24

SUNKEN SHIPS

Otto woke from his Evie dream encounter with an overwhelming sense of joy and new energy. He raced to the top decks to tell his crew the information he had learned. They all shouted with delight and quickly made plans to retrieve the sunken ships. While the crew made preparations for their new mission, Otto, Atlas, and Leo retreated to the captain's quarters to find the scroll with the *aoratis* spell. The threesome spread all the scrolls on the table. Otto looked nervously at the pile, unsure if he could work the spells Evie explained to him, but placed his hands over the pile and chanted the word *aoratis* anyway (hoping for the best). The pile shifted when a single scroll floated up from the stack. A stunned Atlas reached out and grabbed it. Atlas and Otto had been trained for years as protectors and watchers and were experts at what they knew, but it shocked Atlas watching Otto chant a spell only used by keepers. Otto was surprised, too, as Atlas then handed the scroll to Otto. With a little more confidence, Otto once again placed his hand over the scroll and chanted *aoratis anoxis*. Slowly, the scroll unrolled, and there, in the center of the scroll, clear as day, was a passage containing the spell they needed. They didn't have time to think about how amazing it was to have a spell reveal itself to them. Instead, they quickly grabbed the map with the sunken ships' locations and headed to the deck with the map and scroll in hand. They then made their way to the first sunken ship.

Once over where the first sunken ship was marked on the map, Otto and Atlas began manipulating elements. Atlas maneuvered his hands over the water as it began to part. Once the water cleared, the crew could see a ship at the bottom of the lake, fully intact. Next, Otto and Atlas joined hands and chanted the *aoratis* spell out loud, saying in unison, *"Bring to the land what is at the bottom of the sea. Bring to the sky the protection we need."*

After they spoke the spell, a large blast of air came billowing from below, almost knocking the crew to the floor. Otto quickly collected himself and went to the ship's edge while placing his hands together, sending another blast of air from his hands. Otto's air spell went under the sunken ship, slowly raising it into the air, and the whole crew cheered. A few crew members then boarded the new ship, and the team moved onto the next location. They did at each location, each time with more excitement and enthusiasm shouted from the decks of the ships. Once all of the ships had been recovered and manned, they saw a massive orange cloud rolling in their direction. At first, the team was scared, but Otto realized this was the spell Evie had told him of. He then shouted into the air, "This is our way out… Follow me and move quickly."

The crew members on each ship quickly moved to action as the orange cloud approached and engulfed the ships, pushing them rapidly through the air. Otto took the lead on the main ship and followed the route Evie had told him of. Even though it took several days for the team to reach the rock cave and find the Devas ship, in a matter of minutes, Otto and his team found themselves over the town of Davi, directly above Leo's home. As the orange cloud dissipated, Otto and his team looked down and saw the townspeople of Davi coming out from their homes, roaring with cheers and tears. And once again, Alderbard had more hope than ever!

***

Even though Otto and his team made it back to Davi safely, he briefed the head of the Alderbard resistance members that escaping Alderbard would be more challenging now that Balor was on the planet. Elizabeth also informed the team that almost all Alderbard people were in protected areas. This was good news, but she then told Otto and the others that they had seen more Camulus ships circumnavigating the protected areas, as well as many attempts from Camulus forces trying to penetrate the protected cities. She also told them that there were not just weapons that were being used, but there was some new machine they had never seen before being used on a few cities and towns… including Davi. Elizabeth told them that this mysterious machine would shake the barriers of the cities and towns. It hadn't broken the protection barriers yet, but it was still one of the most powerful things they had seen yet. This made Otto uneasy, thinking that Balor must have created a new weapon that was more effective at trying to penetrate the protection spell. Again, the Alderbard resistance began to put their heads together, trying to develop a plan to leave Alderbard safely and destroy whatever new machine Balor had created.

The next few days, the team endlessly worked on different ideas. Many were good, but once again, not good enough. The team also captured a few more ranks of Camulus soldiers, right outside of the protected areas, and again many wanted to defect. When another meeting was in progress about escaping Alderbard, Ben came running in, talking so rapidly and excitedly that they couldn't understand him. Elizabeth told him to calm down, and once he did, Ben, with much enthusiasm, stated, "We think we've figured out how to destroy Balor's weapon he is using."

The Alderbard leaders looked shocked, but before they could ask anything, Elizabeth quickly said, "Go on."

Ben explained that the machine Balor had been using was very large, and it was tough for the Camulus forces to move around. He told them that while he was guarding a group of defected soldiers, one soldier told him that the machine was designed from fire and was supposed to help blast fire spells into the black ships. Ben then told the others that even though it was not originally a weapon, Balor had been using it as such. However, he learned since fire was its resource, the weapon could easily be destroyed by water.

Atlas grinned from ear to ear with the new information and asked Ben if he knew its location. Ben told them that, according to several scouts, Balor was on his way back towards Davi. Atlas looked at Otto as Otto nodded (understanding what Atlas was thinking). Otto looked at the rest of the members and stated, "We will reconvene tomorrow."

Otto and Atlas soon were out the door.

***

The scouts were right. Otto and Atlas had perched themselves on the far side of Davi as they watched Balor and his black ship come near the city. They knew that Balor was aware of where protected cities and towns were because of his inability to see or penetrate them. Due to this weakness, they also knew Balor couldn't see where Otto and Atlas were perched. The twosome also knew that they had a lot more resources than they had ever had, but they decided that it was best the two of them made the attack alone. This would ensure the resources the resistance had procured would be left for the rest of the team if Otto and Atlas were to fail. They also knew it would be too risky to give up what they had found now anyway.

As Balor's black ship hovered a few yards over the land near the water's edge, a cracking noise came from the ship. Otto and Atlas saw that a large device was slowly lowering to the ground. Before the machine reached the ground, Otto and Atlas quickly made their attack. The pair placed their hands outward in a quick, swift motion as blasts of air and water came from their hands. The device pitched back and forth in the air for a minute and then was rapidly pushed backward, weakening the ties that held it in place. Otto and Atlas released another powerful blast, and the device broke off from its ties and tumbled backward. As it fell, it missed the edge of the ground, falling into the water below. Luckily for Atlas and Otto, they didn't have to do much after casting their spells, since Davi was entirely surrounded by water. After the device fell into the water, they heard a shout of anger echo across the sky. They watched as Balor quickly looked off the ship's edge at his fallen weapon. The weapon sank to the bottom of the sea. There was nothing Balor could do. Balor glanced in the direction from where Otto and Atlas had cast their spells when Balor commanded his crew to release a white fire blast from the black ship. Balor followed the white fire blast with a spell he cast from his hands. However, the white fire and Balor's spell were just deflected by the protection over Davi and never reached their intended goal.

Relieved that the weapon was out of commission, Atlas and Otto returned and told the resistance members of their victory. The team was happy because they knew that vanquishing Balor and his weapon would help save the protected areas. However, they knew this would only make Balor more vindictive, making their escape much harder. Once again, the Alderbard team went back to the drawing boards to plan their escape when something happened that they never expected.

Chapter 25

ELLIS TO THE RESCUE

While the Alderbard team was endlessly planning their escape, a young scout came running into the meeting, telling the leaders they had captured a man right outside of Davi. The scout reported the man claimed he knew Otto. Otto looked up with curiosity. Even though he and his team had been on Alderbard for some time, they hadn't had much interaction with the Davi people or the lower-ranking resistance members. So, Otto was stunned when the scout told him this man knew who Otto was. Before Otto could respond, the scout then said, "He is a large, scary, and furious man... do you still want me to bring him here?"

The group exchanged hesitant glances before Leo, Atlas, and Otto headed out of the meeting room and followed the young scout to a small home on the edge of the town. As they approached the small home, they could hear a booming voice, yelling and screaming profanities as well as threatening others that he would pummel them to the ground. After Otto heard this threat, he began to chuckle—he knew exactly who it was—and entered the small home to see a red-faced Ellis, shackled to a chair, attempting to strangle a nearby scout. As soon as Ellis saw Otto, Ellis flinched, curled his fist, and boomed, "Tell these damned idiots that I'm an Antillis resistance fighter an' an heir to Magnus." He then spat on the young scout's foot after the word *Magnus*.

Otto held up his hand and told the young men that it was fine. One of the young scouts went to unshackle Ellis, but as the scout approached him, Ellis shouted another curse at him and yelled, "Yeh're lucky I didn't bring me dog with me… she'd eat yer faces off."

The young man jumped and scampered backward, far away from the large and angry Ellis. Otto grabbed the key from the frightened young scout and unshackled Ellis himself. After the shackles were off, Ellis rubbed his wrist and then fake-lunged forward with a balled-up fist at the other young man as he scampered backward too. Otto and Atlas placed their hands on either of Ellis's shoulders—while escorting him out of the home. They apologized to the young scouts and thanked them for their service.

After they entered Leo's home and gave Ellis some green drink as he calmed down, Otto felt it was safe enough and asked Ellis, "What are you doing here?"

Ellis slurped up the rest of his drink, took a big sigh, and explained, "Funniest thin'. I've been 'avin' dreams fer a while now 'bout yeh an' what is goin' on."

He paused, wiped some Virdis from his lips, and continued. "I thought maybe I could contact yeh in me dreams, but I never could. However, I kept dreamin' 'bout yeh guys, like I was right 'ere the whole time."

Ellis took another pause while shaking his head before he went on to say, "I figured the dreams meant somethin'. So, I decided that I needed to come back an' help, but Callais wouldn't let me." He scrunched up his forehead and continued. "I really didn't like that. So, I did me own recon and investigatin'. Then one day, I found out where Callais 'ad put the chain and fabric."

Ellis sat up a little higher and proudly said, "Of course, Callais placed spells on the vault the chain an' fabric were in, so I couldn't get 'em. Then one day, I followed that ol' guy, Newton, into the room where Callais 'ad placed the chain an' fabric. Well, the vault was open, an' when Newton's back was turned…" Ellis paused and sat up even taller and loudly stated, "… I stole 'em an' came to rescue yeh guys."

When Ellis finished, he had a smile that stretched from ear to ear across his face as the rest of the group sat there in stunned silence. Ellis then gave them a brief overview of how he made it to Alderbard, but he told them he wasn't sure how he got across the star trails. He said it was like the chain and fabric just knew where he needed to go and brought him there. Ellis then told them when he landed, he was light-headed and weak, and everything was fuzzy all around him. He then said, "Me-thinks that's why it was so easy fer those young guys to get me. If I 'ad me strength or me dog, those boys would've been in trouble."

Otto knew he should be upset. However, he also realized this might be their best chance to escape Alderbard now that they had the chain and fabric (as well as knowing the protection spell extended far off the planet). Also, they now had five Devas ships, several staffs, armor, swords, and several newly trained resistance fighters if they had to fight. Otto thought, *Hopefully, the chain and fabric will allow us to leave completely undetected.* So, instead of lecturing Ellis for what he had done, Otto walked over to him and placed his hand on Ellis's shoulder, saying, "Good job Ellis. This is exactly what we needed."

Ellis beamed with pride as Otto turned to the others,

shrugged his shoulders, and stated, "This is it... this is our plan."

That night, Otto made sure to reach out to Callais in his dream to tell him what Ellis had done and that the fabric and chain were safe. Callais was very upset but relieved that it hadn't been taken by someone else. The Alderbard team finalized their escape plan... They were to leave in three days.

Chapter 26
ADDING TO THE ORDER

David was sitting out in Sophia's garden, thinking of everything he had been told since they had left Evie. They had left Evie right before her seventeenth birthday, and now it had been over nine months since they had seen her. He knew that Evie was safe since they could make frequent contact with her after they found the watcher glass. It still baffled David that Evie was in a far-off galaxy, fighting some kind of evil that himself and the others were trying to find answers to here on Earth. Even though Evie had promised him she was safe, he and Ruby had stayed awake many nights wondering if they should call off this search and tell Evie to come home. However, the more David and Ruby learned about Evie and her past, the more they realized that if they didn't continue their journey, the whole world could be destroyed... and them and Evie with it.

David shook his head in disbelief once more and decided to join the others back in Sophia's home. As David entered, everyone was busy poring over books and text, bouncing questions and ideas off each other. David found Ruby and Nadia in the kitchen making some kind of healing remedy found in one of Sophia's books. David kissed Ruby on the forehead when she stopped, turned towards him, and said, "There you are. I wanted to talk to you about something. Can we go somewhere private to talk?"

David nodded as he and Ruby made their way back to the garden. Once in the garden, they took a seat on a nearby bench when Ruby grabbed David's hand and told him, "I was talking with Nadia and Sophia, and they think it might be a good idea to ask some of our other children to join us. What do you think about this?"

David rubbed his head and thought about their conversation the night before with the rest of the group. They had talked about going to Spain, Evie's mother's birthplace, and recruiting Evie's other uncles to help their search. Alvaro also believed that once they got to Spain, he could convince Evie's grandmother to help all of them as well. They were planning to leave at the end of the week. However, David was beginning to wear out from all the information and travel. He was considering taking himself and Ruby back home, leaving Steven and the others to finish the mission. David then turned to Ruby, saying, "I know we need to save Evie and the Earth apparently, but I'm getting tired. Do you still think this is a good idea?"

Ruby could see the concern in her husband's face, "My love, I know you're tired, and every new thing we find just seems to have more questions than answers." Ruby paused before adding, "But we promised The Order, and we promised Evie we would do everything we can to help. We can't give up yet, especially knowing what we now know."

David grabbed Ruby's hand, "I know, but do you think it is wise to involve others, especially our children?"

"Nadia and Sophia believe if we have as many people as we can to help us, it might be easier for us to accomplish this mission before it's too late," Ruby answered before saying, "I think we should tell our children about this and let them decide for themselves if they want to help."

David nodded and paused as he thought deeply about this before replying, "Okay, but I don't want anyone to go who doesn't want to." Ruby nodded in agreement.

David and Ruby then went back inside and told the others they would ask their children to help them. The group agreed this would be a good idea. David, Ruby,

Beth, and Steven left the next day for Colorado to recruit their children, promising the others they would meet them in Spain at the end of the week.

***

Once David, Ruby, Beth, and Steven were back home, they called a family meeting at their house. All of their children came, including some of their adoptive and foster children. Steven then explained to the family everything, leaving out no details this time. Steven believed it was important for them to have all the facts if they were to decide to join them. After Steven told the others everything, David, Ruby, Beth, and Steven spent the rest of the evening answering as many questions as they could. Finally, close to midnight, David stopped the conversation and told his children, "I think it would be wise for everyone to sleep on this tonight before anyone volunteers to come with us." The family agreed and made their way to bed.

The next morning, David and Ruby went to the kitchen and were surprised to see all of their children already up and waiting for them. As David and Ruby sat down at the table, Desi began to talk. "I've decided I'm going with you. I want to help Evie."

David smiled at his brave daughter as several others began to speak up and say they were coming too. Michael and his wife Stacy, Joe and his wife Mary, Leslie, and one of their foster sons Robert, volunteered to go. Jenny and David Jr. said they would stay home and make sure that all of the children and the rest of the family would be taken care of in everyone's absence. David and Ruby held hands as they watched their children discuss who would do what and how everything and everyone would be taken care of. David gave Ruby's hand a tight squeeze when Ruby whispered in his ear, "I'm so proud of all of our children right now."

David gave her a wink, saying, "We made a wonderful and brave family, my love."

Chapter 27

ESCAPE FROM ALDERBARD

After three days of preparation, the Alderbard team was ready to depart from the planet. They had the main Devas ship and two others boarded in the city of Davi, while two other ships had been sent out into protected cities nearby. Otto and Ellis were in charge of the Davi exit. Atlas took a ship to one of the other cities to transport new recruits, while Leo and Elizabeth took the last ship to another town. The other protected cities were near Davi, so they would all leave at the same time and meet in the protected area above Davi (since they knew that Davi was protected for several miles into the atmosphere). Otto gave Atlas the chain to ensure swift travel to the meeting location since the city he went to was furthest away. He believed that maybe Ellis was right—the chain just took people where they wanted to go. Elizabeth and Leo had been given the fabric to cover their ship until they reached the protected area as well. Once the whole fleet was together, the plan was to combine the fabric and chain as they moved out of the protected field into the star trails. Ben had decided to continue to lead the resistance on Alderbard and wait for the Antillis team to return. This saddened Elizabeth because she had to leave her brother behind, but he reassured her that they would be back together again.

The next day, Otto commanded his forces into the air. After they reached the borders of the protected area above the planet, they waited patiently. It wasn't long before Elizabeth and Leo's ship soon joined Otto. After waiting a little longer, with no Atlas in sight, Otto began to worry. Just as Otto decided they couldn't wait any longer, he saw a billow of yellow-and-purple fire flash in the sky. The Hepha fire was followed by blasts of white fire coming from behind Atlas's ship. Otto looked in the direction of the fire blasts and saw that Atlas was firing Hepha at a Camulus black ship behind him. Then, suddenly, Atlas's ship began to fire Hepha in front of them as well. Otto could see the ship behind Atlas but didn't understand why Atlas was also firing in front of him. Otto then turned to look in the direction Atlas was firing to see that Balor's ship was now coming in his direction… Atlas was surrounded.

Otto knew that since he was still in the protected field, Balor nor the other ship attacking Atlas could see Otto. Atlas was close to reaching the meeting location and would soon be protected, so Otto commanded his fleet to begin firing. Leo and Elizabeth followed suit and began to fire as well. Soon, the sky was filled with purple, yellow, and white fire.

Balor couldn't see Otto or his fleet but saw where the blasts were coming from. Balor also saw that Atlas was making his way in that direction. Soon, Balor maneuvered his ship between Atlas and the protected area. Otto saw this, quickly grabbed a Devas staff, and then aimed it in Atlas's direction. Right as Balor released another blast of white fire at Atlas's ship, a massive, electric-blue shimmer shot through the sky from the Devas staff. Right before the white fire could hit Atlas and his crew, a glimmering bubble surrounded Atlas's ship that deflected the white fire and bounced it back at Balor's ship. While Balor's crew scrambled to regain control and figure out what had happened, Atlas quickly cast an air spell into his sails and entered the protected field next to Otto and the others… completely safe from Balor's fury.

Once the fleet was all together, Leo quickly tossed the fabric into the air. When the fabric settled over the ships, in an instant, a loud crack and flash of bright light came from the surrounding fabric. Before anyone knew what happened, the fleet found themselves hovering above the Antillis forest tree line. Otto sat there baffled as he looked across the deck at Ellis. Ellis shrugged his massive shoulders and then proudly said, "Hey, stealin' that fabric an' chain wasn't such a bad idea after all."

Otto released a deep breath he had been holding in. Soon, he could see several scouts scurrying down below on the ground as the ships lowered into the protected field on Antillis.

There was no place to land the ships because of the thick forest, but they docked low enough to stay protected. After the Alderbard team deboarded, Josephine and Newton began to chant spells over the ships, which Otto assumed was to keep them more protected... just in case.

When Otto entered the city of Mari, he was instantly attacked with hugs by Amelia, Emmeline, and Evie. He then saw Evie run to Ellis as she wrapped her arms around him, and Otto could tell Evie was lecturing Ellis about what he had done. As Otto finished hugging his loved ones, he made his way down the path and entered the council room to see Callais—who immediately stopped what he was doing—and came over to embrace Otto. When Callais pulled back and released Otto, Callais, with admiration in his eyes, said, "You did good, boy. I am glad you are home."

Antillis was abuzz with activity for the next few days as they integrated the new people into the city. Once again, the Antillis council members assigned duties and training. Soon, the Antillis resistance was ready for their next move.

Part Three

❯•◦————————•————————◦•❮

The Resistance Begins

Chapter 28
THE NEW MISSION

W hile Otto had been gone, Callais and the elders had been endlessly working on what they would do next. Soon, Callais called for a council meeting to inform the resistance members of their plan. The meeting began like always, as members slowly filed into the council room making small talk. Once everyone was there, Callais stood up and began. "Welcome. Today we will be going over our next steps to take back Antillis."

The council remained silent as Callais continued. "Over the last couple of months, we have gathered information about the Camulus base on the far side of the planet." He paused and then added, "Although we did not let you all know, Simone and I sent spies into the Camulus camp. The spies have come back with information we think will help us gain the planet back."

The council members mumbled among each other

for a minute when Callais held his hand up and went on, "We know that we have gathered and trained many new resistance fighters. Thanks to Otto and the others, we now have several ships, staffs, swords, and armor to help us in our battle. However…" He paused again before finishing. "We will not be attacking Antillis as we had originally planned… At least not for now."

The council members began to raise their voices as some members started to shout.

"Why?"

"Why are we abandoning our plans?"

"What do we do now?"

Otto looked at Callais with confusion and quietly whispered, "What do you mean?"

Callais then held his hand up again as the council members slowly lowered their voices. Eventually, the room was quiet again. Once everyone had settled down, Callais explained, "Even with these new resources and more fighters, we still do not have enough to take down the whole base. There are too many soldiers and too many weapons on the Camulus base. Any effort we make will only be extinguished quickly by the Camulus forces, and I am afraid it will exhaust our forces if we attempt to take them out now. We are still greatly outnumbered."

The room remained quiet as Callais continued. "With

the news that has been brought back to us from the spies, we have found weaknesses on the Camulus base and weaknesses among their ranks that we must take advantage of first. This will hopefully deplete their forces and resources, making a future attack more feasible."

The council began to murmur again as Simone stood up and addressed the members. "The first thing that we have found is that all of the water supply on the Camulus base comes directly from our forests." She paused and then told them, "We have found creeks and rivers that feed into the base. So, our first objective will be to cut off their water supply."

The council members nodded in agreement as Simone continued. "Most of the water that feeds into the base will be easy to cut off by either diverting the creeks back into our forest or by building a dam." She looked around the room and added, "Their main source of water is a large river that feeds into the west side of their base."

Simone nodded, and Callais then said, "We will be sending a large team of resistance members to build this dam so that we can first cut off the main supply. We will also send a smaller team to divert or cut off the water from the other sources that feed into the Camulus base."

The council member once again all nodded in agreement as Simone began again. "We also have found out that there is discourse among their ranks, especially between the lower-ranking soldiers and their head officers." Simone took a deep breath before adding, "We think it will be wise to send a few more resistance members back in with our spies to continue to exploit this discourse and see if we cannot get more of the Camulus soldiers to defect." She paused again before finishing up. "We also want more resistance members to go in as spies to give false information to the soldiers and officers about our plans. Hopefully, this false information will throw them off what we really will be doing. This way, the Camulus forces will have ill-prepared plans against us... I know this will be hard to ask of our resistance fighters, but this will give us the edge we may need to separate their ranks further."

Callais then stated, "Because we hope that more soldiers will defect, we must have an area in the protected forest we can take defected soldiers to hold them for questioning as well as possibly training any defected soldiers that may want to help us." He looked around the room and went on, "So, we will also be building a small base, far from Mari, to detain these soldiers."

The council members once again began to nod in agreement when one member asked, "What if we bring in these soldiers, and they rebel or fight once they are in the protected forest?"

Callais nodded his head in agreement before answering, "Simone and the other elders have figured out some spells that can be placed on the detained soldier base. This should ensure that if there is an uprising, they will not be able to leave the base and can be quickly subdued. Also, with our new staffs, swords, and armor, those guarding the base will have enough resources if the Camulus soldiers do begin to fight."

Several council members let out a sigh of relief as many seemed to have the same concerns about an uprising of defected soldiers. Once the room was calm again, Newton, Marina, and Josephine stood up. Newton then addressed the members, saying, "Even though we have planned for cutting off water, sending in more spies, and creating a base for defected soldiers, these are all land preparations. Since that side of Antillis is not under the protection spell, we became concerned that Camulos or Balor could send in more troops or supplies from above."

The council once again all shook their heads and realized this was a huge flaw in their plan. Josephine added on to Newton's plan and told the council, "I have been reading over several of the scrolls we have here on Antillis. I believe we have found a way to cast protection over the rest of the planet, so there will be no entry or exit from the base." She then added, "This will not protect the base as well as the fourth-day protection spell. However, I believe it will be strong enough for us to accomplish what we need until Newton, Marina, and I figure out a more permanent solution."

Again, several members let out a sigh of relief. Callais then told the council, "Once we have accomplished these tasks, we believe we will then be able to take over the rest of the base. If we can accomplish these goals, when we do invade the Camulus base, we can do so with little or no force. Hopefully, not using all of our resources will ensure once we take over Antillis, we can go out and save the rest of our sibling pack."

Before Callais finished, a council member interjected and asked, "What about the horn?"

Callais then looked around the room, acknowledging their concerns, before answering, "I promise I am still working on that. Every day, Evie is increasing in her powers." He nodded at Evie before continuing. "I believe soon she will be strong enough to read some scrolls we have not been able to, thus, helping us in finding the horn."

The council members seemed satisfied with this answer as they talked about the new plan. Callais ended the meeting by stating they would meet again at the end of the week and start assigning, training, and recruiting resistance members to take on the duties of the new mission.

Chapter 29

ELIMINATE WATER

A t the end of the week, the council met again to begin its mission. The first thing they decided to do, was to begin diverting and damming the water supplies to the Camulus base. Atlas and Lincoln were in charge of the team going to the west side of the planet and would build a dam to cut off the river that flowed into the Camulus base. Leo and Elizabeth were in charge of going to the smaller water sources and cutting off those supplies. Next, they decided Otto would be in charge of building a base for the defected soldiers and guarding Camulus soldiers brought in by the spies and resistance members. Since Otto would be doing this, Ellis and Abe were again in charge of training new resistance fighters. This time, Callais made sure that Ellis would communicate any concerns or dreams Ellis had before deciding to take things on himself. Ellis grumbled about this but nodded his head in agreement anyway. Simone was in charge of sending more spies and resistance fighters into the Camulus base. After everything had been laid out, they all left their separate ways to begin.

***

Atlas, Lincoln, and their team made their way to the river flowing into the Camulus base. However, they were unprepared for how large and rapidly moving this river was and realized that building a dam might be more complicated than they thought. They decided that the best thing to do was command the troops to begin cutting down trees while they thought about how they could build the dam strong enough to hold water. The troops started to cut down trees, and the forest became a clamor of atrocious breaking and hacking noises. Even though they were in the protected forest, Lincoln quickly cast a spell to dull the noise so that if there were any Camulus soldiers within earshot, they wouldn't hear the falling trees.

Atlas then noticed that, although the water was coming down a sloping terrain, there was a small valley to the side of the river that might be large enough to contain the river once the dam was built. Atlas then commanded the team to cut the trees from the valley as he and Lincoln made a plan to have the river diverted in that direction. After a long, daunting few days of clearing the valley of the massive trees, Atlas then began constructing the dam. His first few tries didn't work as well as he thought. The river's flow was so forceful it broke the construction a few times. Lincoln then decided to try a spell that would slow the moving water down. Lincoln knew this would take tremendous energy and strength from him, but he needed to try anyway. Lincoln's first attempt at slowing the water didn't work, and he soon found himself depleted from his spells. Although he was an expert at manipulating water, most of the water he had moved in the past was large, still bodies of water. He became frustrated when a young resistance fighter from Alderbard approached him and said, "Instead of slowing or stopping the water from here, why not find where the river starts and see if you can slow it down from there?"

Lincoln clapped his hands on the young man's shoulders. "Great idea!"

Lincoln told Atlas of his plan and left him to finish the tasks below. Lincoln and the young man with the great idea soon left and followed the river upstream. After a few hours of hiking through the thick forest and uphill, they came to a glacier lake tucked in the tops of the hills that fed into the river. Lincoln then began his spells, and the water started to slow down. Soon, the flow from the lake to the river completely stopped, and a few hours later, Atlas came up, out of breath. Once he caught his breath, he announced, "It's working!"

Lincoln and Atlas remained by the lake for the next few days, casting spells as the crew below finished the dam. With Atlas by Lincoln's side, it was much easier to control and stop the water flow. Although they became exhausted from their spells, they never took a break, ensuring the team below would accomplish their task. Soon, a young woman Atlas left in charge of building the dam was standing next to them, saying the construction was finished. Both Lincoln and Atlas stopped as Atlas then fell to the ground, completely exhausted. Once he regained his strength, Atlas and Lincoln made their way down. They saw that the river was successfully diverted to the valley below as water began to fill up the dam. Relieved, Lincoln returned to Mari to deliver the good news, leaving Atlas in charge.

Elizabeth and Leo found several small creeks throughout the Antillis forest feeding into the Camulus base. Although their task wasn't as large as Lincoln and Atlas, they ran into a few hitches trying to stop the water. Neither one was good at water spells, even though they had some training. With the spells they did know, they were eventually able to hold back the water flow from several streams. Their team then dug trenches and ditches in several areas that diverted the water back into the protected side of the forest. Soon, Leo and Elizabeth's mission was accomplished, and they sent a scout to relay the message back to Mari.

While the others had been cutting off the water supplies to the Camulus base, Newton, Marina, and Josephine found themselves at the very edges of the massive Camulus base and began to complete their plan. Since the protection spell had to cover a whole side of the planet, it took them a couple of days to develop a plan that would work. After a few days of walking around the base and coming up with a solution, they finally found a spot they believed would give them the most advantage in casting the spell. The site they found was a hill that extended slightly above the tree line. From this point, they could see the majority of the base (almost right into the center of the base itself). From there, they were able to combine their powers. As they cast their spell, they watched as a shimmering glow of light shot from their palms into the center of the base, then slowly began covering the remaining side of the planet before fading out of sight. After they were done, Newton turned to Marina and smiled. "You are getting better at using your powers."

Josephine then added, "Yes, Marina, you are getting much better at this. Maybe since you are Magnus's child and you have given up on the things that corrupted you in the past, your powers are coming back."

Marina smiled proudly as Newton and Josephine smiled back, and they made their way back to Mari to tell Callais the news.

Once the news reached Callais from the others, he pulled the people of Mari together and shared the information with the city. The whole city shouted in joy with their first goals being accomplished!

***

With the water cut off from the Camulus base, the whole base soon began to suffer. A small uprising occurred, and several of the Camulus soldiers started to attack their own officers. The officers, completely caught off guard, began to send black ships out of Antillis to send news of what had happened and get water for the soldiers. However, the black ships returned, reporting that they couldn't leave the planet. Josephine, Newton, and Marina's spells had worked, completely grounding all air operations of the Camulus forces. Again, the Camulus soldiers heard of this, and conflict began on the base once more. Silas and his spies then decided it was time to take advantage of the situation.

Chapter 30
THE CAMULUS FORCE UPRISING

The uprising of the Camulus soldiers was small at first, with a few ranks infiltrating the officers' quarters and stealing supplies the officers had reserved for themselves. The soldiers also began to make failed attacks on their own leaders. The Camulus soldiers who made these attacks or stole supplies were soon imprisoned by their officers, leading to more unrest and conflict among the lower ranks. Silas decided this unrest would be an excellent opportunity to use his spies and create more discouragement and conflict among the Camulus soldiers.

The first thing Silas did was send in two of his spies (and himself) to pose as guards for the prisoners detained by their own leaders. Silas commanded his spies to quietly and secretly let the captive soldiers know of the Antillis resistance's willingness to take them if they were to defect. He also made sure his spies told the Camulus soldiers the kindness they would be shown by the Antillis resistance. Before long, many soldiers wanted to defect. Silas relayed this message back to Simone, and she told Otto.

Otto had been building the fort that would hold any soldiers that wanted to defect. Although the fort wasn't much, because of the spells, weapons, and armor they now had, Otto soon told Simone that he was ready to take on the task of bringing in defected soldiers. This information was sent back to Silas as he prepared his team to release the defected soldiers to Otto's control.

Releasing the soldiers from their current imprisonment would be a challenge. Even though a few of Silas's spies were stationed as guards, there wasn't enough of them to release all the soldiers willing to defect. Silas thought about diverting the attention of the other guards, allowing for a few small escapes. However, Silas realized these small escapes would be noticed quickly, and more reinforcements would be sent. Silas then decided that he needed a massive distraction to release all the prisoners at once... so, he began his preparations.

The first thing Silas decided to do was infiltrate the officers' ranks. This way, he could create false information among the higher-ranking officers, keeping their attention elsewhere as he released the prisoners. Silas also thought this might be a good idea because some of the captive soldiers had mentioned that there were a few unhappy higher-ranking Camulus officers. He thought maybe these officers might want to defect as well. Silas also found out that becoming an officer wasn't a hard task since anyone willing to show force and violence quickly moved up the ranks. Because of this force and violence, there was also a lack of trust between the officers, making them isolated from each other to a certain extent. So, when the officers gathered, they only gathered for attack plans and not for support from each other. Silas decided he would be the one to infiltrate the officers' ranks. So, he recruited a couple of his own spies, a few willing Camulus-defected soldiers, and began his own demonstration of force and violence.

***

Silas and his recruits decided to carry out Silas's plan on a day one of the highest-ranking officers came to inspect the imprisoned soldiers. As the officer approached Silas (who was on guard), he and his recruits went into action, starting a fake rebellion. One of the Antillis-fighter spies pretended to be a captive soldier, and a willing captive Camulus soldier who indicated he wanted to defect started the fake rebellion. Silas's recruits began to yell and fight with Silas as the inspecting officer approached.

Silas commanded the two fake rebels to be quiet when the officer was near enough to see this rebellion. The fake rebels refused and began a false attack on Silas. The first recruit lunged at Silas when Silas quickly punched the recruit in the stomach, knocking him to the ground. Soon, the second recruit made his attack, lunging at Silas's stomach, knocking Silas and the recruit to the ground. Silas quickly pinned the second recruit down and punched him in the temple, knocking him out. Just as Silas did this, the first recruit got back up and spat at Silas, saying, "You can't keep us down forever."

The first recruit then made his next attack at Silas. Silas then took out a stun gun, one of Balor's own designs, and froze the first recruit in place. Silas then knocked him out too. The inspecting officer was impressed, and soon, Silas was called to the head commander's quarters.

The head commander was Vlad, and he was well known on the base as a vicious leader. He was similar to Balor in commanding his forces by reinforcing fear in insolent soldiers or those slow to obedience. So, he was notorious for extreme punishment to command loyalty from the Camulus soldiers. As Silas entered Vlad's office, Vlad motioned over to a nearby chair as Silas took a seat. Vlad stared at Silas for a minute and then said, "I like your style. How come I haven't heard of you before?"

Silas then cleared his throat before answering, "I haven't been here for very long. However, as a loyal Camulus fighter and a guard to the prisoners, I've become disgusted with the filthy rebels who think they have a right to question the officers and Camulos's authority."

Vlad was a large man from the Camulus galaxy since he had the physical traits of those from there. Besides being large in stature, he was tall with long limbs, fingers, and pointed ears. His skin was pale, almost gray in color, that was highly contrasted by a thick black beard and mustache twisted up to a point on each end resting on his hollow cheeks. His eyes were black as night, and his eyebrows came to a point in the center of his forehead. Vlad rubbed his black beard between his thumb and fingers as he stared intensely at Silas for a while longer. He then stood up, walked in front of Silas, and told him, "With this unrest from the soldiers, I could use some extra men to exert extreme force and punishment to bring back control." He then paused as he paced in front of Silas before he continued and asked, "Would you be willing to do this?"

"Anything for the King." Silas nodded.

Silas knew this was a common phrase used among the Camulus forces to refer to Camulos and loyalty to him. Vlad smiled and replied, "For the King."

With that, Silas soon became a head officer in the Camulus forces and began to carry out his mission. As with any newly recruited head officer, he had a close eye kept on him for a few weeks. But soon, Silas became trusted, with what trust was given. He had more freedom, thus allowing him to gather information and relay this back to Simone and the others.

While Silas infiltrated the officer's ranks, his spies kept separating the soldiers from their superior officers. The spies were careful not to reveal too much information but enough to cause more discourse. The false information was also valuable. The spies told anyone who was still loyal to Camulos that the Antillis resistance was large, and many weapons and fighters had been recruited. They also told them the resistance was planning on attacking soon and that there would be no way for them to fight since the black ships had been grounded. The spies told the Camulus soldiers no one outside of this base would know of the attack, so no help would be sent. This information caused even more rebellion and conflict among the soldiers. They began to believe that they would soon be attacked and extinguished.

While Silas's spies continued their work, Silas himself found several officers who were also beginning to become uneasy and upset with their current situation.

The supplies were slowly dwindling, and not only were they almost out of their water reserves, but because there was no entry or exit into Antillis, their other supplies were also becoming low. The more the lower-ranking soldiers rebelled, the more forceful many of the officers also became. The officers that Silas had found were becoming uncomfortable with the extreme techniques used by the Camulus leaders. Silas found that (like himself) many of the officers were recruited from other galaxies and forced to become soldiers. Also, like Silas had done, they used extreme punishment on their lower-ranking soldiers to get into higher positions in the Camulus forces. They felt they were forced to use severe punishment to move up the ranks and wouldn't be treated as poorly as when they were lower-ranking soldiers. Over the next couple of weeks, Silas came to trust two other high-ranking officers. Soon, the three of them devised a plan to free the captive soldiers and start a small battle among the rest of the Camulus forces.

Chapter 31
THE CAMULUS BATTLE

◆•————————————●————————————•◆

Silas and his two trusted officers, Albert and Victoria, waited until the dead of night when very few others were awake, and the watch was on low alert. As the higher-ranking officers slept, Silas started a fire in the central quarters, where all the maps and plans were kept. As the fire began, the officers started to wake up from their sleep as they ran around, completely disoriented, trying to stop the fire. As the leaders all ran to the central quarters, Albert and Victoria initiated several other fires across the officer's quarters. Silas had also told his spies of his plan, and they too started more fires across the rest of the base simultaneously.

Simone watched from the protected forest as the Camulus forces ran around the base trying to extinguish the many fires. Once she saw the fires across the base and the soldiers were distracted, she sent Indy onto the base, who dropped an explosive device in the center. Indy quickly flew away as the bomb went off, creating more confusion. The soldiers began to believe that this was the attack they had been told of, and soon, there was complete chaos. The upset Camulus soldiers took the opportunity and began to fight their own leaders. Their officers were still caught off guard trying to put out fires, and soon, a battle started among the Camulus forces.

As this happened, the spies posing as guards quickly released the prisoners. There was so much chaos across the Camulus base that resistance spies were able to flee, completely undetected.

Chapter 32
NEW POWERS

The Antillis spies lead a massive group of defected soldiers to the edge of the Camulus base, where Otto was waiting. Otto commanded his resistance fighters to encircle the Camulus soldiers. He then cast a spell over the horde and led them into the protected forest to the fort he had built. The defected soldiers were soon imprisoned but given food and water (which was needed since the prisoners had been deprived of these simple basics for weeks). After a few days of being captive and Otto's team providing food and water, the Camulus soldiers were pleased with their conditions and the kindness they had been shown. So, the captive soldiers began to freely give information to the Antillis resistance. The information the Camulus soldiers provided proved to be extremely useful. They told the resistance of many more weaknesses on the base, weakness in the weapons, and weakness of the remaining forces. This news was relayed to Callais and the resistance elders as they began their next plans.

***

For the next several days, the resistance council members discussed their next steps. There were still a few spies, including Silas, that remained on the Camulus base. Silas and the spies relayed news that the Camulus forces were beginning to recoup from the fires and attack. Silas also delivered news that there was a man in the Camulus forces (he had only heard of) who was using spells, attempting to make contact to reach someone outside of the base. Silas told the others that he was afraid if they didn't act soon, this man would be able to accomplish his goal, and there would be more forces and resources that would be sent to Antillis. With this news of a man attempting to use spells to contact the outside, Josephine, Newton, and Marina became desperate in their search through the scrolls to find an answer to stop this, knowing that the protection spell they had placed was only temporary.

As they were poring over the scrolls one evening in Josephine's dwelling, Evie came in with Collin and Ellis to see Marina—since they hadn't seen her in a while. Their intent was to take Marina for a few hours so she could have a break. As the threesome entered the room, Collin ran to the table to hug Newton. Collin then pointed to a scroll on the table the elders had been looking over and asked, "What's this?"

The elders stopped and examined what Collin was pointing at. The scroll was a scroll they had been struggling to understand for days but couldn't figure out. Josephine walked to Collin's side and asked, "What are you seeing, boy?"

Evie then came to Collin's side to see what he was pointing out. Since she rescued Collin from the fire in the dream state, Evie had kept a close eye on him. She was worried that he saw something dangerous, and she wanted to make sure he would stay safe. Evie then examined the scroll and saw a shadowy figure of a man walking across the page. The shadow man waved his hands over the scroll as a waterfall appeared. The water then parted, and a small opening appeared in the stone behind the waterfall. As soon as the opening appeared, another scroll seemed to float out of the hole and unrolled. Evie then saw scrambled words appear across the image. Evie looked at the others, then back at Collin, and asked, "Collin, did you see what I saw?"

Collin shook his head yes, saying, "Yeah, the man parted the waterfall, and a scroll came out."

Evie looked back at the others and told them, "I saw that, too."

The group stood there shocked for a minute as Evie thought, *Collin really must have powers like me*! After a minute more of silence, Newton asked, "Well, what do you think it means?"

Evie looked at the others and shrugged her shoulders when she felt a small hand pull on hers. She looked down to see Collin now tugging on her hand, saying, "Come on, guys. I bet it's the waterfall in the cave."

Evie looked at the others and shrugged her shoulders. "We might as well go check it out." Soon, the group was heading to the waterfall cave.

Once they reached the cave, Ellis bolted behind the waterfall, and after a few minutes, he came out, soaking wet, shaking his head, "I don't see anythin' there."

Collin then grabbed Evie's hand, looked up at her with begging eyes, and pleaded, "Evie, I think I can do this. Please let me try."

Evie bent down, so she was on one knee, looking directly into his eyes, "No, Collin. I can't let you get hurt again."

Collin stood taller and boldly stated, "If you do it

with me, I know I can do this, Evie. We have to try…
I think this is very important."

Evie looked up at the others with pleading eyes when
Marina and Ellis came to her side, and Marina said, "He
is right, Evie. We have to try. Ellis, Newton, and I will be
right here to help you. We will not let anything happen."

Evie stood up, and with a bit of hesitation, she looked
back down at Collin and reached her hand out to his.
The small boy took her hand again, and the pair then
closed their eyes. Evie stood there in the dark for a while
when she saw a small bubble float in front of her. As the
bubble approached her, she saw that Collin was inside
it. She was about to ask Collin how he got in a bubble
when another shadow approached the two in the fog. As
the fog cleared, there stood Rosalina. She then nodded
for the two to follow her. Evie was even more shocked
as she and the floating Collin followed Rosalina. Before
she could ask anything, they were standing in front of a
waterfall. Rosalina then told Evie, "He will stay protected
for a while. Nothing can get him right now."

Evie felt a little relieved, but again, before she could
ask anything, Rosalina added, "Collin will stay here with
me in the dream state. While we work on this end to
help you, you must open your eyes and part the water.

Once you part the water, I will release Collin, and he will know what to do next."

Evie nodded. She decided to just not ask any questions and follow Rosalina's instruction. Rosalina then went on to say, "You must be quick about this. I can only keep Collin protected here. Once he opens his eyes, do not let go of him until he is finished. This is the only way he will stay protected."

Evie looked at Rosalina with questioning eyes and then became afraid again for the small boy. Evie was about to protest when Rosalina seemed to understand her concerns, and said, "I will explain everything to you at another time. You must trust me."

Evie, still worried, again just agreed to follow Rosalina's plan. Rosalina then motioned for Evie to start. Evie slowly opened her eyes and placed her free hand towards the waterfall, gripping tightly with her other hand to Collin's. Soon, the waterfall parted when Evie heard Collin begin to chant incoherent words. She looked over and saw the young boy's eyes, rolled back into his head, with only a sliver of white showing. Collin then placed his stub outwards as Evie felt a jolt in her body, forcing her to face the wall in front of them. Evie then felt her eyes begin to roll back in her head when she heard Collin's voice in her mind, and she too began to chant. However, this time, Evie understood what the two were saying. As both of their free arms were stretched outwards, in unison, they chanted,

"*In darkness, we fight. In darkness, we fall. Bring from the dark the light that will help us all.*"

After the words were said, Evie felt another powerful force push in her mind as her body fell to the ground, never letting go of Collin's hand. When she opened her eyes, she and Collin were lying on the ground. Collin then turned his head towards Evie with a huge grin. "I told you I could do it."

Evie grabbed the small boy into her arms. "I'm just glad you're okay."

Collin returned the embrace as the pair looked up at the elders, all staring at them with disbelief. Ellis walked over to the pair holding a scroll in his hand while extending his free hand to Evie, helping her to her feet. Once Evie and Collin were up, the rest of the group described what had happened. They told them that once they had their eyes closed, the whole cave began to shake. Soon, there was a loud cracking noise as the wall behind the waterfall opened, and the scroll floated out—one that looked just like what they had seen on the scroll back in Josephine's dwelling. Newton patted the two on the shoulder as the group went back to analyze this new scroll.

***

Once in Josephine's dwelling, Ellis unrolled the new scroll as Collin and Evie looked over it. They both glanced at the scroll, but Evie couldn't read it again, nor could Collin. Evie's head was hurting, and Collin said his was too. The group decided that Evie and Collin should rest and try again once they felt better. As the pair went to leave, Newton said, "We will tell Callais of this, and maybe we will know what to do when we meet next."

Evie nodded in agreement and left with Collin. As they were headed out towards their separate dwellings, Evie was still holding Collin's hand, which she hadn't let go of yet. She was still worried something would happen to him if she let go. Evie decided that she didn't want to leave Collin or let him out of her sight yet, so she looked down at the young boy and asked, "Do you want to have a sleepover with Amelia and me tonight?"

Collin looked at her with questioning eyes and asked, "What's a sleepover?"

Evie smiled and told him that he could stay the night with her. Collin jumped up. "Yes, I would love that!"

Evie giggled, and the pair headed off to Otto and Amelia's dwelling. By the time they reached home, the pair had returned to their normal playful state and spent the rest of the evening playing games with Amelia and the dogs.

Newton had gone to Callais and told him what had happened with Collin and Evie. Callais was soon at Josephine's looking over the new scroll they had found. The elders decided that there must be something important in the scroll to reveal itself now and agreed that they would have Evie go over it the next day. Like Evie, the elders were also still worried and unsure about Collin. So, they decided to let Evie choose if Collin would continue to help them.

Chapter 33
THE PROTECTION

T he next day, Callais called the elders and Evie to the council room. Once everyone was seated, Callais brought out the new scroll found by Evie and Collin the previous day. He placed it on the table and asked Evie to come look at it. Unlike the day before, when Evie went to look at the scroll, it wasn't hurting her head, but the scroll was still swirling around with whatever was on the page. Evie decided to take a moment and just watch it settle down as she had done in the past. After a few minutes of watching the scroll, it seemed to settle down, but Evie was still struggling with what was on it. She then looked up, shook her head, and told them, "The scroll has stopped moving, but I still can't make it out."

Callais scratched the top of his head when Newton interjected, "Callais, I think we may need to involve

Collin to help Evie, since it was Collin who helped her find this scroll."

Callais looked at Evie. He was also worried about Collin and what had happened to him. Callais hadn't come up with any other answers about Collin, and he wasn't sure if he wanted Collin to help. Evie could read the hesitation in Callais's eyes and told him, "Remember when you said that you think there might be someone helping me we didn't know of?"

Callais nodded his head as Evie continued. "I believe that person is not only helping me but Collin as well."

Callais looked at her with questioning eyes. Evie knew she still couldn't tell the others of Rosalina, but she told them how Collin was protected in a bubble the last time they were in the fog together. Evie then told them she was positive that someone was helping them. Callais seemed to be lost in deep thought for a minute when he finally nodded, saying, "I guess we will have to try."

Newton then left the room to get Collin when Evie glanced back down at the scroll. The shadow man on the last scroll appeared again and started to move across the page. Evie stared at the shadow as it stopped over a jumble of words. The shadow then turned its head and became clear. Evie recognized the face as Magnus. Evie gasped as the others looked at her when she blurted, "It's Magnus!"

Callais and the elders rushed to her side to see if they could see what she was pointing at, but as always, they couldn't. Evie decided to look back at the scroll and follow what Magnus was doing, but he remained in his place by the jumbled words. Soon, Newton returned to the room with Collin, Amelia, and Declan as they approached the table. Collin reached Evie and gave her a hug as Evie looked at Collin and asked, "Collin, do you see what I see?"

Collin looked down. "Yes, that big man there is standing next to words," he answered and then leaned his head in closer before saying, "I think he wants us to read the words."

Evie looked at the scroll again and asked, "Can you read what the words say?"

Collin giggled a little, shaking his head. "Evie, I can't read. I only hear words in my head sometimes when I see stuff."

Evie stood there for a minute as the two stared at the scroll. She then thought, *Last time I looked at the scroll, I was holding Collin's hand.* Evie then reached her hand out to Collin and nervously asked, "Are you sure you want to try with me?"

Collin smiled and placed his tiny hand in hers as the two looked back at the scroll. The words began to move around, and as they began to slow down, Magnus turned his head, smiled, and slowly faded out of sight. After Magnus disappeared, the words stopped and were clear as day. She analyzed the words for a while before she spoke and told the others, "The words seem to be some kind of clue or spell."

Callais nodded his head and asked, "What does it say?"

Evie, still holding Collin's hand, looked back down and read out loud,

"*Protect the soul of our hearts. Free the mind from our evils. Speak the words of love and connection. Bring light to the bodies of the people.*"

When Evie finished, the scroll lit up, and an arrow began to spin around as if it was searching for something. Collin immediately grabbed the scroll and began to drag Evie out of the room, holding the scroll up. Soon, everyone was following Evie and Collin. Collin seemed to be following the direction of the arrow when Evie asked, "Collin, where are we going?"

Collin blurted, "I'm following the words in my head to where the scroll wants to go."

Evie was baffled but continued to follow the excited little boy. They all followed Collin down into Mari when they came to Simone's dwelling, and the arrow stopped, aimed at the table in the center of the room. Collin handed the scroll to Evie as he dragged her again to the table, where another scroll was opened. Evie immediately recognized the open scroll as the one she couldn't read when Lincoln had placed it in front of her back in the council room a while ago. As Evie looked at the scroll, it began to spin, and soon, the whole page stopped and lit up with words that were clear as day across the entire scroll. It was the first time Evie could read an entire scroll completely. Evie looked at the scroll and saw, on the top, the words, *Protection of Antillis*. Evie turned her head to Callais, who was now directly behind her, when she happily stated, "It's a protection spell for Antillis."

Josephine, who was usually very reserved, came running to the table and excitedly said, "This is it! This is what I was looking for to complete the protection over Antillis."

Everyone cheered as Josephine grabbed the scroll, looked down, and shook her head, saying, "I cannot read all of it."

Evie smiled and placed her hand on Josephine's arm. "Well, I can tell you everything it says."

Again, everyone seemed relieved when Collin tugged at Evie's hand and pointed to Evie's other hand—which was still holding the first scroll. Evie moved the scroll up to where she could see it and saw that Magnus was again on the page as more words began to appear. Evie looked diligently at the words, but she couldn't make them out once again. She told the others about what she saw and couldn't read it again. Newton gently smiled, placed his hand on Evie's shoulder, and said, "That is okay, Evie. You and Collin have done enough today. We can always try again tomorrow."

As soon as Newton finished his sentence, Atlas came bursting into the room out of breath, saying, "We have a problem," He took a big gasp of air before finishing, "It seems that there is a Camulus fleet above Antillis right now… trying to enter the protected field."

The excitement that was once in the air shattered as the group looked at each other, and Callais ran out of the room, following Atlas to the council room.

Chapter 34
THE NEWS

After Atlas had told them of the news, Callais called an emergency meeting of the Antillis resistance council. Once everyone was there, Atlas debriefed them, saying, "I was helping Otto with gathering information and training of the defected soldiers, when one of Silas's spies came to the fort and told us that over the Camulus base, several ships were hovering right above the protected field, blasting white fire in an attempt to penetrate it."

Atlas paused for a minute and then explained, "Otto and I went to the edge of the Camulus base, and we recognized the main ship as Balor's vessel. Somehow, he must have received word from the man Silas told us about. It seems he was able to make contact outside of the base and told Balor about what we've done to the

Camulus base." He paused once again and finished saying, "We have to act now before Balor breaks through."

The room was silent for a long time when Callais took a deep breath and said, "You are right. We must act now if we are to have a chance."

Callais paused and looked around the room. "Each team, gather your forces. We meet here tomorrow for battle."

The crowd was solemn as they filed out of the council room, and tension filled the air of Mari that night.

Chapter 35
THE NEW BATTLE PLAN

———————— • ————————

The next day, the council room was filled to the brim with council members and resistance fighters. There was a nervous energy in the room as Callais entered and began to speak, "Today we must fight for Antillis… for our freedom and for our lives."

He took a deep breath as he looked across the room. "Before we head off to battle, I must remind all of you here today to remember the light," He paused before he finished saying, "Remember the love in your souls, and I know that darkness cannot win if we do this."

Callais then placed his hand over his heart as the rest of the people in the room followed suit, placing their hands over their hearts before they slowly and quietly left the room to their battle stations… the battle for Antillis was imminent now.

***

Callais and Ellis reached the far side of Antillis, where Otto had built his fort for the defected soldiers. Callais had decided this was where he needed to be if the captive Camulus soldiers were to see Balor and rebel against their captors. He had also decided to leave Lincoln in charge of Mari if something was to happen to him. Once they reached the fort, Ellis, along with Aphrodite, took a group of fighters and went to the opposite side of the fort while Callais and Apollo remained in the center position.

Otto and Atlas each took a Devas ship with teams of fighters and slowly maneuvered the ships opposite each other on the west and east sides of the Camulus base. Otto and Atlas also had two ground force teams. Leo and Elizabeth also took a ship and a ground team, centering themselves between Callais and Otto.

Like Callais and Ellis, Simone commanded a ground force and positioned her team across the base from Callais's location. The whole Camulus base was surrounded by the Antillis resistance. Before they entered the Camulus base, Callais cast one last spell over the fort to ensure that the captive soldiers couldn't escape. When he was done, he made his command, and the Antillis resistance began to move.

Otto commanded his ground team from his position on the Devas ship, and slowly, they moved out of the protected field. Otto remained in his ship in the protected area as he watched his ground team move further onto the base. Atlas had also made the same command for his forces, remaining in the protected field with his Devas ship. Leo and Elizabeth moved their ship onto the base at the same time as their ground forces. Simone and Ellis soon commanded their ground teams forward. As soon as the Camulus soldiers saw the Antillis resistance move into sight, chaos ensued.

Many of the Camulus soldiers quickly realized they were surrounded and began to flee; however, many soldiers that remained loyal became enraged and began to attack resistance fighters with extreme ferocity. The first team to reach the inside of the base was Simone's team. The Camulus soldiers began to blast fire from their weapons that were quickly deflected by the Devas staffs and armor the resistance fighters were wearing. As the armor and staffs deflected the blasts, the Camulus soldiers became furious and charged in closer. They soon surrounded Simone's team, but Simone commanded her fighters to hold steady in their places. As the Camulus soldiers got closer, Simone made her simple command, "FIGHT!"

Simone's team then began to fight. Silas saw his

aunt's team being attacked, so he and a few of his spies entered the battle as well. As Silas entered the battle, Vlad was standing nearby, became enraged, and attacked Silas. Silas saw Vlad coming at him from the corner of his eye and turned to fight. Before Silas could get close enough for an attack, Vlad pulled out a weapon and shot it into Silas's chest, knocking him to the ground. Simone saw this and became a flurry of rage—and she didn't disappoint with her background as a Denidis warrior. She screamed into the air and made her way through the battle towards her fallen nephew. Simone's skill and rage quickly eliminated anyone in her path as she reached Vlad. Vlad had a mocking smile stretched across his face, and aimed at Simone's chest was the same weapon he had used on Silas. He then said, "Ah, a true Denidis warrior… I will be happy to vanquish you."

Simone stared at Vlad for a minute as a malevolent smile slowly stretched across her face. Vlad, who remained calm, seemed to become uncomfortable with Simone's response and shuffled his feet as his mocking smile vanished. Before he could position his feet into a strong hold, Simone chanted under her breath and made a flying leap across the space between them. Her arms were stretched out in front of her, her fists balled at the end, Indy flying right above her. Indy dove down and turned into a flash of green energy that encompassed Simone. Simone crossed the space between her and Vlad in a split second, hitting him in the center of his chest and knocking him to the ground. The green light faded, and Indy reappeared as Simone landed on the ground by Vlad's feet and looked down. In the center where Vlad's chest used to be was a massive hole punched out. Only dirt, covered in blood and Vlad's innards, could be seen through the hole under his body—it was Vlad who had been vanquished. The Camulus soldiers battling Simone's team saw this and became terrified, scattered away, running as far from Simone as possible. Simone was slightly depleted from using a strong combat move and was glad she had given Indy some of her battle powers. Simone quickly commanded one of her team members to take Silas into the protected forest. She then collected her strength, gave Indy a nod (who proudly cawed), and rejoined the battle.

Otto and Atlas's teams also had a ferocious fight once they entered the Camulus base. Their fighters on the ground were also quickly surrounded by Camulus soldiers, desperately fighting off as many as they could. Their fighters were soon outnumbered as more Camulus soldiers surrounded them. Otto and Atlas simultaneously began to fire Hepha blasts from their Devas ships at the

Camulus soldiers surrounding the resistance ground forces. It wasn't long before many Camulus soldiers went up in flames, running away in all directions. The Antillis ground fighters took their opportunity and charged the soldiers around them, quickly subduing the remaining Camulus soldiers, and made their way further into the base. Otto and Atlas then moved their ships out of the protected forest and followed their ground teams in.

Ellis didn't have as much of a struggle when he first entered the Camulus base. He was able to move his team much further into the base before he encountered any soldiers. Once Ellis was further inside the Camulus base, he saw the hairs on Aphrodite's back raise into the air as she lowered her head and began to grumble under her jowls, looking directly in front of Ellis. Ellis turned to match Aphrodite's stare and saw a line of soldiers come out of the trenches, charging towards his team. Aphrodite made the scariest bark Ellis had ever heard as he watched her muscles tense up and shiver all over her body. Aphrodite then lunged forward and began to charge the oncoming Camulus soldiers. Some of the frontline soldiers saw the massive dog coming towards them and scattered from their position, breaking the Camulus ranks into two. Ellis saw this and made a quick command to his team. Ellis's team split in three. One group ran down the middle, separating the Camulus soldiers even more, while the other two teams went on the outside flanks, surrounding the rest of the Camulus forces. Callais saw Ellis do this and cast a blast of air, knocking several Camulus soldiers to the ground. Ellis and his team quickly took the opportunity, captured the fallen soldiers, and led them back to the fort, where Callais placed them in prison. After the soldiers were captured, Callais patted Ellis on the back, and Ellis and his team headed back onto the base. Before entering the base again, Ellis yelled, "Let's finish what we started." Ellis's team shouted a war cry and ran back into the battle.

Leo and Elizabeth also had made their way much further onto the base than the others had before they were met by Camulus soldiers. However, once the soldiers neared them because Leo and Elizabeth were piloting the Devas ship, they immediately sent blasts of Hepha fire at the attacking soldiers. The Camulus soldiers were set ablaze with purple-and-yellow flames. They soon ran away in all directions as Leo and Elizabeth made their way further into the base.

Balor had been watching the Antillis resistance attack from above and was still desperately trying to find a way to penetrate the protection shield. Since the protection spell the Antillis elders had created wasn't as powerful as the fourth-day protection, Balor couldn't penetrate the spell to enter Antillis, but could still see what was happening below. As Balor watched, he became angry and more desperate. He then stood on his ship, watching the battle unfold below, as a smile inched across his face. Soon, Balor left the deck, commanding his ships to stop firing before he disappeared into his quarters.

Chapter 36
BALOR'S BREAK

———————●———————

Because the protection spell Josephine, Newton, and Marina had placed over the Camulus base wasn't as potent as the fourth-day protection spell, Balor could see the battle occurring on the base below him. However, he still couldn't penetrate the field. He made the assumption that there was some kind of protection spell covering the base, but he also assumed it was a weak spell, and he believed he might have a plan to break it and get through. Balor retreated back to his quarters and picked up a small green mirror that he had been using for some time now to contact Agronas—Camulos's wife. Although Balor knew that he could reach out to Camulos and see if there was a way Camulos could help, the dark leader had become more secluded over the last few months (since Camulos had realized the resistance had found Magnus's heir). So, the last few times Balor had reached out to him, Camulos was of little help because he focused on his own spells and plans to eliminate the resistance. Balor also knew that Agronas was a very powerful keeper and was extremely good at finding ways to break other keepers' spells. So, he picked up his glass and called out to Agronas.

Agronas was soon visible in the mirror as Balor described to her what was happening. After he was done explaining, Agronas flashed him a wicked smile and said, "I believe I have something that just might work."

Agronas then told him a spell she had been working on could possibly break the fourth-day protection spell. Although the spell wasn't complete, she said she believed it would break a weaker protection spell. She then told him how the spell worked, and after she was done explaining, she added one last thing. "Balor, if this does work and you can get through… do me a favor."

Balor curiously tilted his head. "What it is you want?"

Agronas let out a malicious cackle before answering, "There is a woman on Antillis named Josephine. She is very powerful and could possibly lead the resistance and Magnus's heir on a path that could destroy all we have done." She then paused, flashed another evil smile, and added, "So, if you get through, I need you to take that witch out."

Balor, too, smiled a wicked grin. "But of course, my Queen."

With that, Agronas faded out of sight, and Balor took her spell to the top decks and began working on his plan.

Chapter 37
THE FIGHT FOR ANTILLIS

❧ ———————— ● ———————— ❧

As the Antillis resistance fighters made their way slowly across the Camulus base, night began to fall. As the sky grew darker, the resistance fighters began to feel tired. When Callais realized this, he commanded the resistance to fall back. Soon, the Antillis teams retreated to the protected forest as they counted who they had lost. Even though there were many injuries, there were very few fatalities. The Antillis team felt relieved after a long day of battle and were glad they had accomplished as much as they had. The resistance teams took food and rest as Simone made her way to her station to find Silas. As she reached her team's location in the protected forest, she asked for Silas. A young girl told Simone that Silas was still alive but badly injured, so he was taken to Mari for Regina to heal. Simone was relieved he was alive but still worried and told the young girl to go back and give her news of his condition. Later that evening, the young girl returned with news that Silas was awake but badly injured. Simone felt somewhat relieved but was still worried as she finally fell asleep, thinking of what the next day would bring.

***

The next day, the Antillis resistance collected themselves and entered back onto the base, this time with much more ease and less resistance since the Camulus forces had been badly defeated the previous day. As the Antillis resistance neared the center of the base, a multitude of white fire came blasting down from above, knocking several teams to the ground. Otto looked up and saw a large shimmering hole in the protected field above, where Balor's ship was hovering and shooting white fire down below. The hole wasn't big enough yet for the fleet of ships to enter, but Balor had found some way to break a hole in the field. Otto commanded the Antillis resistance to back down as they fell out of range from the white fire blast from above. Otto watched for a while as the blasts continued to rain down when he finally made a command for the Antillis teams to retreat to the protected forest. Once the teams were safely back in the forest, Otto told Callais the news. Callais left Otto in charge of the resistance and made his way back to Mari to discuss what to do next with the elders.

***

Once back at Mari, Callais and the elders retreated to the council room and had another secret meeting. After a few hours, they came out as Callais looked at Evie and told her, "Evie, I want you to go with Josephine and Newton," He paused and then added, "I think it is time we use some of your powers."

Evie stood there shocked for a minute when she felt a light touch on her shoulder to see Declan standing next to her with a worried look in his eyes. Evie began to tear up and said to him, "Oh, Declan. I don't think I'm ready."

Declan gently pulled her into him, gently saying, "Evie, this is what you were born for. I promise we can do this."

Declan pulled Evie back and wiped her tears away as the pair followed Newton and Josephine into the forest. While Evie went into the forest to begin her mission, Callais had called back the rest of the Devas ships and their crews to Mari, leaving only ground forces waiting for their next command. As the Devas crew entered the council room, Callais told them his plan. "We have decided that before we continue our ground attack, we must take out Balor and his ships from above."

The crowd fell silent when Otto stated, "We only have five ships, and they have at least twenty. I'm not sure we can take them."

Callais nodded in agreement before saying, "We have found a way to place protection over the ships using the fabric. This may allow us to take Balor by surprise." Callais paused and wearily rubbed his chin as he continued. "If Balor penetrates the protection field, I fear we will not be able to defeat him. So, taking him by air and by surprise might be the only way."

The room remained silent as they each seemed to be lost in their own thoughts when Callais added on, "This will also help us with our second part of our plan." He paused again and then said, "I have sent Evie into the forest to the far side of Mari with Newton and Josephine. They believe that with Evie's help, they can help cast a solid, lasting protection spell we found over the rest of Antillis, making it impossible for Balor to reach the ground. If Balor is distracted by our air attack, this may give them enough time to cast the spell so we might finish taking over the Camulus base."

Again, the crowd was quiet as they thought about this new plan. Atlas then broke the silence and boldly stated, "Okay. We trust you." He stood up, placed his hand over his heart, and tilted his head in respect towards Callais.

The others in the room once again placed their hands over their hearts and nodded towards Callais as well, and soon, they headed out to their ships and boarded them, more nervous than ever.

Callais also decided that the ships would leave at night so that Balor would be even more taken aback by the attack. As the ships lifted into the night air, Callais cast the protection spell over them as he woefully watched them disappear out of sight.

Meanwhile, Evie, Declan, Newton, and Josephine had made their way to a spot in the forest where Evie could see the Camulus base. Despite the cool, foggy air, Evie could feel sweat had beaded on her forehead, and she knew that she was terrified. Evie wanted to run but knew she had to stay and help those she loved. They were also close enough to the unprotected area of Antillis that Evie could see spots on the ground, covered in blood, where blasts of fire from weapons had left scorch marks in the dirt. Evie shuddered as she thought of the soldiers who must have fought and maybe even died here when she began to tear up again. Declan must have read her mind and placed his hand on her shoulder again as he quietly whispered, "It will be okay, Evie. I won't leave your side, I promise."

Evie looked at Declan and felt relieved as she stared into his eyes, grabbed his hand, and slowly turned and faced the two elders. Newton then reached out to her and held her hand tightly as he explained what they were going to do. Newton told Evie that she must close her eyes as Josephine chanted the spells, and Evie was to listen for the chant in her mind. He told Evie she must repeat the protection spells as Declan helps her cast air and water spells. Newton then hesitated before saying, "Evie, it is likely the spell will lift you and Declan into the air as it is cast." He paused again, looking a little worried, and then added, "You must remain focused, and I promise I will be here if anything happens."

Evie again felt scared as she remembered the last time she was in the air and fell. She became more frightened as she thought of Camulos and how he got inside her head the last time. Evie went to express this fear; however, Newton seemed to read her mind and reassuringly said, "I will cast a protection spell over you before you start, but…" Newton hung his head down and then slowly raised it, looking deeply into Evie's eyes before he finished, "…you will have to remember your own protection spells you worked on, in case mine do not work."

He then handed her the sparkling chain and added, "Hold on to this, Evie. It will help you."

Evie became so scared she began to shake when she heard a breaking noise in the forest. She turned to see Bella, Artemis, Apollo, and Aphrodite, followed by Ellis, bulldozing through the forest branches. Evie ran over to Ellis as he scooped her up, saying, "I told yeh we would wreck hell together, kid." He then placed her on her feet and added, "Now let's go get these bastards."

Evie smiled. A feeling of relief flooded her body, and a renewed sense of energy encompassed her heart, knowing Ellis would also be by her side through all of this. Bella and Artemis then came to Evie and Declan's side when Evie looked at Declan, who puffed up his chest and proudly stated, "He's right. We can do this." He then gave her a reassuring smile and stretched his hand out to hers, grasping it tightly.

Evie rubbed Bella's head, squeezed Declan's hand, and closed her eyes. Again, she could immediately feel the strength of Declan's powers flow inside her, and she began to feel brave. She then heard a voice inside her head, and Evie concentrated as hard as she could to the chant echoing in her mind. Soon, she could clearly hear Josephine's voice and began to focus on the words Josephine was chanting. Before Evie could start to repeat the words, all of a sudden, she heard a loud blast coming from outside of her head. She rapidly blinked her eyes open and looked upwards to see a massive black ship shooting white fire from above to the ground below, only a hundred yards away from where they stood. She continued to watch in horror when she soon saw streaks of purple-and-yellow fire shoot across the air and hit the side of the black ship. The ship soon turned its cannons away from the ground. Evie watched, completely terrified, as the black ship began firing back at a Devas ship. The sky above them was soon filled with white, purple, and yellow fire, followed by a tremendous thundering noise echoing all around them. Evie looked at the others on the ground, feeling frantic and not knowing what to do, when Newton yelled above the roaring noise, "We do not have much time."

Evie and Declan quickly assumed their positions again, and right before Evie closed her eyes, she saw Callais, Lincoln, and Simone running through the forest, casting spells upwards through the hole, aiming at whatever black ship they could hit. It was complete chaos. Evie then felt Declan grab her hand and shout, "Come on, Evie. NOW!"

Evie quickly closed her eyes and waited until she felt Declan. Once she felt him, she began to concentrate and soon heard Josephine's voice in her head. Evie began to repeat what Josephine was saying. As soon as Evie began to chant, she felt a powerful pull in her arms and then a stinging jolt cascade through her body. Evie was scared but didn't open her eyes or lose focus. Evie continued to chant, and as she repeated the last words from Josephine, she felt a powerful blast come shooting out from her head and hands. Evie opened her eyes to see that she was several hundred feet above the ground, high above the tree line, high above the shimmering protection field that was starting to break apart. She then noticed that there was a blueish light coming from her fingertips. She looked over and saw Declan was still beside her when she heard him shout, "Aim the light from your fingers at the hole."

Evie looked below her and saw the massive hole the black ship had been shooting through. So, she aimed the light from her fingers at it. Declan followed her spell with a blast of air, pushing the light from her fingertips rapidly through the sky. A sparkling blue light began to slowly fill the hole. Then a loud, thunderous crack echoed all around them, followed by a powerful blast of light coming from Evie's fingers and eyes simultaneously, illuminating everything around them and spreading rapidly across the sky. Evie then saw the chain float in front of her as it released a powerful flash of air and vibrant blue light, completely surrounding everything in sight. Evie followed the direction of the chain's energy. The gust of energy took out a few of the black ships above her and pushed her own blue energy into the hole below her. Soon, the hole was covered and began to fade, like stardust settling, covering the entire surface below. Evie glanced at Declan, who smiled and nodded. Evie realized that they had done it. She was utterly shocked as the two slowly descended to the ground below.

Once they reached the ground, Evie looked up to see the chain floating downward. She reached up for it as it landed gently back in her hand. She then watched as the shimmering light from the protection spell they had just cast finally faded away.

Several Devas ships dipped below the new protection spell as white fire deflected off the field behind them. Evie could hear a bellowing roar from above as the black ships tried again to break the new protection spell. After another hour of relentless firing, the black ships found they couldn't penetrate the new spell, and the fleet slowly retreated. Evie turned to look at Declan and let out the breath she didn't realize she had been holding. Before she could say anything, the elders came to their side, looking both tired and proud. Callais placed his hand on Evie's shoulder. "I knew you could do this, Evie."

Evie then turned to look at the rest of the elders, each with a look of pride on their faces. Josephine then shook her head, saying, "I have not seen that kind of power since Magnus." She then dropped to her knees and began to cry. Through her sniffles, she was able to barely push out the words, "I cannot believe we might finally have a chance to defeat Camulos after all these years."

Evie still couldn't say anything and was shocked by her own powers and the response she received from the elders. She thought they were all very powerful, but now, she finally realized that she was more powerful than she knew after seeing their reactions. Ellis broke Evie's thoughts, came over to her side, and scooped her up. "I'm so proud of yeh! I love yeh so much, kiddo!"

Evie wrapped her arms around Ellis's massive neck and began sobbing, exhausted from everything. Ellis then scooped her up again and carried her back to Mari, the others following silently behind.

Chapter 38
PLAN FOR THE END

I t was dark when the Devas ships docked near Mari after the lasting protection spell was cast. The majority of the Antillis resistance had returned to Mari to recoup after a long day of battle as well. Although they hadn't completely taken over the Camulus base, they decided to reconvene and go over their final battle plans to finish what they had started. The Camulus forces were badly defeated, and many of their resources, soldiers, and weapons had been extinguished from the battle. And now that Balor couldn't come in with his fleet to help the Camulus forces, the Antillis resistance knew they had a real fighting chance.

Although Callais knew it would be much easier for them to take over the rest of the base, he wanted to ensure that his resistance got some rest so they wouldn't make any mistakes in their next attack. Simone and her team remained on watch over the Camulus base, and Otto returned to his station with his team to ensure the newly captive soldiers were taken care of. Evie and Declan had retreated to Regina's dwelling, while Callais and the council elders met to ensure their next plan would ultimately defeat the Camulus forces.

Evie and Declan were feeling depleted themselves after their last encounter. Regina had called them to her dwelling to ensure that they hadn't sustained any issues from using such powerful spells. Once Regina gave the pair the all-clear on their health, Evie and Declan went to the council room to meet with Callais and the others. When they entered the council room, there weren't as many people as Evie had expected there would be. The elders and a few others in the room talked in hushed tones and didn't notice when Evie and Declan walked in. Evie cleared her throat as Newton motioned for the two to sit down. Evie and Declan sat at the table with the others when Callais turned to Evie and Declan and said, "We have been discussing the best approach to take over the rest of the base." He paused for a minute and then continued. "We think it would be a good idea to have the remaining Camulus forces see your strength and powers."

Evie and Declan exchanged nervous glances when Josephine added on, "We still have not been able to figure out who was able to communicate to Balor through the use of spells." Josephine also took a long pause and then finished, saying, "We believe that if this person is to see you demonstrate your powers as our resistance carries out the rest of their mission, word may spread among the Camulus forces of your strength, and hopefully to the rest of the Devas system as well. We want you to do this, so all will know we have found Magnus's heir."

Evie took a deep breath and nervously said, "I understand that this is something that you need me to do, but I'm worried about Camulos finding me again."

The elders looked at each other when Newton nodded. "We understand your fears, but we will do everything to protect you. Since he is already aware of your presence, we need to ensure that the rest of the Camulus forces and our sister pack understand that we have a fighting chance now that we have found our savior."

Evie took another deep breath and forced a weak smile. "Okay, tell me what I have to do."

The elders began to explain to Evie and Declan their plans for the resistance and what Evie and Declan's roles were. The meeting lasted well into the late hours of the night. Once it was over, they concluded that they would begin their attack the next evening and sent Evie and Declan off to get some rest.

Evie retreated to Otto and Amelia's dwelling that night as she lay awake for a bit longer, thinking of the challenging task ahead of her. She finally fell asleep, and once again, the starry dream fog rolled in, and Evie found herself in Rosalina's cave.

Chapter 39
ROSALINA'S HELP

Evie was in Rosalina's cave for a few minutes before Rosalina came in through the back door. Rosalina slowly inched her way over to a chair nearby, and Evie took her seat next to her when Rosalina said, "I understand that tomorrow you will be fighting the Camulus forces."

Evie nodded and wondered how Rosalina knew this and how she even knew so much of what was going on without being there. Evie pushed the thought out of her head, realizing now wasn't the time for more questions, and answered, "Yes, I'll be fighting the Camulus forces tomorrow, and I'm so scared. What if I don't succeed, or what if something bad happens to me… or even worse, to the others?"

Rosalina placed her hand gently on Evie's arm and told her, "I promise I will do everything in my power to help you and your young man." She paused for a moment and then said, "When you go tomorrow, I need you to trust yourself and listen very carefully for my voice in your head when you start to fight."

Evie gave a nervous smile and then asked, "Why can I not tell the others you're helping me?"

Rosalina returned a weak smile and said, "There is a lot you do not know yet, and I promise that someday, when there is more time, I will tell you, and I will make myself known to the others. However, for now, I need you to trust me and believe in yourself."

Evie nervously nodded again before asking, "Are you helping Amelia and Collin too?"

"I am helping you all, child," Rosalina replied, smiled, and added, "Amelia and Collin are special because of the torture they endured as children. The torture they both endured unlocked certain parts of their minds. They are both so resilient and strong in their own powers. This is why they are more aware of my presence than the others."

Evie sighed and thought again of the pain and suffering her two friends had gone through but was glad that Rosalina was taking care of them. Evie looked into Rosalina's ancient eyes and told her, "I promise I'll do everything I can, and I'll be sure to listen for you when the time comes."

Rosalina removed her hand from Evie's arm and gave her a reassuring smile. "You are so much stronger than you think. Just remember that, child, and know that you are capable of greatness."

Evie then watched as Rosalina crept slowly to the back door, and soon, the fog rolled in again, taking her back through the stars, back to her body. Evie woke up, shook off the nervous feelings flowing around her mind, and took a deep breath before she headed out the door to the council room to begin the last battle.

Chapter 40
FINISH IT

✦•─────⬤─────•✧

Before Evie went to the council meeting, she stopped by Regina's and used the watcher glass to contact David and Ruby. When Evie contacted them, the first thing Ruby and David said was happy birthday. Evie had been so distracted by everything going on that she didn't even realize that it was her eighteenth birthday. Ruby then promised they would have a fantastic celebration as soon as they were back together again. Evie smiled and said, "I can't wait to see you again. I miss you so much."

They then told her they missed her and loved her as they talked for a bit longer. David also told her they found an uncle of hers, her mother's brother, and were going to Spain to meet her other uncles and, hopefully, Evie's grandmother as well. Evie was shocked by this and asked to speak to her new-found uncle. Unfortunately,

David said he had already left for Spain but promised to let her talk to him once they got there. They spoke more about their adventure and asked about what Evie was doing. Evie didn't let them know she was going off to battle. She didn't want to worry them. However, Evie just told them how much she loved them—just in case something terrible happened to her. After the conversation, Evie shuddered and handed the glass back to Regina. Regina could tell Evie was nervous and reassuringly stated, "Evie… you are so much stronger than you know. If you feel scared today, just remember all those you love. Love will give you more strength than any other power or spell in this universe."

"I promise, Regina," Evie replied, giving Regina a weak smile and added, "I'll do my best to remember love."

Regina returned her smile and gave Evie a hug as Evie left and made her way to the council meeting.

***

As it was once before, the council room was filled to the brim with council members and resistance fighters, waiting in anticipation for what was to happen next. Callais and Lincoln entered the room, followed by the rest of the council elders, as the crowd fell silent. Callais approached the center of the room and looked intently at all the members before he took a deep breath and said, "Today, we hopefully fight our last battle on Antillis, and we will finally accomplish our goal of taking back this planet."

He looked around the room again and finished saying, "We will be infiltrating the Camulus base mostly with our ground forces. While our ground forces engage and distract the remaining Camulus forces in battle, Otto will be piloting a Devas ship into the center of the base with Evie and Declan on board."

He paused again and nodded at Otto when Otto added on, "Once we have reached the center of the base, all the remaining ground forces will be sure to protect Evie and Declan as we lower them to the ground." He also paused and took a deep breath before finishing, "It's extremely important that Evie and Declan reach the ground. Our main objective is to not let anything happen to them as they carry out what they will do next."

Otto then nodded at Evie and Declan as the pair stood up to speak. Evie became flooded with emotions and found she was unable to speak. Declan looked at her, realized she was frozen, and spoke for the two. "Once Evie and I reach the ground, and we are safely covered, Ellis will give the command for our forces to back down.

This will allow Evie to demonstrate her power to the rest of the Camulus forces, hopefully taking many out… or scaring the rest into surrendering."

Declan now took his deep breath as Lincoln stood up and took his turn to speak. "The power that Evie and Declan will demonstrate will be powerful. All of our fighters must stand back at a great distance so Callais can cast a protection spell over our own forces. We do not want our fighters to be caught by Evie and Declan's powers."

Lincoln followed suit like the others and took a long pause before finishing, "The rest of the council elders will be within reach of Evie and Declan and will guide their powers with the use of spells. So again, when Ellis gives the command, all fighters fall back."

Once he was finished, Marina and Josephine approached the center of the room when Marina told the council, "We not only hope this will defeat the Camulus forces, but we also hope that showing the remaining soldiers our power will spread word to the rest of the galaxy about the resistance and Evie."

After Marina finished her sentence, the crowd remained silent, all in deep thought. Elizabeth and Amelia then stood up and placed their hands over their hearts as the rest of the room did the same. Then something happened that hadn't happened before. Everyone removed their hands from their hearts and joined hands as many began to weep. They all then raised their held hands to the air as Josephine began to sing. It was a song that Evie thought she had heard before and sounded much like a lullaby. Even though Evie couldn't remember where she heard it, the song was so powerful she soon began to weep with the others as well. The song began to resonate outside of the council room and into the underground city of Mari. The walls of Mari echoed with the sound of the lullaby as the people of Mari also raised their hands to the air. A feeling of peace and calm soon filled every person's heart. When Josephine finished the song, the whole city was silent. The silence was quickly broken by Otto, who then yelled so loud, it also echoed through the city of Mari, "Familias nostrais vitais sempris!"

The rest of the city then echoed back, "Familias nostrais vitais sempris!"

The people of Mari then went to battle.

***

Evie and Declan plodded slowly behind Otto and his team to the Devas ship docked near the Mari entrance in silence. Evie was still feeling very nervous about what would happen next. So, Declan kept pace with her slow trot, gently squeezing her hand every once in a while, attempting to give her courage. Once on the ship, Evie approached Otto before they took off and asked, "What did you shout back in Mari before we left?"

Otto gave Evie a loving look and answered, "Well, in words you may understand, it means 'to the life of our family forever.'"

Evie smiled. "I like that."

Otto returned the smile and embraced her. "For our family."

Evie felt warm all over and realized, for sure, that this was what she was fighting for. Evie was fighting for everyone she loved, and for the first time, Evie felt brave as the Devas ship took the air and made its way to its destination.

***

It was dusk when the resistance fighters made their way onto the Camulus base. Once again, since the Camulus forces had been so badly beaten, and with Balor's fleet gone, it was fairly easy for the Antillis ground forces to reach the center of the base. Once the resistance fighters reached the center of the base, to their surprise, it seemed empty. The resistance fighters all looked at each other for a minute in disbelief. Suddenly, hundreds of Camulus soldiers came charging out from under the ground. They had dug trenches all across the center of the base that they had covered themselves in. The Antillis fighters were caught off guard, but not for long, and soon, the final battle began.

The battle raged for hours as both sides took enormous hits from each other. It seemed to the elders, who were still waiting on the outskirts, that no side would win. Callais became concerned that once Evie, Declan, and Otto got to their position, there wouldn't be enough room for Evie and Declan to reach the ground safely. Just as he thought this, Callais saw the Devas ship carrying Evie and Declan approach the center of the base... and the center of the chaos.

Otto looked down at the battle below, and he too became concerned that they wouldn't be able to accomplish their goal. Callais and Otto seem to share the same thought as both men charged to action. Callais started to cast spells into the center of the battle as Otto began to shoot small blasts from his cannons downward. Both tactics seemed to work as the people in the center of the battlefield began to scatter from their places, leaving a space large enough to bring Evie and Declan to the ground.

Evie watched in horror from the side of the ship and

once again began to feel overwhelmed and terrified. She then remembered Otto's words, *For Our Family Forever*. The feelings of horror and terror soon dissipated as Evie once again felt brave and knew she must save her family. Evie looked at Declan and grabbed his hand. Declan looked at her as he squeezed her hand and gave her a wink. Evie saw in Declan's other hand he was holding a Devas protector staff. Otto then motioned for the two to take their positions as they went to the ship's side, and Otto began to lower them down. As they were lowering to the ground, Evie was still watching the battle unfold. Suddenly, a blast of white fire came from the side of her and almost hit her in the head. She began to panic but then quickly remembered her protection spell training. She quickly chanted under her breath, and she and Declan soon fell out of sight as they continued their descent to the ground.

Once they reached the ground, Evie looked around desperately for Ellis but couldn't see him. As she looked, she heard a loud bellowing noise. She soon saw Ellis, Aphrodite, Bella, and Artemis, charging and trampling through a line of Camulus soldiers. The dogs began swarming after the soldiers in a frenzy, making a path for Ellis to get through. Evie watched in awe—she was amazed by the dog's bravery and with her valiant and courageous Ellis—as they finally reached the center of the battle. Evie then released the protection spell over her and Declan, making them visible to Ellis… and now everyone. Ellis saw her and yelled over the battle sounds, "Let's do this, kid!"

Ellis then motioned his hand in the opposite direction as a loud trumpeting noise echoed over the battlefield, and soon, the resistance fighters began to fall back. The Camulus soldiers had no idea what was going on, and some began to follow the retreating resistance fighters. Others realized that Evie and Declan were standing in the middle of the battle and began to charge in their direction. Evie held her breath as the soldiers charged. She then saw a multitude of air and water blasts coming from all directions, aimed at the Camulus soldiers. Soon, Hepha blasts started coming down from above, aimed at soldiers that weren't hit by the air and water spells. The Camulus soldiers who followed the retreating Antillis fighters saw this and began to charge back to the middle battlegrounds.

Although several spells and Hepha blasts came from all directions, it was not enough to contain all the charging forces. Evie became scared when she looked nervously at Declan. Declan then held out his hand with the Devas staff, and instantly, a glimmering blue light shot out from the Devas staff. Evie watched as several soldiers near them began to levitate in the air. Declan then made a swiping motion with the staff, and the levitated soldiers went flying backward. Evie watched in amazement and once again felt the power and strength return to her watching Declan's bravery. Declan then slammed the Devas staff into the ground, and a shimmering blue bubble surrounded the pair. He then nodded at Evie and boldly stated, "It's time."

Evie held tightly to Declan's hand as she closed her eyes and began to feel the power inside her increase. Soon, she felt Declan's powers as he started to chant spells—which Evie knew were water and air spells to help her. As she felt Declan cast his spells, she remembered to listen closely for Rosalina's voice. It was hard at first because all she could hear was the sounds of battle surrounding her, but she began to concentrate harder and clear her mind. Soon, she couldn't hear anything, and there was complete silence. Evie became nervous in the silence when she began to hear a faint voice, speaking in a slow, rhythmic tone. The voice slowly became louder and louder, and Evie was then able to hear it clear as day, and she began to repeat the melodic chant. The words were beautiful. It sounded to Evie like a Native American spirit chant she once heard when she went to a powwow with David and Ruby. She then thought of her loving adoptive parents and all the people she loved as she continued to repeat the chant over and over. Suddenly, the powerful feelings of love released a prevailing shiver all over her body, and she felt a force push her eyes open.

As Evie opened her eyes, she saw that she and Declan were several feet off the ground. Evie then felt the love and power from the chant shake her body as sparks of light began to come out of her fingertips. She looked down at her hands and saw the sparks become rays of light. Evie looked at the surrounding battle and saw that the Camulus forces were trying desperately to penetrate the Devas staff protection field, in which Ellis, Aphrodite, Bella, and Artemis now stood. She looked up again and saw that most of the Antillis resistance fighters were out of range. Those who weren't fighting Camulus forces were just watching her and Declan in awe. There were also a few Camulus soldiers outside the central battle, watching them as well, but with more horror than awe. Evie then heard Ellis shout from below, "Now, kid!"

Evie looked down once more at her beloved Ellis and began to release the light rays from her hands. At first, the light rays only began to knock down a few soldiers when Evie heard Declan say, "I can't hold the spell over the staff much longer."

Just as he said this, a group of Camulus soldiers found

a way to penetrate the Devas staff protection shield and rushed towards Ellis and the dogs. Evie instantly became enraged, thinking about anyone hurting Ellis or the dogs. She then screamed into the air, "NO!"

Evie quickly aimed her hands down at the soldiers charging Ellis and the dogs when a massive blast of light discharged from her fingertips and blew the soldiers back. Evie then aimed her palms outwards at the remaining forces in front of her and sent another powerful blast, knocking more Camulus soldiers to the ground. Evie began to spin in a circle in the air as the powerful energies released from her open palms. Declan was now lowering himself to the ground next to Ellis... and they watched Evie.

Evie then closed her eyes and thought of everyone she loved as her body began to shake and spin. Light began to crackle in the air around her, and Evie could feel the energy of the elements in her soul. She saw how rays and streams of light would form and split apart and then merge together inside her body, as if her body was the source of all power. The lights then began to surge in her body and mind. Evie then thought of her dream of Magnus and how the energies inside him increased before he released his power. She could feel that same energy inside her reach its peak, so she looked back down and released all the power she held inside her at once. Light, wind, earth, and air came rushing from her body, shaking the ground and vibrating the air all around. Rays of light streaked across the sky, as bolts of electric blue flashes crashed on the ground, burning up and eliminating pockets of Camulus soldiers nearest to Ellis, Declan, and the dogs. Wind whipped through the air, as billowing squalls of light and air energies flung soldiers ferociously around. Cracks in the ground spilt open as more soldiers were swallowed up by the earth's thick, heavy, black dirt. The energies then converged and engulfed all Camulus forces left standing as the elements relentlessly pounded against them. Suddenly, a massive surge left Evie's body and cascaded across the battlefield. The force knocked any remaining Camulus soldiers to the ground...instantly ending their lives.

Once all the soldiers were down, Evie felt the energies drain from her body as she slowly lowered to the ground. When she reached the ground, she stood next to Ellis, Declan, and their faithful companions. She saw that they were completely surrounded by fallen Camulus soldiers. Soon, they heard a cheering roar come from all around them. Evie looked up and saw the Antillis resistance fighter who had fallen back come running onto the battlefield, yelling and cheering. Many resistance fighters began to capture the fallen Camulus forces as

Otto lowered himself to the ground from the ship above. Otto, Declan, Ellis, and Evie all grabbed each other and began to jump up and down, tears of happiness falling down their cheeks. Callais soon reached the center, where the joyous foursome continued to bounce around and cheer. Evie suddenly felt weak as she thought of all the soldiers she just killed. He soul began to ache as she cried out and fell to the ground. Just before she passed out, she heard Callais yell, "Someone, get Regina!"

Evie's world then went dark.

Chapter 4

THE END AND THE BEGINNING

◆•————————●————————•◆

Evie's mind was spinning in the darkness. She could remember the battle had ended; however, she couldn't understand why she wasn't able to wake from the darkness that now surrounded her. As she spun in the blackness of her mind, she tried her hardest to focus and find a path that would lead her anywhere. The more she focused, the more she began to spiral. Evie finally decided to stop trying and just fell into the shadowy nothingness. As she let go, a small light started to shine in the distance, so she focused on the light as it got closer to her. As the light finally reached her, a hazy figure began to appear. Soon the figure came into view, and she saw that it was Magnus. She couldn't see what he was doing or what was around him, so she weakly called out, "Magnus."

After Evie called out his name, the large man turned around and looked directly at her. Magnus smiled at her, and Evie realized that this was a much younger Magnus than before. In the drawing she had found, and all the other times Magnus had appeared to her, he was a much older man. This time, Magnus had no gray in his hair and was much bigger in stature than she had seen in the past, and his face seemed to beam with happiness and peace. As he smiled at her, Evie instantly became comforted when Magnus turned back around, and the surrounding room became clear.

Evie could see that Magnus was standing in a room, similar to the one in "the stacks" back in Ireland where Marina lived. Although it was fairly similar, many differences made Evie realize that this might be the home Callais had mentioned that Magnus had on Antillis when he was younger. She watched Magnus hover over a table filled with scrolls and books when she heard a knocking noise coming from behind her. Both her and Magnus turned around when Evie saw a man enter the room, followed by a young Rosalina. Magnus walked over to the pair and embraced them when, in a joyous tone, he said, "Ah, brother and sister, I am so glad you have joined me. I have something exciting to share with you."

Evie realized the man was Camulos and was shocked. She watched as Camulos and Rosalina followed Magnus to the table where he had previously been looking at the scrolls laid out. Evie looked at the three in awe. Not only was Magnus much younger, but Camulos didn't look as horrid as he had appeared in past visions, and Rosalina was absolutely beautiful. Although Magnus was a large man, covered in red hair everywhere, Camulos was tall and lanky with deep gray eyes, gray skin, and long, wavy black hair. Camulos also had pointed ears and long spiked fingernails, and Evie noticed his eyes were a little closer together than Magnus's eyes (he kind of looked like Atlas and Abe, and Evie assumed maybe they were both from the Camulus galaxy). Evie also noticed that Rosalina still had her cat-like features, but her eyes were much more of a sparkling yellow color. Rosalina's hair was extremely curly and almost matched the color of her eyes. Evie wondered how they were all siblings looking so different from each other, but then she remembered that there were many different kinds of beings in the universe. Evie thought, *Although they all kind of look human, the mother and father must have created these differences on purpose.* As the threesome looked at the table, Magnus began to speak. "I have found an ancient text that the mother and father must have written themselves."

He paused for a moment before continuing. "It seems that there is a passage in the text describing how

340

to manipulate an element in our universe, that, if done right, can eliminate all that is bad in the universe. If we can figure this out, we can have complete peace in the universe like at the beginning."

Both Camulos and Rosalina smiled when Camulos said, "Brother, this is great news. The universe can finally be free of darkness."

Magnus happily patted his brother on the shoulder and went on to say, "There is something else…" He took a deep breath. "It seems the passage is incomplete and is missing the second half of this spell. If we do not find this text, this passage we have now, if it is used without the other half, I am afraid it could cause darkness and destruction instead of peace."

Rosalina then asked, "Do we know where that other half might be?"

Magnus closed his eyes for a minute before answering, "That is what I have been trying to search for, but to no avail." He paused again, then added, "We must keep this scroll a secret. If this half of the passage is to fall into the wrong hands, I am afraid of what could happen to our universe."

The three of them then made a pact to keep the scroll safe until they were to find the other half. After talking for a bit longer, they all left the room. Evie tried to follow, but she couldn't and was left alone in the room. After being alone in the giant room for a while, she heard the door slowly creak open. She turned to see that Camulos had reentered the room. He looked cautiously around and then slowly crept over to the table. Camulos then quickly snatched the scroll the three of them had been looking over and darted rapidly out of the room. Evie gasped as she watched this and tried to yell out 'stop' and attempted to follow Camulos. But again, Evie was trapped where she was and couldn't follow him or yell out. At one point, she thought she saw a young blond girl come out from behind a stack and chase after Camulos, but the room quickly went dark, and Evie was, once again, left in the room alone.

Shortly after waiting in the empty room, Magnus and Rosalina reentered. Magnus went over to the table and turned to Rosalina with horror in his eyes. "It is gone."

Rosalina looked back and shook her head. "So is Camulos."

Magnus roared at the top of his lungs and turned the table over, knocking everything to the ground, scaring Evie. Rosalina approached the large and angry Magnus and placed her hand on his arm, "Magnus, we must find him and stop him. You know how powerful he is, and you know he has been questioning our path for peace."

Magnus began to weep, turned to his sister, and sadly shook his head, saying, "I thought there was hope, Rosie. I thought that finding this would bring him peace."

Rosalina wrapped her arms around her brother. "I know you did, Magnus. You always see the good, even when there is none to be found."

For a while, the pair held each other. Then the room, Magnus, and Rosalina slowly fell out of sight. Evie was left once again in the darkness and shadows when another light began to shine, and Magnus's face appeared in the light. He looked directly at Evie and said, "*You must find the missing scroll that connects the two passages together. Please, child, you must, or the universe will end at the hands of my brother.*"

After Magnus said this, he faded away, and Evie began to spin back into the darkness and fog.

***

Evie spun in the darkness and fog for a while when she could hear voices in the distance. She focused on the voices when, to her relief, she could clearly hear Ellis's voice and the bark of her beloved Bella. She called out their names from the fog, and soon Evie could feel a hard surface under her body. Evie then began to bat her eyes and slowly open them. As she opened her eyes, when the grogginess lifted, she found herself in Regina's dwelling with Ellis and Bella right by her side. When Ellis saw that her eyes were open, he yelled out to the room, "She's awake. Come quick!"

Ellis then wrapped his arms over her body and began to cry, saying, "Good god, girl. Yeh gave me a fright."

Soon, everyone she loved was around her as Regina rubbed goo on her forehead, and Evie slowly perched herself upright to see all her friends and family. Evie sat up and looked at them with a huge smile stretched across her face. One by one, everyone came to embrace Evie, happy that she was okay. Declan was the last to approach the table, and when he did, he bent down and kissed her deeply. Evie fell into the kiss like it was something she had done for a thousand years—it felt perfect to her. As Declan pulled away, tears were streaming down his cheeks when he said, "I love you, Evie."

"I love you too," Evie said, smiling from the deep love she felt for Declan.

Declan reached back down and embraced her once again. When the pair finally released, Evie looked over at Amelia and saw her flash a big toothy grin followed by a wink. Evie returned the wink when she suddenly remembered what she saw while in the darkness of the dream. She turned to Callais, saying, "I have something to tell you."

"I am sure you do," Callais replied with a small smile and then added, "We have great news for you too, but for now, get some rest. We will be meeting tomorrow in the council room."

Evie nodded as Callais and a few elders left the room, followed by Otto and Emmeline. Marina, Declan, Collin, Amelia, and Ellis refused to leave, so Regina again put them to work. Evie laid back down, snuggled Bella into her chest, and fell asleep (with no dreams or fog). And for the first time in a long time, she felt happy and peaceful.

Chapter 42

CELEBRATE

·•────── • ──────•·

Evie woke the following day to see that everyone was eating breakfast at the table in Regina's dwelling. She sat up, and immediately, Amelia, Collin, Declan, and Ellis came running to her side. Declan helped Evie get to her feet, and surprisingly, Evie wasn't in as much pain as she thought she would be. They made their way over to the table when Marina got up and hugged Evie tightly. "I am so proud of you, child."

Evie returned the tight embrace and earnestly admitted, "I couldn't have done it without you guys!"

The two released their tight embrace as Evie sat down and ate breakfast when Declan and Ellis began to tell her everything that happened. They explained that the Camulus base and forces were all taken down, and the protection spell that Evie had cast was lasting—Antillis was completely safe. They also told her that many

Camulus soldiers defected and wanted to join the Antillis resistance. Once they were all trained and trusted, they would have greater numbers than ever. Evie felt relieved that she hadn't killed all the Camulus soldiers. They also explained that Balor hadn't returned. Declan and Ellis told her that Josephine was able to find the man who had been using spells to communicate with the outside Camulus forces, and they were questioning him as well. As the excited pair finished telling Evie the great news, Callais entered the room and stated, "We are ready to meet in the council room."

Callais flashed Evie a big smile, which Evie admired for a minute since she had only seen him do that one other time. Seeing Callais smile made Evie so happy, she got up, walked over to him, and gave him a giant hug. Callais held her and chuckled, saying, "I knew you could do it."

The group then left the room and headed to the council meeting. Once everyone was there, Callais began to speak. "Council members, brave warriors, and our beloved Antillis family. Today we celebrate, for we have won a great victory on our path to defeating the darkness in this galaxy."

The room roared and cheered with excitement as many members began to hug each other and shake hands.

Once the room settled down, Callais finished, "Thanks to our brave fighters, our plans, and our courageous Evie, we now can to go out and rescue the rest of our siblings… the rest of our family."

Again, the room cheered with joy, and soon, everyone was standing with their hands placed over their hearts. All eyes in the room fell on Evie. One by one, the people in the room dropped to one knee and bowed their heads. Evie stood there in shock, realizing that they were all honoring her. She turned her head to Callais, who was also taking a knee and bowing. Evie looked around the room at the bowed heads and held her hand up, saying, "No, please don't bow to me. I didn't do this alone; I couldn't have done this without each and every one of you." She paused and told them, "You are my family, and we did this together. I should be bowing to you, your love, and your faith in defeating the darkness."

When Evie finished, the members in the room slowly raised their heads when she heard Newton say, "Evie, you are what will keep this family together."

Then the crowd then all stood to their feet when Ellis yelled, "To Evie!"

The room roared back, "To Evie!"

Evie smiled and yelled out, "To Devas!"

The crowd then jumped up and down and yelled even louder, "To Devas!"

Once again, the room filled with cheers and joy as Josephine approached Evie and said, "You are truly Magnus's heir. Your kindness and compassion are why they honor you."

Evie smiled at the old woman and hugged her. Josephine returned the hug when Ellis came over to Evie, lifted her up on his shoulders, and yelled out, "To hope!"

The crowd shouted back Ellis's call, and that night, Mari celebrated.

Chapter 43
NEW MISSION TO ALDERBARD

◆•————— ● —————•◆

After three days of celebration, Callais called another council meeting. The room was filled with nervous energy when Callais and the elders entered. This time, instead of Callais talking, he nodded his head at Otto as Otto stood up and addressed the council, "We have had a great victory here on Antillis, but now, we must plan for our next steps. We will move forward to save Alderbard."

Otto nodded his head, and this time, Elizabeth and Leo stood up when Leo added, "We have a resistance on Alderbard. It's not as great as the resistance here on Antillis, but we have enough people there, and with the fighters and resources we have here, we know that we can take Alderbard as we have done with Antillis."

Elizabeth then began to speak. "We have made a plan, but there are still many holes in it, and we need to pull together once again and find the best way to save and protect Alderbard as we have done here."

The room all nodded in agreement when Newton stood up and told them, "Although we have more people and resources, the Camulus forces now know that there is a resistance that can defeat them since we have proven this here on Antillis. We are sure that this defeat will only increase the Camulus forces' rage, and we will be met with great resistance. We may face more challenging obstacles as we go out into the Devas system."

The room remained silent as the members thought deeply about this. Callais then stood up and said, "Once again, I know that we are outnumbered and will face great resistance from Camulos and his soldiers as we carry out our next steps. I must remind everyone here that with the love in our hearts and the willingness to defeat darkness, there is nothing that we cannot do if we remember who we are and what we are fighting for."

The crowd murmured among each other when Otto placed his hand over his heart and said, "For our family forever."

The room then followed Otto and, in unison, repeated, "For our family forever."

As Evie left the council room, surrounded by her

friends and family, she knew that this fight was worth it… because family was always worth fighting for!

Glossary

ANIMALS/COMPANIONS

Fenriris/ Dogs (Assigned to keepers)

Aphrodite: Magnus's and then Ellis's dog. An English mastiff (female).

Apollo: Callais's dog. A pit bull (male).

Artemis: Declan's dog. A blue Cane Corso (female).

Bella: Evie's dog. A medium-sized black dog with tints of brown and white, similar to a mix of a Jack Russell terrier and a boxer (female).

Darwin: Newton's dog. A golden retriever (male).

Delila: Clara's dog. A golden retriever (female).

Indy: Simone's black bird (raven) (female).

River: Collin's dog. A cattle dog with one blue eye and one brown eye (female).

BUILDINGS/MACHINES

Devas Temple: Located on Canopiuis where the Devas keepers performed their separation ceremony

extraction machine: The machine created by Balor,

entwined with Agronas's tracking spell, and cast with devious spells from Camulos to extract memories, thoughts, and dreams from the Devas beings. Many who have extraction marks have cut off their lower arm (like Collin) to avoid being tracked and controlled by the Camulus pack. The dealers also provided many Devas beings fake extraction marks to fool the Camulus pack, but charged high prices that often couldn't be paid off. So whether fake or real, those with the mark live in fear.

senate tower: Located on Polgaran in the Darthus galaxy. Purplish in color to match the Darthus environment.

CHARACTERS

Abe Alexopolis: One of Otto's and Atlas's friends, trained to be a watcher by Callais. Fighter for Antillis resistance.

Agronas Fortias: Camulos's wife (Strife and Slaughter Keeper), comes from Darthus galaxy.

Albert: A officer in the Camulus forces that joined as a spy for Silas and the resistance.

Alvaro Diaitz: Evie's uncle and part of The Keeper's Order

Amam Kalb: Part of the Keeper's Order. From Egypt.

Amelia Vegas: Evie's friend (close in age to Evie). Otto's younger sister. Originally from the planet Sirios in Devas galaxy and is now on Antillis. She is mute because she cut out her own tongue to protect her brother Otto.

Atlas Vili: Otto's friend and right-hand man. Trained by Callais to be a protector. Fighter in the Antillis resistance.

Balor Kronius: Camulos's right-hand man (Death Keeper), comes from Camulus galaxy.

Ben Abebis: Elizabeth's brother from Alderbard. Fighter in the Alderbard resistance

Beth Anderson: Evie's social worker and part of The Keeper's Order

Callais Baldais: Head of the Antillis and Devas resistance. Lower keeper with strong powers and resistance elder.

Camulos: From Camulus galaxy. God of war, darkness, and destruction. Keeper/Ruler of the Camulus Force.

Clara Bellatrias: Declan's mother and a head keeper. Lives on the planet Canopiuis in the hidden city of Kali. Is missing and thought to be a spy for the Camulus forces.

Collin MacDunleavy (father): Evie's biological father (killed in an accident).

Collin Junaius (boy): Lost boy found in Canopiuis, the hidden city of Kali (six years old). Has no left hand, presents scar from the left eye down to the left shoulder. One of Evie's friends. River is his dog, and he has keeper powers, but no one is sure what happened to him or why he has keeper powers.

Constantine: Lost head keeper of Antillis and Terran.

David Jones: Evie's adoptive father. Now part of the Keeper's Order.

Declan Bellatrias: Clara's son and Evie's friend. From Devas galaxy from the planet Canopiuis and found in the hidden city of Kali. Now Evie's right-hand man and a keeper.

Dermot Kelley: Head of the Keeper's Order on Earth/Terran (now deceased).

Desi Jones: David and Ruby's daughter.

Ellis Ó Murchadha (Murphy): Descendant of Magnus, found on Terran by Marina. He inherits Magnus's dog, Aphrodite. Fighter in Antillis resistance

Elizabeth Abebis: Escaped from Alderbard. Sister of Ben and a resistance fighter.

Emmeline Freyas: Otto's girlfriend and Regina's daughter. One of Evie's friends. Trained as a healer.

Evangelina MacDunleavy: Also called Evie (eighteen years old). From Magnus's bloodline on Terran. She is true of heart. Now has powers and trained by Antillis resistance elders.

father: Original creator of the universe (along with the mother).

Jafari: Bad dealer who Elizabeth and Ben were to be turned over to, but they escaped before it could happen.

Josephine Januis: Head keeper who comes from an

unknown ancient bloodline. From the Devas galaxy. Elder of Antillis resistance.

Leo Kimathis: Head resistance fighter and dealer on Alderbard.

Leslie Jones: David and Ruby's adoptive daughter.

Lincoln Hektoris: Callais's right-hand man on Antillis and previous head Keeper on Alderbard. Part of the resistance council, not only a keeper but trained as a watcher and a resistance elder

Magnus (Deae) Ó Cuinn: The most powerful head keeper of Devas galaxy and all galaxies.

Maria Borbón MacDunleavy: Evie's biological mother (killed in an accident).

Marina Ó Cuinn: Evie's lost ancestor and Magnus's daughter. She found Evie. Lives on Terran. Now has more powers and is an elder of the resistance on Antillis.

Michal Jones: David and Ruby's son.

mother: Original creator of the universe (along with the father).

Nadia Lebedev: Part of The Keeper's Order and a watcher.

Newton Evander: Head keeper who is powerful with air spells and elder in the resistance.

Nox Guard: Balor and Camulos's private guard (created by Balor).

Otto Vegas: Amelia's older brother and Evie's friends

in the resistance. Trained to be a protector by Callais. Originally from Sirios and is right-hand man to Callais as a resistance fighter.

Regina Freyas: Emmeline's mother and healer on the planet Antillis.

Rosalina: Magnus and Camulos's sister. She is hiding in a secret place, and only Evie knows of her existence.

Ruby Jones: Evie's adoptive mother. Now part of the Keeper's Order.

Silas Scorpuis: Captured Camulos soldier who defects. He is Simone's nephew and now resistance fighter and spy.

Simone Scorpuis: Originally from the Denaban galaxy and a Denidis warrior. She is now an elder in the resistance and a fighter. Leader of the Antillis resistance spies.

Sophia Murphy: Evie's aunt and part of the Keeper's Order.

Steven Jones: David and Ruby's son and part of The Keeper's Order.

Victoria: Officer in Camulus forces that turned spy for the resistance.

Vlad: Head commander in the Camulus Forces stationed on Antillis base.

Zane: Dealer who had Elizabeth and Ben before making a deal with Jafarai.

CITIES

Candor: Capitol City on Canopiuis in Devas galaxy. Where the temple was located.

Davi: Protected city on Alderbard and head city of Alderbard resistance.

Donegal: Located on Terran, in the country of Ireland. Where Marina's home is located.

Kali: Hidden underground city in Canopiuis.

Mari: Hidden underground city in a mountainside on Antillis.

ELEMENTS

Air, Water, Earth, Fire, and Light: Elements that keepers can manipulate to enhance their spells.

dark matter: Found in the Camulus galaxy. Not innately a bad element, but because of Camulos's manipulation, it became a dark and powerful force. Made of the darkest and empty parts of space and time. Originally thought to hold an ancient time memory of creation, as to why the manipulation of this matter can cross time faster than any other element.

Desmodias: Found on Antillis. A rare plant that is used to craft almost indestructible fabrics. Used in Devas sails and the Fabric of Space and Time.

Hepha: Yellow-and-purple fire used in Devas protection

and weapons. Created by several Devas galaxy keepers. Stronger than white fire.

light matter: Found in the Devas galaxy as the galaxies' main element. Used to store memory and ensure connections with the seven siblings in the Devas system, as well as connections to the rest of the galaxies and universe. Made mostly of stardust and remnants of the mother's powerful love.

vegars: Metal found in Camulus galaxy. Enhanced with Camulos's spells. Used in armor, ships, and swords of Camulus's forces.

white fire: Created by Camulos and enhanced by Camulos's spells. Used to enhance weapons. Found in Camulus galaxy, enhanced by fire from the planet Sirios.

GALAXIES/PLANET

Adarais: City on Alderbard where Elizabeth and Ben grew up

Aldebard: Planet in Devas galaxy. Made of water and land bridges. The main element is water.

Alpharman: Planet in Devas galaxy and is the land of spirits. The main element here is spirit. The planet in Devas system where souls store their memory and spirits. One of the hardest planets for Camulos to control. Agronas stationed herself here after the invasion. Also where the rare bird, Andeais, is located, whose feather helps with the staff levitation power.

Antillis: Central planet in the Devas galaxy. Main elements are flora and fauna because the planet is inhabited mainly by plants and animals. Mari is the lost city in the forest, full of survivors. Many of the watchers, protectors, and keepers reside here because the forest is vast, and it is easy to hide where the fourth-day protection spell covers. The resistance is strong on this planet, so there are many Camulus soldiers stationed on the unprotected side of the planet.

Darthus galaxy: Thought to be the most central galaxy, where the intergalactic senate was held in early years. Home galaxy of Agronas.

Denaban: Galaxy system where Simone is from.

Devas galaxy: The last galaxy that wanted peace and attempted to separate from the war and darkness. However, it was invaded by the Camulus pack. Furthest galaxy from the rest of the other galaxies.

Denidis: Planet in Denaban galaxy where Simone is from.

Canopiuis: Capital planet in the Devas galaxy. Capital city is Candor, where the keeper temple was located before the invasion. The hidden underground city of Kali is also here. The main element is air. Because it is the capital planet of the Devas system, the Camulus force is strong here.

Regulusa: Planet in the Devas galaxy. The main element

is fire. First planet that Camulos invaded because he needed the main element of fire to help him enhance the elements he brought with him from the Camulus galaxy.

Sirios: Planet in the Devas galaxy. The main element is metal, with Skyclad being the most powerful one. There is thought to be a lost mountain city where survivors live. Hostile desert lands.

Terran: Planet originally in the Devas galaxy cast out after the ceremony break. Now located in a far-distant galaxy. The main element is earth. This is where Magnus escapes to, where he creates his own bloodline, and where Evie is found.

RELICS

The Chain of Reality: Made up of stardust from the Devas galaxy system. The stardust chain leaves trails of light between the seven siblings. Can be used to travel among the siblings in the Devas pack. It is enhanced with water from Alderbard to highlight powers of the spells and star trails. The spells cast on the chain ensure it could only be used for good and protection for anyone who held it.

The Fabric of Space and Time: The fabric can change shape so that it can be small enough to fit in the hands of the smallest being or become large enough to cover an entire planet system. The fabric is made from the element in the Devas galaxy called light matter. Light matter can only be used for good and has the extra benefit of controlling time. The fabric was also infused with Desmodias, the planet on Antillis, which is almost indestructible. The spells cast on the fabric ensure that it is completely indestructible.

The Horn of Infinity: Made of a sacred crystal matter connected to the very first planet the mother and father had created. The horn is transparent but has a shimmering glow of light that illuminates from within it. The light is thought to be the first seeds of the mother and father's love. This horn serves two purposes: to warn the seven siblings if the war is to find them, and to destroy darkness. Given that love is more powerful than evil and darkness, the horn could vanquish all that was evil and dark. Anyone could blow the horn to alert all in the Devas pack, but only one keeper and that keeper's bloodline could blow the horn to vanquish the darkness. It is currently lost.

The Sacred Circles: These are circles cast with spells and inscribed with sacred text to help find the ancient city on Terran. Two have been found, which are Evie's parents' gold wedding bands. The sacred circles are also made of gold, a powerful element to help with casting spells. Not all the sacred circles are rings like the wedding bands, and three more must be found.

KEEPERS, WATCHERS, AND PROTECTORS

head keepers: Are found in each galaxy, with one head keeper per planet in each system. They are born with their powers.

head watchers: Do not have the full power of keeper, but the head watchers have training and apprenticeship with a head keeper for ten years. The training focuses on how to manipulate control of the elements and time. The head watchers also have the special assignment of keeping an eye out for any approach of the darkness before and after the separation. So, the head watchers have the special gift of sight beyond the Devas pack, as well as sight through time. Only have powers for half of their lifespan.

lower keepers: Also found in each galaxy and vary in number according to need. Some may have an original bloodline and may be born with innate power, but often they are trained by a head keeper to have powers.

lower watchers: Exactly like head watchers but only trained for five years, and only have powers for a quarter of their lifespan.

protectors: Trained by Callais in the Devas system and found on the central planet of Antillis. The protectors were given the gift of travel among worlds. Their special gift was to manipulate space to move rapidly among the planets in the Devas system. The protectors were also given special tools to help protect the Devas system. These tools were ships that could help them travel among worlds on the stardust trails in the Devas galaxy, and metallic staffs that had spells of protection from the sacred texts cast on them.

SHIPS AND STAFFS

black ships: Used by Camulus forces to navigate and control the Devas galaxy. Created by Camulos and fueled by fire elements.

Devas ships: Used for protection by the protectors in Devas galaxy. There were 100 ships, made of the finest metals from the Sirios planet, including Skyclad. The metals were cast with spells to make them lighter than air yet almost indestructible. The metals were specially crafted into the ships, so they could manipulate space around them. This gave the ships the ability to match any environment they were in, making them naturally camouflaged (so they could be close to invisible). The sails on the ships were made from a plant found on Antillis, called Desmodias, finely crafted into fabric, and could withstand even the harshest of climates (so the sails would never break).

Devas staffs: Given to the protectors in the Devas galaxy, the metallic staffs were made of the finest metals found on Sirios and had similar properties to the ships. The staffs had protection spells that could be used to protect anyone around them within a fifty-mile radius (like a large shield). Each staff also had a feather of a special bird found on Alpharman, the spirit world, embedded into them. The feather comes from a bird sacred to Alpharman called Andeais. This feather helped the staff to elevate objects for temporary periods.

CPSIA information can be obtained
at www.ICGtesting.com
Printed in the USA
LVHW080621130522
718522LV00012B/133/J

9 781735 593234